SCREEN

Martin Miller works for <the welfare department?> But his attention to his job is wandering. <He isn't sure> he can work there anymore. What Martin really wants is to be in the movies. Not as an actor, not quite. He wants to be *in* the movies. He sits in the theater, and he becomes Marcello Mastriano to Sophia Loren. He becomes Roger Vadim to Brigitte Bardot. He has sex with these women, and knows that this world is better than real life. His boss, Mr. Poirier, warns him that he will very likely be fired. His girlfriend, Barbara, warns him that Hollywood isn't real. But Martin knows what he knows—that in a darkened theater, he can be whomever he wants when he enters the screen.

CINEMA

"Susan has had a full day in New York. She has participated in the making of a pornographic film, she has had intercourse with the agent of the film's producers, she has been offered a leading role in a forthcoming production by the same company, she has come to terms with herself in perhaps ways that she was not accustomed. At the end of all of this she stands in a hotel room fully dressed somewhere between retention and flight... She senses that if she were to tell the men in the street who stare at her what she had been doing that day, they would be amazed but, then, they might be perfectly matter of fact. People in New York accept all sorts of things as matter of fact."

SCREEN
CINEMA
BARRY N. MALZBERG

STARK
HOUSE

Stark House Press • Eureka California

SCREEN / CINEMA

Published by Stark House Press
1315 H Street
Eureka, CA 95501, USA
griffinskye3@sbcglobal.net
www.starkhousepress.com

ISBN: 978-1-951473-11-2

Book design by Mark Shepard, shepgraphics.com
Proofreading by Bill Kelly

First Stark House Press Edition: June 2020

7

Screen
By Barry N. Malzberg

110

The Jewel and the Madonnas
By Barry N. Malzberg

115

Cinema
By Barry N. Malzberg

197

The Commercial Culture
By Barry N. Malzberg

200

Barry N. Malzberg
Bibliography

SCREEN

BARRY N. MALZBERG

For RJD

"…You ought to be in pictures…"
Popular Song

I

Friday, it was YESTERDAY, TODAY AND TOMORROW. It was playing at the Jewel, a battered, faintly odorous theatre somewhere near the slaughterhouses in the business district of the borough, but the business of slaughterhouses didn't bother me at all. I was not, after all, purely on a pleasure trip.

YESTERDAY, TODAY AND TOMORROW, all things taken into account, isn't too bad. It's the least titillating of all the truly hot movies of the 60's but then again it's in fast company. There's the Sophia Loren breast feeding business in the first part and all those fine necrophile overtones in the second and the theological overtones of the third are really dirty. Putting an ecclesiastic of any gender in proximity to the likes of Sophia Loren is in itself promising. All in all, it isn't a bad deal for the kind of film it is. Of course, there was nothing much else playing in the city that night; I had checked it out. There was the underground stuff, of course, but I'm no pervert. My purposes are not frivolous.

So I went out to the field, then, at about two in the afternoon, visited two dreadful old men living together on Old Age Assistance for fifteen minutes—getting credit, then, for two visits that way instead of one which would almost get me through the afternoon anyway, even if I was playing it straight—and got back to my apartment at about a quarter after three. I opened a can of beer and watched a panel show while I checked the movie clock to see that the most convenient showing would be the one at 4:30 because then I could see it through three times and still have the evening ahead—and then, at about four, just when I was getting ready to go, the phone rang. I knew right away that it was Poirier, the supervisor, calling to check on me, waiting for me to pick up the phone so that he could ask me why the hell I wasn't in the field; what I was doing at home over an hour before clock-out time. That was all right with me. I didn't mind hearing from him in the least at that point. I picked up the phone and making no attempt to disguise my voice—an old, usually successful trick but too damned childish—said hello.

"That you, Miller?" Poirier said.

"That's me. I'm right here."

"You're supposed to be in the field."

"I finished up early."

"You checked out at 2:00 and you're home already? That's pretty serious, you know."

"I got sick in the field," I said. "I'll take sick leave from three on, which is when I finished my visits. So I'm not trying to steal any time from you."

"You declare sick leave before you leave the office, not after; you know that. You know all the ropes. You've been with the department for three and a half years so how do you expect me to believe that?"

"It was my gut," I said. "I got sick to my gut. After I saw those two old bastards sitting together in that room—"

"A lot of people here are gunning for you, Miller. There's a lot of heat on you now. Why are you making more trouble for yourself?"

"Why did you call me? There'd be no trouble if you hadn't called, isn't that right?"

"You know better than that. I've got to protect my unit, the clients it services. You're in trouble, Miller. You're in bad trouble. They had a conference here this morning upstairs about a lot of people and they want to let you go. They want to bring charges."

His voice had that flat, hard, anxious edge which always came into it when he was either trying to give one of his investigators a hard time or trying to close a client's case. I could imagine his hand, moistening slowly to the excitement of it all, grasping the receiver even more closely to his ears. I had dealt with Poirier for a long time, with middling success. Now we were approaching the last act.

"Well," I said, "let them bring charges. It takes a long, long time to make a dismissal stick in this department, Poirier. Besides, I don't even know if I care to have the job anymore. I might just save all of you a lot of problems and quit. Become a freelance researcher."

"You're a fool," he said, his voice moistening along with the hand, as he thought of the Department. "You're a fool to throw over a good, secure job like this. If you get fired you'll never get another position in civil service. Besides, you know how the department is coming along; how improvements are being made in services, how salary increases are in the works. I can't see a man like you—who has nowhere else to go anyway—doing something like this to himself."

"How do you know I have nowhere else to go?" I said, taking up a new can of beer and opening it one-handed, not a very difficult thing to do if you have any practice and any serious interest in getting at the beer. "For all you know, I might have something in industry all set up for myself. It so happens that one of the largest movie producers in the country and I are talking right now about a position in the east coast casting department. It could come through for me any day. How much difference can it make to me what you people do?"

"Well, listen, Miller," Poirier said, stopping to think that one over only slightly; there is not, among supervisors in the Department of Welfare, a great interest in the arts or crafts, "if you want to go, you go. But you go clean now: just put in your resignation form and quit. Don't play around, have them making me call you Friday afternoons to check you out. Stop complicating my life and everyone's, okay?"

"Well," I said, "well, we'll see. I'll be by on Monday morning and I might just have a surprise for you; I might even have a little two weeks' notice. We'll see. We'll see."

His voice went to a new level. "You quit, you have your caseload absolutely cleaned up, you understand me? No loose ends, no evictions, no new pregnancies or anything like that."

"No problem," I said. "I've got the neatest caseload in the whole east side. I'm on top of it like a big, throbbing drum. Be talking to you on Monday, then, Poirier; have a good weekend."

I hung up on him.

It put the tag end on the week.

After that, and because I already had the can opened, I figured I might just as well sit and finish off the beer; I could still make it to the Jewel on time or only a little bit late and since I was going to see it through three times anyway it wasn't as if I would miss much. Of course, it would leave a few loose ends in the plotting, but nothing I couldn't work up fast. All that I wanted to do was to sit and think quietly for a short while, try to purge Poirier, his conversation, the people upstairs, and the whole Department of Welfare out of my system for the weekend. Never a man for fast transitions, I needed a few more minutes to catch up on it.

About five minutes after that, some publicity stills came special delivery from Warner Brothers anyway and it was fortunate that I was there to sign for them; I had obtained them by advising the studio that I was publicity director of a large freelance critical bureau and it would have been the end of me at Warner Brothers if the envelope had been returned UNKNOWN or NOT AT HOME. So I thanked the mailman very much and gave him the thirty cents postage due and put the stills in the bottom of my dresser drawer with everything else to be sorted out sometime later and then I went downstairs to my car and went over to the theatre.

I was practically the first person into the place. The old woman in the window gave me that peculiar intense look mixing stupefaction and contempt which only ticket takers in neighborhood movie houses truly know and went past an even older man guarding the inner doors who was so numbed that his hand was barely able to reach out and make connection with the stub I handed him. Then, at last, I was inside the cool spaces of the theatre itself; irrelevant preparatory music bleating out from the lighted space under the closed curtain—they were holding back the start after all—and with a feeling of gratitude I found a seat in the middle of a middle row and camped into it. There were only two other people in the house; a teenage couple sitting down in the first row, already necking. The girl had long, thin arms which, coming bare out of the sleeveless sweater to encircle the boy assumed, in the muddled light, the aspect of chains; I wondered how he could stand being in there. But before I had too much time to think about it, the music cut off with the kind of high whine which meant that the needle was being drawn over the record and the lights went down and the different kind of music began.

So I leaned back, taking my shoes off, and propped them on the back of the seat in front of me looking at the screen, at a higher, more intense angle now, suspended above the people in the front row so that, for all intents and purposes, they no longer existed; suspended above even my own memory and the dismal events of the afternoon. Now, in the blackness, all things were truly possible: it was possible that I would go in to face Poirier on Monday morning and hand him my identification card and say, *listen, kid, I've had it; after three and a half years of escape and loss I've found my own private way out and I won't be taking this on anymore*; it was possible that in the mail on Saturday or at the very latest on Monday, before I went to work, there would be a letter telling me that my application for a position in the promotion department had been carefully considered and found to be acceptable and that I could report for work one week from the date of the letter; it was even possible that not once this weekend would the phone ring and the girl named Barbara, the one in my case-unit, would be on to ask me if I had any particular plans for that afternoon and whether or not I didn't want to try to straighten out and make a go of the job. Everything was possible in that first darkness of the theatre; that was the lesson I had learned a long time ago and held closely to me ever since; the permanence of dreams in the first fastening. Now the curtains were parting and past the title I could hear the voices of people, could see the people themselves, could see the girl, the first intimations of her breasts coming through the angle of the dress she was wearing: could hear the music, the sounds, could hear the bands playing and the familiar sweeping passed through me then, all the way through and out to the other side, and I was suspended somewhere in the overwhelming continuity of history moving forward, moving forward, always moving forward. I must have cried again with the shock of it, and then I had passed through.

In the mirror of the bedroom I could catch the reflection of what I had become and it was fine; it was completely in order and I had to think of it no more. Sophia turned to me, the harsh blackness of her dress striking against the whiteness of her arms and legs and the bedsheets and said to me, "what are you doing with yourself now? Can't you ever pay any attention to me? You look perfectly all right, now stop it!" Her voice speaks English with only the slightest laboring on the vowels whereas my own English is marred by harshness on the consonants; this strangeness somehow improving the way that we go together.

"I merely want to look well," I said to her, clucking slightly. "This is not an unimportant party you know. Possibly, my entire future in the organization hinges upon the impression which you and I give before these people tonight; so pardon a fastidiousness which is only a question, this one time, of being sensible."

"But Marcello, you are always this way. A big, big peacock." Over her face comes the familiar pout, half-leer, half promise. It is really too bad that I have long ago lost most of my passion for her, because she is a splendid looking woman. Time was when I could induce an orgasm—a very strong orgasm—simply by thinking about her for a long time and then touching her, very lightly, on the flesh of the shoulder; the stored release would come with a mingled sigh of pain and necessity. But for the last few months there has been a distinct falling off; a clear feeling that whole areas of thought and connection to her have been blocked off as if by slamming doors. It is a thorough pity, of course, but there is really nothing that I can do about it; I have other things on my mind.

"I am not a peacock," I say. "I am an executive ascendant which is something entirely different. The one makes an end out of appearances. The other makes an appearance out of his destination. I guess that that didn't come off very well, did it?"

"No," she says, "it didn't," and tumbles back on the bed, now, all hair and flesh, a whiteness on whiteness, her breasts, undisturbed by the fall, peaking tightly from her dress. "Why don't you come here and make love to me now?" she says with a smile. "We still have plenty of time."

"Because we would have to take our clothes off completely and it would ruin everything. You know how long it took me to dress."

She draws a finger over her lips. "No we don't," she says. "We can make love with our clothes on. All we have to do is to make certain adjustments." She hitches the skirt delicately above her legs, places a finger inside her exposed panties. A splendid woman, she has no need whatsoever of other undergarments.

"I wouldn't even have to take them down," she says. "I could just turn them to the side." She does so, showing me a slight patch of her pubic hair, the dark circle concealing the darker circle within. She raises her other hand, squeezes and envelops her breast, motions to me. "All you would have to do," she whispers, "is to let down your fly and support yourself on your hands with your feet hanging over the bed. We wouldn't disturb a crease in your jacket then; you exercise more drinking a cocktail. See, I'll even do all the moving." And her thighs began to gesticulate subtly, their curved inner surfaces coming together and parting, a suggestion of moisture trapped between them, then spiralling out onto the bed. Yes, I cannot deny it; despite myself, despite my cold, focussed perception of what she is trying to do to us, I am excited by her. And yet with the idiot temptation to move upon her whatever the consequence to the evening's appearances, is the realization that if I do I have truly conceded some point to her; a point which is such a mystery that I will not be able to understand her victory for a long time but which, nevertheless, has sent her in this way on the evening. "Sit up," I say, trying to be reasonable. "We have other things to do this evening. Later tonight, who knows?" It is true; later tonight, now, I would go to bed with her with joy and completion as if for the first time but now, despite the rising throb of my genitals there is a darker undercurrent, need, persuasion, the events to come. But it goes beyond her.

She drops the hand covering her breast onto an inner thigh; begins to curve and stroke it alternately, moaning slightly. "Marcello," she mutters to me, "are you such an entire fool that you cannot see my need?" And elevating her hips slightly she draws the panties down below her knees.

And now I see the whole of her; I see the whole of Sophia Loren exposed before me, her rounded ass, the soft curvature of the thighs, the secret of the *mons veneris* pulsing out its slow confession on the bedsheets and even though I am a movie star it proves to be too much; entirely too much for the likes of me ... even though the party tonight will be splendid and magnificent and crucial to any definition of my outcome, it is still too much for me. I remove the cigarette from where it has been dangling all this time between my pursed, quizzical lips, and putting an indolent but quivering hand on my fly, I move toward her. Now, in that intensity of anticipation I can feel the room itself contract, literally contract around me and there is that feeling of slow contraction in space which I have felt so often in screwing Sophia, and maybe this is one of the primary reasons why I originally lost interest in her; she is too intense. But those are all post-coital thoughts; what has seized me now is the outspokenness and idiot need of lust itself and, kicking my shoes off tentatively, one by one, I vault myself onto the bed and hang carefully above her, my body suspended on my clattering knees, reaching for my fly. She moves a hand upwards and helps me with it; there is an almost fatal snag halfway down and I think for an instant that I will have to wrench off the pants themselves, commit all of the evening to a kind of penance, but then the fly comes down easily with a slow wheeze, much as if it had made a difficult but determined choice and resolved to cooperate.

Hovering above her now, swimming in want and retrospection, I see her face. The eyes are closed and she once again has entered that slow passage where only the connection matters; I wonder, absurdly, as I poke and pry below, how many men have seen Sophia like this. Certainly, both in and out of the worlds she portrays in the cinema, both as creation and reality, she has never been seen like this; the eyes shuttered, the cheeks faintly puffed, the mouth itself curled in that slow, blinking sex-smile which both denies and implements what is going on below. For a moment, I would reach my hands out to seize her breasts, hold and remove them slowly from the low bodice but I must be firm, firm, so I think of her nipples one by one instead and remembering that we must be leaving for the party in no more than ten minutes, now, I hasten myself into need.

"Oh, don't you like this?" she murmurs, my actress, my nemesis, my wife, my tool, as I hover over her, "isn't this nice? Don't you wish, Marcello, we could just screw all the time and not get involved in those silly, contrived plots; this childish nonsense?" and her arms come around slowly in procession to enfold me as I plunge deeper and deeper into her network, finding an obstacle, withdrawing from the unseen, push, getting it past another way and now at last I have moved inside her all the way and delicately, tentatively, have begun my dance upon her, still wondering absurdly about creases in my clothes, loss, need, urgency, as I feel the convulsions from below. "I just wish we could get out of this movie and live our lives without things always getting in the middle," Sophia murmurs to me and I open my mouth to tell her, then, that she is wrong, wrong: that only the interception and contrivance matter, that only the interruptions are meaningful, lending taste and balance to this other, darker side, but I am unable to speak. Her breasts rise against me, her dress glides against my pants with a tearing, zooming sound and I feel myself spend to the last inch and then begin to drive clear in the high, white, detailed sensations of orgasm. I poise out over her, extended now in the need to plant, to generate and she spreads even further before me and then begins to reciprocate with a slow unfolding of her juices; I hear her moan and grunt and ease out below me. I feel the shudders of her hands passing slowly over my shoulders and the exhaustion comes on top of the coming but I cannot collapse over her; I cannot ruin my suit and thus my reputation and so I manage to part from her quickly, already overcome by the old revulsion, the old boredom, and pass off her side to the floor itself where I stand already instinctively rearranging my clothing. Her body curls out on the bed and then unwinds slowly. I can see between her thighs the first trickling indications of what we have done together.

"Oh, my," she says, "oh, my, my, wasn't that good?"

"Get dressed," I say, "we have to go to the party."

"But wasn't it? Wasn't it? Didn't you like it?"

"Yes," I say, "yes, yes," feeling that I must comfort her or the evening itself will be lost in the aftersulk. "It was all right, Sophia. But now I insist that we leave; we have things to do."

Drums clatter behind us and I sense we are ready for a transition. We hang in an undefined space for a time while I feel her assemble beside me, something that seems to be a thick, continental fog embraces us and takes us to its center. When it releases us from that grip, we are standing in a ballroom with several hundred people around us, being introduced. Sophia's garments cling to her now, it is apparent that she has done one of the most effective of all her reconstructions. In the crowd there seem to be some people I know: Fellini, Magnani, a couple of minor British directors and perhaps—although I cannot be sure—Elizabeth Taylor and Richard Burton themselves are there, entrapped somewhere between the *hors d'oeuvres* and a group of large, red-faced men who seem to be alternately shouting at or clawing them. It is that kind of a party.

It is precisely that kind of party; now, as I assemble myself toward its unfolding I can feel the decay slip through me, the corruption, the loss, the waste; the feeling of a Europe gone far and irretrievably past its best possibilities, now useless and irrelevant in the heart of its industrial wastes, sinking deeper and deeper into crime, pollution and elegant parties which can barely shield the rich, indolent and beautiful from the pain of knowing they are themselves. I inhale this feeling with a stricken and rising feeling of familiarity; this is what I know best, this is what I do best. Next to my increasingly provocative stream-of-consciousness, and my superb if rather mechanical performances with Sophia, the thing that I do best of all is to center myself at such parties, accepting with my swollen, descending eyes both the best and worst parts of myself; moving through them like the idealized tome of conscience itself as I drift into the rising inebriation, the rising despair, the settling remorse that these parties become. Casual, inflating slowly to the cloak of my attitude, I turn to Sophia who has stood loyally beside me, lifting my elbow slightly and say, "This is one of the worst parties

I have ever seen in my life. The bankruptcy, the depression; the waste of all of this. Where have all the real people gone?"

"You insisted that we go. You said it was vital to your professional career. Now that we are here, stupid, it should be quite clear to you that no one takes any interest in us at all; they are all playing their own pursuits." She is holding a very large martini in a glass the shape of a barrel and she takes a slow, dramatic sip, looking at me. "I could have told you all of this but you never listen, Marcello."

"Listen, listen, nobody listens!" I say, rather loudly, and feel the old rage move in somewhere under my mood, vitiating the situation, at a stroke, of the best of its possibilities. "Nobody listens to anything anymore at any time whatsoever; we drift ever further into obscurity, into masks, wine and chatter; the reality only a sceptre to guide us, staggering, through the last door of night. No, I cannot say that I like this. Why did the partners insist we come? Why did the partners say my appearance at this party was so vital to them? Surely, we would be better off in a small room, holding one another, moving past one another, looking slowly into one another, looking slowly through one another, blending and joining in the silence of postwar Europe, moving forward to creating itself; the candles whickering past the bedside, the moaning of doves—"

"Marcello," she says, giving my elbow a jog, "you are sometimes full of the most paralyzing kind of misconceptions. Really, you often make an impossible thing of yourself."

I am hurt. What Sophia does not understand; what she has never understood, is that this particular kind of plot imposes certain exigencies which, while they make the actors unhappy, cannot be helped. It is a postwar sequence with which we have very little to do; we are, after all, only there to commit a certain portion of imagination to reality. But this would be too deep for her. Everything is too deep for Sophia; all the publicity to the contrary, she is a simple, religious creature, numbed to the first level of response, more comfortable with ritual than with manner and thus obsessed with the need to define everything with which she comes into contact in terms only of a kind of ceremony. As this intricate thought hits me—and with it a kind of depression that I will, in no way, be able to make Sophia see this; were I to seize her breasts from behind, cup them urgently and do a tattoo on her buttocks she would still think that the world was a kind and simplistic place—I feel a severe depression and with it a necessity for flight. The fact of the matter is that I am sick of Sophia. I have been married to her for several years, I have done my duty; past routine fornication I have no more interest in her and I have already taken care of that for the evening. What I want to do now is to dismiss her.

This is less easily accomplished than thought; we are at a party populated by most of the reigning personalities and libertines of the continent but she is, nevertheless, my wife, and I am condemned by the contrivances of the plot to work out the evening with her at some basic level of contact. But there is a way around this, of course, which has to do with the accessory of plot. This is something which ordinarily I dislike trying because it breaks a certain consistency; causes even my handsome, knowledgeable features to grey with a kind of insecurity, but on the other hand, there are alternatives here which I feel it is vital for me to pursue. Besides, I need make no apologies; I have already gone to bed with her. I have performed sublimely, that is to say successfully. Past obligation, I assure myself, I have no further commitment.

So I walk away from her rather quickly, balancing a cocktail glass which someone has placed in my hand unevenly in the curve of my fingertips, heading for the cluster of people in the area of the Richard Burtons which, as I approach, dwindles; red-faced men with dim expressions of woe scurrying for the sides as they witness my coming. It is usually that way; it is not so much that I consciously want to be mean to potential rivals as it is a profound kind of inequity which embarrasses other men into retreat at my faintest gesture. It is not something which I would have willed that way; it simply happened. Behind me, through the haze and gloom and the thump of two prematurely copulating bodies already settling to the floor in a huddle of coats, I imagine that I can hear Sophia crying to me: *Marcello, Marcello, why must you wander? Cannot I alone satisfy you; there are so many people who think I am an entirety of woman,* but I pay it no heed. Sophia is like that. One must be very determined to escape her, as my superfluity of appearances with her in the public domain should long since have proven.

I am standing by Elizabeth Taylor herself now; her husband, shrunken by this engagement to realistic proportions stands grinning rather vacuously at the two of us and, attempting to show that he is not discomfited, awkwardly gobbles an *hors d'oeuvre,* most of which glances off his cheeks and onto his clothing. Demolished by this—the more so because he has been betrayed by manners rather than choice—he shrugs vapidly and says, "this is just one of those terrible, terrible parties. It would drive you to drink, that is what it would do. Drive a man to drink, that is if he had a drink fit for the drinking which is precisely what the scum here will never offer you. I recognize you; you come from this country, don't you?"

I shrug, not committing myself and reach out a finger to caress Elizabeth's shoulder lightly; coming out of the blue, strapless gown she is wearing it is enormous, an explosion of near-white rippling skin against the tighter sheen of her throat, the pearls casting their mysteries in reflection off the chandelier. "I come from all countries," I say to her. "Decay, waste, loss are universals rather than particulars, at least in the society which we have come to inherit. Wouldn't you think so?"

"Oh yes," she says, looking at me quickly, then back to her drink which is a muddy orange in color; it sets her dress off nicely, to say nothing of those large, bursting, Madonna's breasts fighting unsuccessfully through layers of bone to reach an accommodation with the good free air. "I couldn't agree more with that. Richard and I were saying to each other just before you came over that we hadn't the faintest idea why we were at this party at all; someone sent us this silly invitation by mail and because we had absolutely nothing better to do this evening we came. But it's so American, the whole scene here, that you could just throw up, that is if you were the kind of person to get easily nauseous. There is something about what Americans do to every place they tenant that can kill a good party."

"Nothing else to do?" I say, stroking the softness of her arm again and letting my eyes glance off her breasts; sensing dimly in the background her husband's recession. It is almost as if, in the extremity of this contact, he has ceased to exist: despite all his contracts, all his notoriety, all his literacy and fame, some complex apprehension has stripped him to the soul and left him vacuous. "Do you mean to say that you had nothing else to do this evening?"

"Well," my madonna says, "we could have done all kinds of things. But we didn't. Richard likes to go to parties and drink. That's his worst fault."

I look upon her fully now, let her see the knowledge growing in my eyes, the sensitivity of my face, that strange, piercing, glowing quality which reduces contacts with others to the level of a uniform and depressing pretension. "It all depends on the marriages, yes?" I say, "and the persons who are married to one another. Sometimes there can be too much to do, am I right?"

"And sometimes not enough."

I finish my drink in a remorseless gulp, my eyes like glass now, inspecting her, looking through the sheen and fullness of the dress to the skin underneath; the tired, workmanlike honesty of her body which I know, now, waits to receive me. I crumble the glass to ash between my fingers, cupping it beneath my hands, feeling the fragments sift like ash and silt over the corruption below. "Let's get out of here," I say.

"And go where?"

"Does it matter? To some clear quiet place by the sea, perhaps, where we can look upon the purer spaces of the moon and grasp ourselves. Anything away from this sadness."

Her eyes twinkle and I remember, gazing at their lost translucence, how beautiful she was in NATIONAL VELVET; how far she has voyaged from there and yet how inextricably, how peculiarly, she is bound to her past; like all of us doomed to act out small parodies of her history in lighted corridors. "My husband," she says. "You must understand how Richard feels about this kind of thing."

I shrug, another inexpressible, consuming Italianate shrug. "Where is he?" I ask. "I haven't seen him around for a long time, now. He seems to have disappeared."

"He drinks. He drinks all the time, Marcello. May I call you Marcello?"

"Yes. And I will call you Elizabeth Taylor."

"You can call me Liz."

"No," I say, liking the fullness, the rightness of it; the enormity of that devouring. "You are Elizabeth Taylor."

"He drinks more and more. I don't really know how to control him. It's like he goes out into a world of his own and I can't even touch him. Sometimes," she says, running her palms over the surfaces of the dress, the flesh of her upper arms trembling slightly at the effort, "well, sometimes I don't even know if he thinks of me as a woman."

"That is terrible," I say. I take her hand. It is time. "We cannot have you go on feeling like that, it does not befit you. We must show you that you remain a woman."

Her palm glides into mine, rapid, discrete, somehow self-enclosed, but she comes with me quickly. "Oh, I wouldn't say that I don't think I'm a woman," she says. "You've got to understand that a woman of my background doesn't have too many worries that way. No, it's just that sometimes, I think, the whole American corruption has gotten to poor Richard and it beats him down."

"Disastrous," I nod, with a journalist's briskness. "Absolutely disastrous."

We pass from the party that way, the two of us joined by our hands, her gown trailing over the floor; the rapid patter patter of my expensive shoes setting the basic rhythm of retreat. The crowd, which has been assembling in an ever-increasing horde around the now invisible copulating couple on the floor, moves aside slightly for us to pass through, purring in acknowledgement. Sophia herself is huddled somewhere near the *hors d'oeuvre* table, two pieces of toast clasped to her breast, her glass somewhere in the invisibility of the spaces between her breasts, tentatively balanced there. Once again I think I hear her reproach, sense her dimly saying something to me above the sounds of pain and mingling on the floor, the faint crows of delight that echo through the room,

but I am secure now, centered to my purpose, far beyond her capacity
to reach me. Besides, I wish to do nothing to embarrass Elizabeth Taylor; we are, after all, on a first date. So I leave a smile and a wink in my
wake for Sophia to pick up and interpret as she will and we pass
through the clattering, shuddering doors of the ballroom, into something
that looks very much like the corridor of an apartment building and out
into the cool, desiccate air of a muddled landscape.

"Take my car," she says urgently, producing some keys from the space
between her breasts. "I want you to drive my possessions; it will excite
me far more than anything else you could do."

"Where shall we go?" I ask, taking the keys, feeling their weight in my
hand, reaching up a palm to graze her shoulder.

"Away from here. I know an old couple in the next town who rent out
this room. We can go there and be alone."

"Well," I say, "that's perfectly all right with me." Old couples, young couples, middle-aged couples, I think ... when will this corruption cease? We
get into her car, a large Cadillac, from opposite ends and she slides close
to me on the plastic of the seat; I insert the keys and start the motor.

There is no transition. We are on a long, flat grey road moving past
the parking lot, moving past refreshment stands, past used car auctions,
past drive-in eateries where adolescents turn numbed faces in the twilight to watch us glide past, food poised at their mouths. If it were not
that I knew so much better, I would take the scene for an American
rather than Continental embroidery and this fills me for an instant with
distress—is the reel breaking up, are they about to jolt me from the camera's flash?—but it occurs to me that in the broken loss of the postwar,
all landscapes have become America, a generalized country of the
heart, and this idles my anxiety, fills me with a questing peace. I have
a fine, analytic journalist's brain even though, from my performances,
one would never think so: I perform vaguely "creative" duties I know and
have even written some essays upon the metaphysics of decay. Someday, far away from all these useless women, I will have to think more
on this.

We pass through forests ringing us on either side, the lights of cars
halving our bodies with their beams and Elizabeth drifts over to me,
takes my hand again, leans her shoulders heavily on my chest. I can feel
the throbbing of her heart through the even rising of her breasts and
on an impulse I free my right hand from her embrace and slip it into
the cold crack between her breasts. The smoothness and fullness of the
skin assaults me, a faint crack and smell of gunpowder drifts through
the car. It is not every day, after all, that one touches the breasts of an
Elizabeth Taylor; even though she is thirty-eight years old she was very

beautiful as a young girl in NATIONAL VELVET and won an Academy Award for having such large breasts and almost dying with them in the bargain. I feel my lean, perceptive loins quiver and she drifts a hand over them, pauses at the outer ring of my genitals and then works a tender thumb into a crevice she has created. I begin to bounce upon the seat in childish glee, pumping the brake pedal furiously, my despair and disillusion for the moment—for all moments, perhaps, while feeling and being felt by Elizabeth Taylor—forgotten.

After a long time, a long slow passage through this connection, the car seems to slow of its own volition; I see that we are approaching a large, twinkling farmhouse on the near side of the road from whose windows two absent, unrecognizable faces peer like doughnuts, looking down upon us. Elizabeth takes her hand away from me and stretches on the seat, moves up to a more proper position against me. "That's it," she says. "That's the place. They're always waiting for visitors here."

Superbly, careless of my accomplishment, I bring the car imperceptibly into the curve of the access highway, move it slowly through rubble toward an enormous gate which swings open before us, move through the plowed, brown spaces of the field into a small parking cubicle which sits before the house. I cut the motor and the two of us get out slowly; an old woman confronts us from the porch.

"Good evening," she says, before I have had a chance to properly introduce myself, to say nothing of Elizabeth Taylor. "Have you come to pay us a visit?"

The crone's features shift in the twilight and she assumes for me, then, an aspect of familiarity; if I were not absolutely convinced otherwise I would be sure that I had met her before; perhaps in one of my earliest comedies playing the role of a vaguely religious character. It is evident too from the way in which she looks at me that she feels this connection. But she passes through the moment with a gesture of dismissal which implies in its totality almost everything which I have been thinking this evening and says, simply, "how long do you want to stay?"

Elizabeth huddles more closely to me, her face against my shoulder. "As long as I need," I say, and then, as I feel her tremble, I say, "I mean, as long as the lady wants to."

"Is this lady your wife?"

"Of course. Do you wish me to produce evidence?"

The woman shrugs and turns away. "It is not necessary. The two of you will want the master bedroom, of course. That means that I will have to displace my husband for the moment."

"Oh, listen," Elizabeth says, "we wouldn't think—"

"Nonsense. You people come; you take the master bedroom. It is only fitting. Pepe is quite used to it by now; besides, he needs the air." She calls his name twice and a large man wearing loose-fitting garments, peers from an upper window, motions to her.

"Come down," she says. "The people are here again."

"I was just doing the crossword—"

"You do it in the kitchen. Hurry, Pepe, we do not wish to offend these young visitors."

The man withdraws, moves away and Elizabeth, still against my shoulder gives a small cry which might be pain or pleasure mingled; might be simple embarrassment. I fold an arm more tightly around her, watching the woman inspect us, possibly for signs of infestation. As she recognizes us—and I can see the knowledge sifting into her honest face with the interminable slowness and inevitability with which the sun must huddle, every evening, behind her house—a twitch of an eyebrow affects a shrewdness and she says, "of course, it will be very expensive."

"What will be expensive?"

"The use of the room. Pepe is a sick man; he is under doctor's orders not to come out of doors except during the evenings and then escorted, always escorted. Really, the quarters are quite pleasant, even luxurious. We will need at least several billion lire for its occupancy."

"How much would that be?"

"Twenty dollars."

I take out my wallet, give her two tens clutched against one another with tender familiarity, brush my hand over Elizabeth's shoulder. "We must not be disturbed."

"Of course not. We are very discreet people."

"Nothing must disturb us," Elizabeth says.

Pepe emerges from the house now, a small, spry man whose spirits and demeanor seem to render questionable his wife's gloomy medical report. He smiles at us, waving the newspaper. "Visitors!" he says in a shrill voice. "I love visitors. They are so profitable."

"Quiet, Pepe," the woman says.

"Perhaps you would know a four-letter word synonymous with *egress*? The puzzle is very challenging today."

"Later, Pepe," the woman says, showing him the tens and taking him by the elbow in a gesture similar to the clutch of my hand on Elizabeth but lacking the urgency of lust. "These nice people must not be disturbed. We can wait by the trees."

"I am merely trying to be friendly. The word is not *door*; I tried that already. I think it begins with—"

"Now, Pepe," the woman says determinedly and leads him away. His little legs scuttle over cobblestones, alternately losing and reasserting their balance; he weaves unsteadily in their wake. "I'll talk to you later," he says.

"Have a pleasant time, children," the woman says, leading him somewhere behind our parked car and from then on, as far as we are concerned, out of our lives forever. I increase my pressure on Elizabeth, lead her slowly toward the house. We move into its cool, small interior, feeling surrounded by wool and old odors, up a thin, dangerous stairway and get eventually to the room itself, a neat room with a bed, a nightstand, two ashtrays, a washbasin and a strange contraption which might be a toilet or some kind of purging mechanism. I close the door and turn to Elizabeth. She is shaking slightly.

"Oh, no," I say, feeling the old, creeping, Sophia-dismay rising within me. "You're not going to get nervous or depressed now and spoil everything, are you?"

"No," she says, sitting on the bed. "You know me. Of course not. I love good times. The only thing is that it makes me feel kind of cheap and spoiled."

"There's no reason for you to feel that way. We must find our love where we can and this is a lovely room."

"That woman knows. I tell you, she knows."

I am distressed that Elizabeth Taylor, of all people, is behaving in this manner. It makes me suspect her publicity, not that I would be so unkind as to say anything of this sort to her. Instead, I lean forward and kiss her gently on the forehead, at the same time working with my hands to free my belt, feeling it part with a crunch and underneath it, somewhere in obscurity, my pants. "Of course, she knows," I say. "That woman knows more about the human soul than Stendahl or the very famous Alberto Moravia. That woman has entertained, in this very room, the cream of Continental and American society."

"That crone? That hag!"

But this does not disturb me because I know that Elizabeth is known for her sharp tongue and cutting judgements of people; it is a blunt honesty which I expect to see complemented by frank and open passion in the bed. "She is a very wise, understanding woman," I say, "and she has done more for the betterment of society than even Freud himself."

"Well, it makes me feel very cheap."

I kick myself considerably out of my pants, working now on my shirt. "Come, come, Elizabeth," I say. "Free yourself of your clothing, as I am, and it will be beautiful. In the early gathering of sunset this room takes on the rich and dark hues of an immortal Autumn."

She sighs at this—I know her taste for poetry—and stands limply from the bed, begins then to work on her garments. The dress, which I had envisioned to be astonishingly complex, turns out to be a very simple, almost childish kind of thing similar to those bathing suits which small boys and girls will wear to the paddling pools on Sundays, for there is a zipper concealed in the folds of a side panel, and with one truly majestic sweep, she has taken it all the way down, the dress parting itself completely to reveal her standing before me only in her brassiere. She has worn no pants or other undergarments whatsoever. The rich, light scent of her—what I had taken to be in the car the smell of sweet auto grease between the axles—comes out frankly to fill all the spaces of the room and I look upon her with wonder, struck, even in the center of my own reputation and accomplishment, by the beauty of this international movie star. She bends a hand back awkwardly behind her brassiere, shaking her head slowly.

"Sometimes I wonder why you men are so insistent upon having all the clothes off," she says. "Richard is the same way. He won't do a thing unless we're both naked with the door locked somewhere. Just because animals make love without any clothes, must humans as well? Clothes, after all, are what bring us closer to the Divine; why can we not accommodate ourselves to them?"

I let this speculation pass. My shirt off, stripped to my multicolored garters and socks, I have found myself seized by excitement at the sight of her breasts tumbling before me; the nipples bursting to flower, the strange, hardened surfaces of the areolae a mystery themselves; the thick whiteness of the underbreast trembling slightly in the heat of the room. Now, as she raises her arms over her head, I find that I can literally no longer control myself; as debonair, assured and despairing as I must surely be, my cock sings a different tune at the sight of my lovely Elizabeth, kept for joining in this room, and I whisk toward her, both calves flying and grip her in a hard embrace, feeling her body slide up and against me. I hear her mumble something about the shade, about the need to get the shade down, about the light that is coming into the room but I cannot permit myself to release her—it is like a dream; were I to release her I might awaken and all of it would be gone—and so, instead, I sidle over to the shade still maintaining that grip, our surfaces bumping and jogging against one another, the touch of our toes and calves adding a not unwelcome and highly relaxing air of *commedia* to the proceedings. With my left hand I manage somehow to undo the string from its place on a post and get the shade down; I manage to do all of this while, below ships, my cock is making urgent, tentative contact with the hard, moist surfaces of her sex. She gives a squeal, somewhere between dismay and need, and still locked in that joining we prowl to the bed and fall upon it like a pair of assassins, her hands groping to raise her breasts to my lips. I stretch my palms into the small of her back to raise her into me and then, for a very long time, I feed upon her, feast upon her juices, swaddle my contemporary despair in the darker fluids that are rising all within and without us.

I am doing it to her, then, and with the keener, finer, more histrionic and detached part of my mind I am able to depart from the linkage to the degree that I can look upon it almost as a voyeur—I have always had this streak of perversity; it shows even in the mildest of my films— and this thought; this realization, rather, that I am doing it to a very big star, to a very important actress: that I am doing it to Elizabeth Taylor herself, enters me much as my cock must be beginning to prowl her and I swim with excitement and lust. There are not many people, after all, who have been fortunate enough to have been in this position with Eliz- abeth Taylor: this is something that has been restricted to relatively few men and it increases my excitement to no small degree. Thinking of this, lapping on her huge breasts, making myself believe that there is milk in them that will emerge in a matter of seconds and fill my mouth to bursting, I speculate what most men would think of me now; men, that is, who possess dull wives and no outlet—as could have happened to me if I had not known better than Sophia—men who had no wives and less outlet, men who came alone in the darkness to movie theatres and watched this woman on the screen, trying somehow, in an extension of their muddled hopes, to place themselves against the celluloid and so find the softness. As I bite her nipple, hearing her small whickering cries I think now of men who sit in movie theatres all over the world, men with grey coats covering their laps to conceal the frantic busyness of their hands from view; men who, immersed in the terrible economy and brutality of image, try to flog themselves through and into another level of feeling while I, Marcello, have the reality itself poised against me, sob- bing something about the dense air in the room as I move further and further on top of her, deeper and deeper into her spaces. I think about these men and as I do so it is not with arrogance nor even with pity but only with the kind of massive resignation and sadness with which one thinks of a brother fallen upon an evil, disastrous end, an old friend fallen into an unsuccessful speculation. It is, after all, partly luck that I myself am in this hole; I came from a very mediocre background.

Elizabeth shifts against me, her breasts still seized in her hands but pulled out of my mouth and as she begins to work on my ear with in- sistence she is whispering about her thighs, the necessity to go to her thighs, to enjoin them for cooperation, and so I move below, blindly now, shutting my eyes against this good fortune and bury myself, all the way to the tongue in the fur and odor of her necessity. Her lips thrash wildly, her thighs straining to engulf me and for a tense moment I think that I might actually be immersed; that I might swim and die in those foreign spaces but then another rocket of energy tears me loose, my tongue clinging to bits of hair and I return to her breasts, feeling like a voyeur's dummy—because all those departed brothers and friends indeed might be looking at me—but no less excited for all this explosion of good luck. Her breasts are before me again, this time without the benefit of support from her hands and in their massivity they roll off her chest, diving into sheets and pillows as I seek to recover them, all willing and neat, with my agonized mouth. She begins to murmur to me again; this time she is murmuring gracious obscenities with a hint of Brooklyn practicality behind them and so, then, I rise a little; I rise upon my knees; I swim in the channel of darkness I have created, I rise up all the way and then I plunge into her, the first strokes vapid and languid, then, as I accommodate myself to her contours, picking up in rhythm; moving faster and faster in that invisibility, the visitation coming to a clamorous end and I feel myself moving up all the way in her. Her face is turned to one side, her eyes closed against the load of Italianate ardor which I am about to place in her furthest spaces and then as she sighs and stretches back, her stomach and genitals pulsing in a lostness of their own I squeal—I can distinctly hear myself squeal but it is a delicate European shout; there is nothing animaline about it—and throw my load all the way into her, gasping.

And yet it does not stop there; this is Elizabeth Taylor and for her I carry on the longest sustained orgasm I have ever had in my life; far, far longer than the ten or twenty-second specials which I have managed for Sophia; it is as if the mysterious hidden triggers are blocked inside me on OPEN and I hang at the very crest of it for an incredible, for an almost frightening extension of time, feeling that because this is Elizabeth Taylor herself this time, I may literally never stop coming and my hands reach again for the remote hugeness of her breasts and I subside finally, breaking upon her, all sobs and shouts, mingled in the warm and sheltering spaces of the room.

After a long time, we disentangle. There is really nothing to say. We have solved our anomie in difficult and separate ways, blended together for an instant's shout. I light cigarettes and hand her one, slightly chilled by our excesses and trying to show her, now, by the poise and control of movements that I could not possibly have been the one who squealed like a goat; no Mastroianni would be capable of something like that. No, it must have been an illusion, must have been her own shout hurled back at her; it is known that I come silently and with great force and control, my face twitched at the crest in a quizzical, correct, interrogatory sneer. She begins to fumble for her brassiere, her face open now with the renewed knowledge of love. There is a knocking on the door. We are both beautiful people; there is nothing to fear from our discovery. I get up from the bed, go to the door and open it. Pepe is standing there, a newspaper flapping. His face apprehends slowly the state of our clothing and condition but it does so without lust; rather the multifarious creases and curves seem to settle even more deeply upon his skull. He shows me the newspaper.

"I found the word," he says, showing it to me neatly written in in a painful, senile hand and I agree; he has certainly found the word. "Can I come back in now? I'd like to rest on the bed."

"Well, we could use a few moments—"

"Doctor's orders," he says and puts a wiry elbow into my ribs, brushing me to the side and proceeds toward the bed.

I look back of me to tell Elizabeth that it is perfectly all right; to comfort her but—not surprisingly—she has already gone, disassembled completely and vanished. This is not the least of her witchery. I would think upon it further but I feel a wrench at my own vitals.

Creased into the seat, so deeply riven into the folds of it that it took me a long, wrenching effort to get free, I slowly reoriented myself, hearing the thud of music behind the screen, the sound of iron curtains closing. Before me, the teenage couple seemed to have disappeared below seat level, only an occasional flying ankle or arm indicating that, like me, they were still with the picture and themselves, but my view was cut off by the heads of two old ladies, who had, apparently, come in sometime during the movie and it was difficult to see. It was even more difficult to move but self-discipline was vital—it is only by a deliberate excess of movement after a movie that I find myself able to be restored and I have no desire, even at this point, *not* to be restored—and I managed to get a wrist up, check my watch, which said in sly luminescence that it was 7:00 and that, apparently, I had already sat through two showings of YESTERDAY, TODAY AND TOMORROW. Between my stomach and head there was a vague feeling of disconnection, probably caused by the beer I had had with nothing following—it is a very bad idea for me to go to a movie having had nothing to eat—but I was able to fight my way through that and forced myself into a standing posture, and then into a vague, shambling, somewhat terrified walk which took me out into the empty aisle and through into the lobby. It was an unusual day, there was no question about it for I had rarely felt so drained. Usually a double feature or a consecutive showing of one film will leave me vaguely chilled and in severance from any real sense of past for a few moments, but the weakness, the sense of drainage this time were something entirely new. It had been one of the most powerful exercises yet; a sheer vault past the extraneous into the center of need itself and abetted no little by the women themselves; it was very rarely that I possessed more than one woman during the span of a movie, let alone two beauties such as these. It was too much for me. It was, all things considered, simply too much for me. I had the feeling that one of my clients might have had if his welfare check went scuttling from him on payment day, lost purposes dwindling down the street, his feet in hopeless comic flight; in just such a fashion did I feel myself trailing, unsuccessfully, after my consciousness. I paused before the candy counter and looked at the glow and winkage of the popcorn machine for a few minutes, then decided that it was probably not popcorn which I was after at all. There seemed to be a wind in the lobby; a feeling of being a gnome trapped in a small, bat-strewn cave. I turned and saying *the hell with it, the hell with this; I'm tired, I don't really know what I want to do so I better get out*, left the lobby and came into the warm, dim spaces of the street and finding my car in the parking lot, starting the motor and moving out slowly, I decided that all the experiences of the evening having been equal—as they usually, usually were—I might as well get the hell home.

II

Which I did in fair order.

Underneath my door, shoved half in and half out was a note from Poirier. It was about what I would have expected from the louse; a 40-year-old Unit Supervisor who had spent fifteen years in the field before his promotion six months ago and who took every action of a subordinate as a deliberate, premeditated attempt—probably in collaboration with higher levels of the Department—to put him right back there again.

Dear Mr. Miller:

The ordinary kind of Unit Supervisor would let you hang yourself and forget the whole thing but since I was heading out your way anyway and since you're one of my most experienced workers, I thought I'd drop this brief note off under your door and try one last time to help you see the light. I won't even try to talk with you; I have nothing to say, I don't want to get personally involved with anybody here at all.

But you should understand that your conduct can lead to no good, either within or without the Department. Your dreaminess, your laziness, and the clear suspicion I have that you are falsifying visits and leaving the field earlier lead me to believe that you are undergoing an emotional crisis of some sort; probably with something that I have no knowledge of whatsoever at all. That's perfectly all right because it's none of my business but we must learn to separate our professional lives and our emotional lives; you've got to keep one in the one place and the other in the other as I have learned from long years of work and living, Mr. Miller. I have no interest in helping them to bring charges against you so why don't you devote this weekend to straightening out whatever seems to be bothering you and come in Monday with a fresh attitude and ready to work.

Your Supervisor,
JAMES POIRIER

That was fine. I took the note and cross-sectioned it absently, tossed it into the basket in the kitchen and seeing that it was 9:30, decided that it was time for another beer. I got one and sat down in the grey chair in the center of the room resolved that I would have a quiet evening, that I would just let the week drift over me and assemble itself at some obscure place in the rear of my mind, but I couldn't. I was jumping, still jumping; the images sweeping over me, the power and passion still throbbing within; a circle of need that worked between my groin and skull and drenched itself nowhere. I had gotten more than I had bargained for at the Jewel; perhaps it was the peculiar, slippery nature of the seats, perhaps it was only the long-delayed and therefore explosive release of tensions which had accumulated; in any event, I did not feel like a quiet evening at home—although this was probably what I needed more than anything else; I needed to contemplate, I needed to reassemble. There was the question of how I would handle Poirier on Monday to say nothing of the stream of offers from the talent agencies and movie promotion departments that I was expecting.

I put the beer away under the chair—I didn't need to drink; drinking would either ignite something dangerous within me or, worse yet, drown the fire, leave me numbed and absent, ready only for the cove of sleep—and went into the bedroom, opened the bottom drawer of the bureau. Looking at the thickness of the package they had sent me, its weight and substance, I thought that I had hit something strong but when I opened it, tearing strips front and back, I found that it was only some kind of combat picture—some kind of liberal combat picture because it was a mixed cast and nobody seemed to be enjoying shooting in the stills—with very few women and, as far as I could see, absolutely no action whatsoever. I went through all of the stills carefully and it was true; there was nothing to it. The flack copy was an equal kind of dullness, having to do mostly with the biographies of the nonentities who were in the film and with disgust, I put the whole mess back into the drawer—I never throw out a thing, not a single thing, not ever—and went back into the living room.

I was jumping. I was on edge. For a moment the perverse impulse to call Barbara was strong at hand; she lived with her parents for one thing, and for another, she did not seem to be the kind of girl who would be going out on a routine Friday night. What I would say to her and precisely what I would do when I saw her I didn't know although it would have had absolutely nothing to do with sex. I was looking for diversion. In some unwanted pocket of the mind I could see a small figure fleeing, darting down a long corridor, its pants askew, going in search of connection.

It was that kind of evening.

In ordinary circumstances—there was precedent for it; I had felt this way before—I probably would have gone out again, found something to watch in the all-night theatres on 42nd Street where even though the company was distracting and the films jumpy in the palsied hands of the projectionist, it was possible, sometimes, to do something decent. But things were more or less resolved for me when the phone rang. Strangely, I was glad to hear it. I would even have talked to Poirier. *Hey, Poirier*, I might have said, *I'm just going crazy for tail this evening, do you have any ideas? Maybe you could get free of your old mother and come over and talk about it for a little while.*

But it wasn't Poirier at all. It was Barbara. A proper *deus ex machina* to save me from a dangerous evening.

"Martin?" she said. "This is Barbara."

"Oh, hello," I said. "How are you?"

"How are *you?*"

"Pretty good. Feeling no pain."

"I understand you had quite a day."

"Now and then. Now and then."

"They're really out to get you, Martin. They were having conferences all afternoon and I guess it was about you."

Barbara was in Unit 83, two rows behind me, a location which gave her a good view of Poirier's broken profile most times, to say nothing of my shoulders and back. Despite the fact that I knew exactly who she was and had even had lunch with her twice—long, dull lunches in the liquor-license luncheonette across the street surrounded by dishes filled with pickles and the haze of exhausted gossip from the welfare center—it was hard for me to recall, at this moment, exactly what she looked like. The connection was not there; to say nothing of any comprehension of why she was calling me. I hadn't called her; what was the difference?

"I don't care," I said. "I couldn't care less. Me, I came home and had a beer and went to the movies."

She giggled, a shade hysterically I thought. "You're too much, Martin," she said. "Those things that go on with those people don't disturb you at all, do they? I mean, it just doesn't have any effect on you."

"I just put in my time there. I give them the six, seven hours a day and that's it. I punch in and punch out. When I come home, that's when my life begins."

"But they're trying to fire you, Martin. They really are." It sounded as if she was squeezing her face against the receiver, almost absorbing the mouthpiece with her lips as she said this; an image whose absent lasciviousness filled me with such horror that I had to move the phone away from my ear.

"So I'll go on to other things. It's just a stopping point; just a stopping point. Who stays with the welfare department?"

"Well," she said. "Some people. I have. But the thing is, I wanted to check on you and see if you were all right, that's all. I was thinking about you. I'm concerned. What if you got fired? Where would you go?"

"I think I'd manage. I'm angling with a couple of movie studios for a promotion job. There are other things. I don't think I'd starve, you know."

"Oh, I didn't mean that. I didn't mean that everything wouldn't work out. I just meant that it's tough to lose a week's salary, two weeks' salary before you get straightened out."

"Well, I've saved a little," I said.

There was one of those thick, deadly pauses when a conversation has worked out its best possibilities and can only hover between cancellation and a kind of choice with neither being, in any sense, connected back to what has already happened. I let it hang, weighing things, letting the movements shift in my mind and heard the sound of her breathing stirring in my ear. Back in a far distance I could see Sophia's face: it was leaning toward me with a look of concern suffusing the features with something approaching woe, as she moved it forward, the lips curved, her neck and then breasts came into view, bare, shimmering. A hand reached out through an infinite space, moved to brush me then fell back, and the face receded, receded. I could sense myself following that diminution, trying to chase it through some telephone wire of need and loss and desire but it was gone; become stone in some vanished place.

I could hear her voice murmuring: *Martin, Martin* but then it faded.

"Martin?" she said. "Are you still there?"

"Yeah. I was thinking."

"Oh."

"Look," I said, and for a dull instant could not recall her name and then when it came back to me it was with such explosive relief that it triggered the sentence without any difficulty at all, "Look, Barbara, you want to get together this evening?"

"Oh?"

"You want to come over and we'll have a drink or something?" She lived with her parents; I could distinctly recall that much and that made the ploy clear; to the degree, that is, that I wanted any ploy at all; what I really wanted was wandering in the dim spaces, untouched, but I wasn't going to get it; I wasn't going to get it any more this evening.

"Well I don't know. It's kind of late."

"You can take a taxi. I'll pay for it; no problem. I've been having trouble with the car, getting it started and so on or I'd pick you up."

"Oh, that's not necessary. I could make it over there all right. But it's very late, Martin. I just called to find out how you were feeling, what you were doing."

"So come over and I'll tell you about it some more."

"I don't know if I should. It's been a long day. And I don't know if I should go out for the night."

"Come on," I said. "It'll be nice to see you outside of that office and talk."

"Well," she said, "All right. But you don't have to pay for any taxi. The subway is right here and it's direct. I'll see you in a little while, then."

"Okay."

"Do you want me to bring anything?"

"Just yourself. That'll be fine."

"Well, okay," she said and hung up. I hung up too after a while, shoving the phone back into its receptacle on the couch, getting up to look at the walls and the grey patches of light that showed under the curtains. The point was that I didn't really know what the hell I was after, anyway.

She lived in a dull, lower middleclass residential area near the sea with a direct but incompetent subway line between us which meant that at this time of the night I could figure on twenty-five, thirty-five minutes before she came into the door full of questions to say nothing of advisements about my future in the Department of Welfare. I was still trying to remember what she looked like and under the new intensity I was almost sure that I did but it wasn't worth it; I would see her soon enough and the evening would proceed on its way. I supposed that I would end up laying her; it would be the second time and if it was anything like the first I could be spared this one, but the concern she seemed to be feeling might lend some kind of urgency to the conjoinment so it would beat anything else that I could do; not that there was anything much on my mind. There was nothing at all on my mind.

I had about half an hour, then. I decided, for the hell of it, to take a quick look at Sabrina while I was waiting.

The small eight millimeter projector came out of the top shelf of the closet quickly enough; the reel was right where it should be in the cannister neatly marked: SABRINA—44-26-38. I set it up on battery, put the reel in and cut the lights, using the closed wall of the kitchenette for the projection space. There was the usual clicking and whirring and the film jumped a couple of times so that I had problems with shaking fingers getting it in right but finally everything was set in tight and just for the hell of it, I was gliding, gliding in: a slow, murky viscosity seeming to settle down upon me from some dwindling spaces and coalescing me, almost painfully, into a kind of attention.

I have finished with the shooting, finally, the camera put to one side, contented that what I have got is no better or worse than what I am supposed to have; swaddled in my professional photographer's pride of office even to be held out against the flower of temptation that is still stretched before me on the rug, thighs crossed heavily over one another, breasts, even in this posture thrusting more upwards than out, the nipples open and vulnerable to the harsh lights. I switch them off and look at her with a professional appreciation that, in the aftermath of the shooting, turns to another kind of awe, and I say, "Well, Sabrina, we're pretty well packaged up. I guess you can get dressed."

"You've got something you want?" Her voice is high, almost piercing; it would be irritating were it not that it comes from the full, dark complexity of her throat, the colors of the skin played off against the brightness of her breasts. There is no question that she is very limited, even a child, but I still find her enticing. There is no reason to deny it.

"Everything. Absolutely everything. It will be all over London a month from now and all through America in six months and throughout the world a year from today and you and I will be very, very happy. The magazines will be waiting in line to buy pictures of you, Sabrina."

She stretches her arms over her head. "You're quite sure now," she says, manipulating her breasts so that they bobble uneasily yet gracefully in that precarious position, the nipples tightening slightly. "There isn't anything more that you'd like to take."

"We have every possible angle covered."

"How about my breasts? Were they showed off to their best advantage?" She cups them, moving her buttocks slightly, now. "Wouldn't you like to get a few like this?"

"We have several sets like that. You'll get cold there now, with the lights shut off. Why don't you get up?"

"Well," she says, letting her breasts subside and pulling herself to her knees, the high crown pulsing against the slight fold of her belly. "If that's the way you feel about it."

Despite myself now, I can feel the urgency rising within me, can feel my genitals pout and protrude. I try to sweep the excitement away with an index finger, because I am a professional nude photographer specializing in pornographic and semi-pornographic sets and yet I find this very difficult, feel the bob and twitch against my finger to indicate that this time I am in real need. I have seen very few women like this; even though Sabrina came to me with unusual credentials, I admit that I did not anticipate that she would be like this. It has been a very difficult set.

She comes up to me, rests the softness of her inner arm against my cheek, caresses my lips, while another vagrant hand grabs my genitals gently and begins to manipulate them. "Why I believe you're excited," she says. "I really think you are."

"Only a little. Not as much as you would think."

"It's perfectly all right, you know. All my photographers go to bed with me. All the directors of those films they make me appear in end up in bed with me too. I'm not embarrassed. I love to fuck. It's the only thing I really care about." She inserts a nipple delicately between my teeth; looks at me with a kind of contented astonishment as I inhale it, rub my tongue against it; explore deeper communion. She raises herself on her toes and embraces my risen crotch with the vise of her legs.

"You don't even have to take your pants off," she says. "Not if you don't want to. I know how we can do it standing up and all you have to open is your fly. Believe me, it's all the same to me. I'll take it any way I can get it. I love fucking. I love to feel it in me. My breasts hurt me all the time unless they're getting sucked. My thighs itch unless there's a big cock lying somewhere in the center. Don't be embarrassed. Everybody does it. It doesn't mean you're a bad photographer. Go ahead; go ahead, baby, bite it."

I bite down further on her nipple: helpless, floundering, underneath this a current of dim rage that she, this woman, this property can do such a thing to me and yet behind all that is only a vast immersion; I am lost in her flesh, in that dark softness, in the vanished folds, turning slowly, beginning that basic insertion with the turning feeling of a corkscrew. Somehow—I am not sure exactly in what manner—my fly is opened and I feel myself being sucked slowly straight up, my prick rising at an almost ninety degree angle from its base, some genius of accommodation enabling her to greet me at that angle. Her lips move over my face, loose, wandering, absorbing and my hands rise to touch her breasts; I hear faint gruntings and she begins to pulsate on me.

And so, then, surrounded by all the network of camera apparatus: by rods, by flashbulbs, by stems and wirings, by klieg lights and by the priceless load of equipment itself I begin to come, feeling myself moving from the storm-center of need into a fruition of contact, her breasts bobbling in my hands, possessing enormous flexibility in this posture; rising, virtually to be dumped, one nipple at a time into my mouth. *Oh, you're so good, Bill,* she murmurs and for an instant I wonder who Bill is; my name is not Bill; I sign all my photographs ANONYMOUS so that I will not be blamed for the inanities of my models, the venality of the publications in which they appear, the peculiarity of the audience that savors them. But I have no time left for wondering, the time is ripe for rising and so I move the last tortured inch into her, hearing the pounding, feeling the pounding: all inside and outside of me there is pounding now, thudding, a feeling of entrance and I try to push past it to the last glow of fire but the pounding gets louder; it gets louder still, it racks and overwhelms my being, moving down to my muddled cock and forcing it to dip and swerve at the last crucial instant. I groan with rage, trying to move past it but the pounding increases; it is getting louder and louder, now, and it is apparent that it is more outside than in; more discovered than central and as I try one last time to merge past it it becomes louder still and I realize that I am wrecked and stifled and Sabrina must feel that too because her breasts turn to glass, pulpy glass that shatters in my mouth and her frame turns to water coming unglued and dripping in my hands and then the light, the final explosion of light crashes down on me, leaving me stiff and pinned to the floor.

I got up slowly, listening to the click! of the projector, hearing Barbara's bumps and shattering on the door increase in volume, not to say franticity. It was as if, standing there, knocking for me, it had come to her for the first time now—the possibility that I was not at home; that I had constructed an intricate ploy for no other reason than to shame her. Feeling the shooting pains in my genitals, the feeling of looseness and uncoupling so rare and yet so known and yet always so terrible I feel a perfect rage for this girl sweep through me but I put it down, turning off the switch, putting on the lights.

"Okay," I said in a dwarf's voice, and then it moderates to a more credible level. "I'm coming. I'm coming." I left the film in the projector—there was no time for niceties of concealment—and staggered to the door, opened it, looked at her. She looked no different; in that moment of locked composure it came to me that I still wasn't sure exactly what she looked like. It was not her fault. She was just that kind of girl.

"Well," she said, coming in, "what happened to you? Where were *you?* I was beginning to think that you weren't home."

"I was in the bathroom."

She entered with that air of familiarity which women incur for any apartment that they have fucked in, no matter how briefly or unceremoniously, looking absently at the furnishings and at the projector. "Why do you have that out?"

"Some rushes. Part of the interviewing process, the studios send you some clips of forthcoming movies and you're supposed to write your opinion on them in about 500 words. It's one way in which they find out how you're qualified."

"For a promotion job? They want you to act like a critic just for a job in promotion? You said you were looking for a job in the promotion department. I can't understand it."

"It's pretty competitive. It's a tough industry to break into. I've been trying for quite a while but I'm just beginning to get somewhere."

"What's the movie?"

"Just an eight millimeter reduction of something. A western."

"What's the title?"

"You've never heard of it."

She shrugged and sat on the couch while I fumbled the reel all the way out of the projector—there was no sense in being an ass; there was no sense in taking any chances—and crossed one leg over the other while I put it back into the can and shoved it all under the machine. Now, from this perspective, all of her was coming back to me; the totality of Barbara's appearance: the bright cheeks with freckles faintly imbedded on them, the thin, somehow graceful body with small, desperate breasts that prodded their way through an indifferently hung sweater, the large, vague luminosity of the eyes that seemed to take in everything and comprehend nothing. She had looked to me that way before; in the instant of sexual completion and at all the other times, a girl who somehow was a denial of all the richness going on within and without me and yet one of those girls with such a positive conviction of her sexual identity—I had known the type—that absolutely nothing could shake her; a dim aura of desirability, imagined or not, seeming to whirl slowly around her. She crossed her legs. "Can I have a drink?" she said.

"Why not?"

"Only if you will, though. I don't like to drink alone. But sometimes, cooped up in that house with my parents on a Friday night I could scream. The weeknights aren't too bad. But usually I try to go out on Friday night. I can't stand it; they just haven't any understanding of what's going on."

"I've already had a few beers," I said. "I don't really feel like drinking. I could have one, though, and watch you, I guess."

"That would be lovely. I'll have a scotch."

I found the almost unused bottle on the bottom shelf and poured her a drink, straight. When I turned to ask her if she wanted ice or anything else, I found her looking at the projector.

"Well, I think it's pretty silly too," I said. "You would think that they'd ask a promotion man to take a test promoting something; give him a screenplay and ask him how he'd plug it. But you know those studios. It's not the most rational industry."

"Nothing is."

"You want anything with this?"

"I'll drink it straight."

I gave it to her, went to the refrigerator and took out another beer, sat down on the couch a good distance away from her. I could feel the strain rising, rising in the room; a strain, perhaps, that I could break simply by reaching for her and immersing myself in the qualified battle that would follow, but I couldn't do it. Sabrina was still in my loins; the night close around me. So I opened the beer and drank about half of it as quickly as I could, noticing with gratitude that she no longer seemed to be interested in the projector now that I was sitting next to her.

"I really want to talk to you, Martin," she said. "That's what I came over to do. There's something very wrong with your attitude and I don't want to see you get into trouble."

"My attitude is fine. That's why I am in trouble."

"No it isn't. I've been watching you. It's like you aren't even there in that welfare center any more. You're always someplace else."

"I should hope so."

"It isn't a question of the job. Everybody hates the job. I hate the job. I wanted to be a teacher but I don't have enough education credits and they wouldn't give me a special license so I've got to sit around there and take evening courses. But that doesn't mean that I don't do my work."

"I've been there for a long time, Barbara."

"Well, I've been there for a long time too. I've been there for six months which is long enough to know everything that's going on. I don't know, Martin; I just don't know."

"Look," I said, "look, Barbara, what's the difference? What do you care what I do? I tell you, I'm on the road to another job and none of this matters any more. I can laugh at it."

"Are you laughing?"

"All the time."

"Well," she said, taking the glass inexpertly and finishing off the fair amount of scotch left in it at a single gulp; all things considered, she took it pretty well although her next sentence started with a gasp, "well, Martin, I just care about you; about what happens to you, there, I mean. Is there anything wrong with that?"

"No. Of course not."

"Then you've got to straighten out. If you don't, nothing's going to work out for you."

And suddenly, then, I was tired, tired; I was tired of the inches of manipulation, the rhetoric of defeat which would move slowly, inevitably to a weary coupling; I was tired of solicitousness, tired of the girl sitting across from me. I wanted to be only in a small theatre somewhere, a gnome huddled in darkness spinning my life away; I wanted to be in my old car on a highway leading from here to there, a clean, white space where all things would fit. But I was past that too; I was past any hope of huddling, or flight ... not with this girl in the room. So what I did was quite simple. I put the beer can on the table and took her scotch glass from her hand and, landing both with a clatter, I moved forward and put an arm around her. In that posture she looked at me, almost sullen, unresistant, and then her face broke open with that knowledge which had always been hiding there, waiting for just such a trap, and I put my hands firmly on her shoulders, hoping that I had enough spirit left in me to see the scenery through and then I drew her toward me. I kissed her, working my lips quickly, I moved a hand down to search for her breasts, I clambered against her. *Haste, haste.*

And so what we did then; what Barbara and I did was to have a kind of sex; an equivalence of sex it could be called, I suppose, bearing as much relation to the act itself as my position in the Welfare Department did to the career in the movies that I was sure I was going to make. I brought her sweater up to neck level, unfastening her small, straining bra, and took the short length and weight of her left breast in my hands, feeling the nipple pulse; I rose under her buttocks until she fitted against me and then, praying for function while I suckled and wandered for the other breast, I gave her what she wanted; I gave her what she needed, locked in some other space far above her, watching all of the water recede. Her breasts spread over her chest like small, dotted pools, her thighs spread and spread until the accommodation was so easily made as to be shocking and poised over her, I came to a final kind of resting, feeling everything within diminishing.

After it was over, she lay beside me for a while and said, then, that she had to get home; her parents would ask questions. I told her that she could stay the night if she wanted and she said, no, no, it wouldn't be right but there would be other times; other places where it would be beautiful. So I helped her dress and gave her her coat and another scotch while she pulled the various segments of her being back together again and told me that I was a perfectly reasonable man but I had to understand the realities of situations; I could no longer deny them, and then she allowed me to guide her to the door, the surfaces of her body huddled against me fishlike, until I gave her a kiss and set her on her way. She clutched my hand in the hallway and asked me if it hurt and I said no, it didn't hurt at all; nothing hurt as much as you thought it would if you only came to terms with a situation. So she touched me again and left me, taking the stairs, disappearing down them bumpily and when I knew that I was alone in the hall I sighed once, twice, heavily and went back inside and did the little cleaning that needed to be done and then for a few minutes I watched Sabrina again but although it was pretty good it was, necessarily, not the same. So I went to bed and entered the final cove and thought of nothing for the next ten hours, thought of nothing at all.

That was Friday.

So much for Friday.

There were other days.

III

Saturday, the Strand had an old Bardot film which I had no intention of missing. They were running a retrospective that month, the best from the hottest, so to speak, and since this film had been one that I had missed on the first go-round and since the Strand was almost nearer to me than anything else on the local circuit, it figured to be the anchor point of the day, something really exceptional. I picked up some more stills out of the mailbox and a letter from Hollywood telling me that my request was under consideration and then, without even a cup of coffee, I went downstairs. My car was parked directly outside—sometimes, on Friday nights, if you get back early enough, you can pull off a stunt like that—and for no clear reason, I had the obscene feeling, when I first came to it that somewhere on the opposite side, on the two doors, would be scrawled obscene statements and warnings; some sentences that would be so poisonous as to force me to come to terms with the fact that I lived in a Very Bad Neighborhood. But the surfaces of the car were as blank, that morning, as the interior of my groin seemed to be, and I got in without ceremony and as unobtrusively as possible, got away from the curb.

The Strand started running at eight o'clock on Saturday mornings and then went straight through so there was no problem in timing; none at all, I was on a fully rational journey to a meaningful destination. Nevertheless, I could not get over a dull feeling within me as I drove that morning that there was something entirely disreputable about what I was doing, that I had no business being on the streets at that hour; that I belonged either in bed huddled next to a girl or out on a sports field doing something useful. What it came down to is that I found myself thinking vaguely about exactly what the hell I was doing and I found that I didn't like it that damned much. It is not possible to like too much in the world early on a Saturday morning and I tried to tell myself that it was all a generalized woe, a generalized depression come out of too much pressure, too little sleep and the purposeless joining with Barbara the previous night but somehow I couldn't quite duck it, not all the way. The question, above and beyond everything, was: *why the hell was I doing this, anyway?* And I wasn't entirely sure that I knew.

I didn't know for the same reasons, clearly, that nobody knows why he ultimately finds himself in a given position; our condition at any point in our lives—barring natural catastrophe or what are referred to coyly enough as "acts of God"—is a compound of everything that he has done or wanted to do, or failed in doing and I was no exception; I was only a kind of totality, an obscure working-out of numbers. But I could feel the numbness and depression working through me; moving through in circles until it camped behind my ears, squeezing itself there into an obstacle of woe, then working behind my eyes until I could feel the apprehension of tears. Yes, it was going to be a bad day; there was no question about it because there was no fighting the seizures when they came, I had had too much experience the other way. The only thing to do was to ride with it; once every other month or so everything that was within me was going to back up into a slow, muddy, dripping flow and until it passed beyond, there was nothing to do. I found myself thinking vaguely of Barbara; repressed a mad impulse to pull the car over to a street telephone and get her up from bed and say: *listen, baby, nothing that happens between you and me touches me in the least little bit; not any of it at all, so you just better come off this*; better than that, I could phone and get her father instead, rouse him from the Saturday-morning sulk that seemed to be the normal state of any regular working man and say: *what do you know, I screwed your daughter in my apartment last night and I didn't even like it that much; I seduced her right into my bed and had her all the way and for all the difference it makes to me she might just as well not have been there at all because who the hell needs her?* But that would have been as pointless as the first way; I wanted nothing to do with them, nothing to do with either of them, nothing to do with people at all.

Near the Strand there was a small pornographic bookshop, nothing special but well-stocked and interesting enough for something way outside the main stem of the industry and on impulse I decided to drop in there; I was in no hurry to get to the movie and the way things worked out at the movies it didn't matter what time I got into them anyway; what part of the plot I walked into because it all worked out the same. The point was to look over some good pornography and jolt myself out of the mood in that fashion; it had worked before. So I parked the car at a meter, hoping that my friend would be open and he was, a feeble bit of light glinting through the shaded windows, books and pictures swaying slowly in the windows, a sound of thumping within. I went inside and, of course, it was completely empty; the proprietor probably in the back room checking over some new merchandise, some stills, perhaps, that he had been mailed from California. I looked it over disinterestedly, not really interested in buying, just trying to get the flavor of it all in, the easy relaxation, the cold numbness that a store full of this stuff always seemed to induce in me.

He had changed his setup slightly since the time, some months ago, when I had been there last; at that time, things had been arranged more or less by publisher or by category so that the paperback books were ranged on one side of the room and on the other the photographs and small pamphlets nestled against each other, surrounded by marriage manuals and recordings of natural childbirth. This time, though, things had been changed so that they were arranged, instead, by category: the heterosexual stuff was on the near side of the store both left and right and in the back, on a series of long shelves, the more or less perverted stuff was set off by various divisions: the whipping, leather and flogging stuff was on the far left, the necrophilia and bestiality and natural childbirth were toward the center and all of the homosexuality and lesbianism was on the right. The way he had done it—and it was ingenious, you had to give him that; nobody had any business in the field at all unless they were ingenious—it was possible to go over to exactly the kind of fetish you wanted and make your choices, rather than wander aimlessly all over the store, getting into embarrassing predicaments when you were chasing heterosexuality and found yourself looking too closely at ADONIS. Also, the customers could be segregated by type which would lead to far less embarrassment and mixing; the homosexuals could take one position, the leather and flogging boys another and the few trembling heterosexuals that peeped into the store could stay far away; could avoid being contaminated and sacrificing their tentative and probably very hard-won interest in girls. It was a very strategic arrangement indeed; not without aspects of originality and I could appreciate it because if I ever decided what I was truly interested in in relation to pornographic bookstores, my friend would make selections very easily for me. But now that I was in the small, humming cave of the place itself, I realized that I hadn't the faintest idea of what I wanted or why, precisely, I was there in the first place. It was very puzzling.

Perhaps the clanging sounds of that puzzlement attracted the proprietor; at any rate, he emerged from the rear of the store slowly, looking at me without much interest and took up his station at something that looked like a podium a few feet above floor level. I tried to show more absorption in the materials as he sat unsteadily and looked at me but it wasn't easy; furthermore, as it became quite clear to me that he not only didn't remember me but hadn't the faintest intention of talking. I felt an acute embarrassment slide over me, a feeling of enclosure and final entrapment and I had to put down a maniac's impulse to grab two or three of the nearest packets of pictures and run giggling from the store. I didn't know what the hell I wanted to do; that was precisely the point but somewhere on the far rim of consciousness swam Brigitte Bardot, looking at me from some enormous height, her soft breasts reduced in their fullness by the distance, her eyes all-encompassing, somehow knowledgeable.

"You looking for anything special?" the man said in his elf's voice. "Anything you want I may have."

"Nothing in particular. I just came in to browse."

"Well, why don't you give me some kind of idea; maybe I could help you. We just got a whole shipment in from California the other day. Plenty of stuff in the back we haven't even unpacked yet."

"No," I said, "I'm just in here to browse, to look around." Pointlessly I added, "I'm really on my way to see a movie."

"Oh? Well, we got movies here too. Sixteen millimeter stuff, anything you want. Give me an idea."

"No, a regular movie. A commercial movie."

"Well, I got movies that'll give you a lot more than you could see anywhere downtown. Why don't you let me know—"

"No," I said again, "I'm not interested. I just thought I'd have a look, that's all. Don't you remember me?"

He leaned forward slightly, peering at me as if from a far greater distance than a few feet, then straightened up again. "Sure," he said, "I remember you."

"Yeah."

"I remember all of my customers. You come in last week, almost every week. You're one of my regulars."

"No, I came in last about three months ago. I don't come in very often. I bought a film from you, then, the Sabrina clip."

"Oh yeah? Well, you look like one of my other regulars. Oh, sure, I remember you. You bought the Sabrina clip in here. Well, what can I do for you today, anyway, son?"

I couldn't answer that. I wasn't even sure why I was there; why, with Brigitte Bardot already moving slowly, densely, across the old, pitted screen of the Strand, I had come into this place. To think about it was, perhaps, to edge deeper and deeper into an area not worth consideration. So instead I said, "how's business?"

"Oh, you know; you know." He moved back slowly against the chair, folded his hands, looked at me cunningly. "What's the difference?"

"Just asking."

"Why ask?"

"Forget it," I said, putting back the plastic-wrapped photographs of some obscure 45-26-33 model I had been looking at. "Just making conversation. I'll be on my way."

"Well, listen, anybody comes in here asks how business is might have more than business on his mind. You follow?"

"I'm not a cop," I said. I resisted an impulse to take out my welfare identification card and show him that one: *I'm in a different branch of slaughter*, I'd say. "Just an old customer."

"Well, no offense at all. No offense meant, no offense taken. What I'm doing is perfectly legal anyway. You can look it up, anywhere. I even got a license."

"Okay," I said.

"Besides, the fact of the matter is that business ain't too good. In fact, it's lousy."

I drifted past a row of magazines showing young boys on the cover, blots of darkness against their genitals, and into the more rewarding area of lesbos where on the front of most of the magazines, girls appeared to be doing violent things to one another. "Why would that be?"

"I can't answer that. I've been around too long to know any easier answers than that. I think there's too much competition."

"Competition?"

"Other things, other interests. The guys got too many other things on their minds, now. Always chasing here, chasing there. You can't build up no steady clientele anymore."

"That's too bad."

"Time was, you had a nice steady group of customers that came in time and time again; repeat business, you know? Now, a guy comes in once, buys or doesn't buy and you never see him again. And that's another thing. You got too many browsers now. Guys just don't come in and buy the way they used to. Now they stand for hours and look at the stuff until they go crazy. Does it take so much guts to just pick up something and buy it? What's the big deal?"

"Couldn't imagine," I said. "When I want something, I just take it. Nothing to it."

He half rose from his seat now, gesturing to me; apparently he had wanted to talk almost as much as I had although not, evidently, to the same purposes. "Trouble is," he said, "that the word got out that this stuff is for perverts, that only perverts come in; a guy gets himself labelled as some kind of sickie if he touches my stuff. So he doesn't want to identify with it, you know what I mean? It didn't used to be that way. But the newspapers and the magazines and all those sociologists got hold of it and now, automatically, if you buy a picture of a little piece of tit, you're a homo or a rapist or out to get a gun. It isn't fair. Guys can't put up with that."

"It doesn't bother me."

"I could tell you about all the customers I used to have: the nicest guys in the world; married men with families, fine people, businessmen with orders to meet and big salaries, and they'd come in all the time and pick up a little something and they'd be happy; I'd be happy. College boys used to come in here; boys with scholarships from the best backgrounds, and they'd be happy to have a little something. With their responsibilities they didn't have the time to chase tail; they just needed a little something to keep them off the streets, that's all. But now, you go into a little place like this and you buy a pocketbook to read on the subway going home and you're a madman, a pervert. The whole thing's changed."

"It has," I said. "It's changed a lot."

"And it's changed for the worse if you ask me. What's wrong with the whole business anyway? I ain't bothering a flea. But you keep guys from getting something they want in a place like this and they can get themselves in real trouble; they get full of tensions. *Then* is when you get your perverts and rapists. Not when they come in here and get a little something to ease their minds."

"But look," I said, putting back a lesbian magazine and drifting over now with a dark sense of relief to the heterosexual section; looking at the covers of magazines with names like BROAD and BURSTING which in the context of the other things in the shop now seemed innocent, naive almost, less numbing. "There are a lot of places in midtown, you know. There are more and more than there ever have been. So maybe—"

"It's not the same," he said, "it's just not the same at all. Sure, you got a lot of those places opening up; you got a lot of those places closing down too. They don't stay around. They're just fly-by-nights; got no loyalty to their clientele, they just try to grab a buck and another buck and then pull stakes and move somewhere else. What you got to do is to build up customers through the years, have a real relationship with them; give them some place where they know they can always go and get exactly what they want. These guys don't figure that way at all. Besides, they ain't really selling what they say they're selling. It's mostly an under the counter racket with the stuff used just as a front."

"What kind of stuff?"

"Now, how would I know? I'm not running that kind of business. Drugs, numbers, heroin, all that kind of stuff. The merchandise they sell up front doesn't have anything at all to do with the real business. Now, how can I compete with that? I'm a businessman, what I sell I sell and everything you see around here is for sale and there's nothing hidden that ain't. What's good enough for me is good enough for my customers; I'm not pushing anything else. You want to buy something, son? You just can't stand around there looking at things; it just soils the merchandise and makes it hard for me to sell to the other guys."

I took a copy of something called STROKER off the stand and told him I would take that, then went over to the other side and got an eight-photo set of the model with the forty-fives just to show him that I wasn't trying to buy conversation cheap; just to show him that I wasn't any kind of pervert. Whatever I had wanted to find in the store I had either gotten or not because it was clear that it was time to leave; I needed to get into the air, back to my car, and off to the movies. There were other, if somewhat dimmer worlds. So I bought the magazine and the set and he wrapped them in grey paper with scotch tape and told me that because business was slow, he would knock 20% off anything else that I wanted to buy, now that I had those two.

"No," I said, "that's all right. I think that these are fine. Nothing more right now."

"You buy something else now; you don't have to come back so soon. You can use this stuff up pretty fast, you know. It seems like a lot, now, but by the time you get right down to it, there isn't so much. You want to get a special price on some film?"

"I've got film at home."

"Yeah, but you're a movie fan; you said you were going off to some place downtown. You can always use another little something."

"Not just now," I said. "Maybe later."

He leaned toward me, showing me the crevices in his face; the small, deep wrinkles under the eyes, the hard cheekbones of his special insight. "We got some clips of something in from Australia; you've never seen anything like this girl in your life. I'll guarantee you. And she has some strange habits who she likes to do it with."

"I tell you, I don't need it. I don't want it now."

He leaned back, clicked his feet underneath him. "Okay," he said, "that's your loss. I could have made a nice price for you; a really nice price. But it's the customer's decision."

"Maybe some other time."

He was already far away from me, his eyes moving toward the ceiling, backed into his skull. He waved a hand. "Anytime at all. No hurry. See you again."

"Thanks for the fill-in."

"Oh, yeah. Just a question of my opinion, you know."

I went out quickly through the open door; on an impulse yanked it closed behind me, sealing him up in his cave. Then I went into my car, tossing the package underneath the front seat so that even in the event of a serious auto wreck, the cops would have a hard time pulling it out and tracing it back to me. Then I went over to the Strand, driving slowly, feeling that faint distension and elevation at last; the old pre-movie feeling that I had not yet had this morning and which probably had been the center of my difficulties. I felt calm, calm; the calmer for the package underneath me which I knew I would never need because I had something far, far better. I got the car into the almost empty parking lot, locked it up and went inside, past the beaten old lady in the window who looked at me without interest, past the thirteen-year-old ticket-taker and into the cold spaces of the theatre itself. I had had nothing to eat so I bought a box of popcorn at the counter, tipping the girl five cents so that she would forget about me instantly and then, holding the popcorn under my arm I went into the theatre itself which was even emptier than the Jewel had been yesterday; really drafty, abandoned, a feeling of blasted hopes hovering around the wide, dim spaces penetrated only by the ticking of the projector and the hollow voices in the huge room. Brigitte was on screen, doing something innocent with her thighs and calves as she immersed them into a small pool of water, surrounded by trees and birds and the tiny sounds of spring and as I slid into my end seat in a near aisle, clutching for the popcorn so as to not drop it, I was lost already; I was already lost, sharing fully with her that tentative and graceful commitment which exists at the borderline where dreams and memory touch, never to part again.

We are walking on a beach, the two of us, a long, abandoned, salty trail of sand and earth somewhere in some nameless part of the continent, our hands linked, our eyes moving toward and then past one another as the gulls cried. Because Brigitte, on one of her mad, gay impulses, had plunged into the surf further up the beach and had gone into the water up to her careless neck, the dress now clings to her with the desperate embrace of a sinking lover; showing in its subtle transparencies the outlines of her body as she sways with me. For a woman in her early 30s she does not look bad at all; in fact she looks extremely well—better, perhaps, than Brigitte has looked since she was thirteen and knew nothing about movies whatever—but even in the face of all this beauty, this devotion; even in the aimless lover's pose we have concocted out of Brigitte's necessity and my cooperation, I can feel the slow, hard roiling of withdrawal within me; a kind of retreating which, even in the contact of her hands, makes me feel that I am not so much reaching toward her as withdrawing, withdrawing into some cold, hard chamber of self. It has been this way for several weeks now; despite all the despair of our passion and all the lies which my French soul has tried to whisper to my brain, the fact is—and can no longer be avoided—that I am tired of Brigitte; that in some obscure way she bores me, and that I need desperately to get away from her. I would not have believed this when our affair began a year ago, when the frantic marriage culminating the affair was performed in the small chapel three months after that because at that time Brigitte's flesh and spirit had entered into the most necessary, because hidden, crevices of my being and swimming in some complex compound of envy and desire, I felt myself literally unable to survive without her but—as with most of the women with whom I have dealt since adolescence, in or out of marriage—my accomplishment has muddied those fine emotions down to a kind of tired necessity and, to be fair about it, I am sick to death of Brigitte. She is so Gallic, that is the trouble; Gallic and wasted and irrelevant; it is the American women who, like their country, are so vital and deadly and more and more I find my creative and directorial thoughts turning to those fine, young postpubescents who would surely galvanize me into an approximation of my old energy. But I can tell none of this to Brigitte; none of it at all. The major problem is that my kitten is not only insensate but stupid; we deal only at the lowest order of communion which tends to make our whole relationship faintly poisonous, faintly superfluous. I wish desperately, at this moment, that I were in Cannes; surrounded by starlets, displaying my latest film at a massive gathering while small, ingenuous girls circled around me, wine glasses in their hands, showing me and me alone the fine, deadly lines of their breasts.

Brigitte pauses for a moment, letting her feet sink into the sand and dabbles in the water. "Roger," she says in her small voice, "Roger, I feel that I'd like to swim again."

"Don't be ridiculous," I say. "The water is cold and besides, it is the late fall, now, you would get a deadly chill. Hold my hand more tightly and let us walk."

"But when I want to do something I always do it, Roger. Besides, this vacation was supposed to be a way in which we could gratify all of our impulses and really get to know each other. You said it yourself, Roger; I'm not telling you anything that you didn't say." Already her mouth is edging into the familiar, the hated pout that with Brigitte either signals the beginning of sex or its end or the involution of her limited personality into some area that has nothing to do with sex at all; of all these, I do not know which is the worst. So, in compensation, I clutch her hand more tightly and try to hasten her walk; try to hasten her toward the cabin in whose direction we are headed, hoping that by the time we get there all may be forgotten—this small, child's whim—and that we may be able to find oblivion one way or the other for several hours; tonight there will be a large party on the other shore at which Brigitte and I are guests of honor. But she will have none of it, crouching to her knees in a small pool of water that the sea has thrown onto the shore, putting her palms in that water, running them through it and then passing the fluid onto her hair so that it runs down to her face, giving her a blotched, off-center appearance; something which my director's heart finds vaguely repellent.

"I want to swim," she says. "Maybe if I go out into the water like this I will get very chilled and get pneumonia. Then you will have to hold me, Roger; you will have to hold me very close in my chill so that I won't die. Wouldn't that be nice?"

"Brigitte, please don't be ridiculous. We have things to do this evening and, besides, it is very cold out here. Let's go home and sit by the fire, together."

"But I don't *want* to sit by the fire," she says petulantly, cupping her breasts in one industrious hand and examining them, through the material, carefully while with the other she flicks some sand in no particular direction. "I want to do what I want to do and besides, Roger, you're no fun anymore. We used to dance by the shore; we used to touch each other very much in the night. It was like with Sacha at the beginning, even better because you're more famous. But now, it's entirely changed. I don't think that you love me anymore, Roger."

"Of course I love you. Brigitte, will you get away from that surf; you will get terribly chilled and we'll have to see the doctor and you will be very unhappy and I will be very unhappy and our vacation together will be spoiled. Brigitte, you must be an adult and stop indulging yourself. How many times must I tell you this?"

She stands slowly, her fine eyes regarding me, her hands moving to brush her forehead; the small, womanly slope of her breasts framed in profile against the sea. Now, almost, almost, I regret what I have said; regret what I have meant, because Brigitte is a child and there is no point in hurting a child, but before I can say anything—before I can raise even a tentative hand and tell her that at the root level of communion, no matter what else happens, we are still lovers—she darts from me and, her buttocks swaying energetically from side to side, she plunges into the sea, moving quickly toward the furthest of the waves.

For a moment I am stunned; I do not realize what has happened. It is like one of the slow or stop-actions in my many famous films; the freeze of motion where, for an infinitely extended moment, there is only the slow pattering of limbs toward disaster against the frieze but then, as it becomes apparent that Brigitte has truly plunged toward the ocean, into the ocean itself—and Brigitte cannot swim—I feel the fine shreds of panic enveloping me like cords. I really cannot afford any scandal; not with my reputation and with various unsavory—and completely false—jokes circulating around me because of my marriage to Brigitte; not with the pre-festival favorite already entered in the Cannes and Lincoln Center film festivals. As it becomes clear to me that this child, this nymph, this bitch might actually try to drown herself and in the doing destroy the two of us forever—both the living and the dead—I feel the rage coming over me and beyond that the panic; I tear my sweater from me and not even bothering to undo my pants, I race out after her into the sea. Behind her, behind me, drifting back to the vacant shore, I can hear the crow-cries of her child's laughter as she diminishes into the surf.

I plunge after her, feeling the cold and darkness of the water tearing at my ankles almost absently, from some far distance, concentrating only on that removed, diminishing dot in the sea. It seems for a while that it will be far, too far; that I will never reach her before she brings the water up to her chin and dodges on the precipice of suffocation and my movements, somewhere between swimming and running, become increasingly frantic; I feel myself being gripped below in a hold as solid and essentially unremitting as Brigitte's own convulsive embraces but then I am free, floating, thrashing, swimming on top of the water and Brigitte herself has stopped because I can see that I am approaching her at higher speed; the distance between us diminishing with every gasp as I immerse myself in the water. When I come upon her, she is completely halted, looking absently toward gulls in the far distance, her hands joined clasped before her, and she turns upon me with the indifference and blandness with which she might greet an aged, frantic relative speeding out after her for reunion on the Metro. Brigitte is that volatile; there is really nothing that can be done with her. This may be the primary reason why I really cannot stand this marriage anymore and feel that I must have given into the oldest and most juvenile impulses of all by letting her entrap me.

She folds my hand into hers and then into her stomach. "Isn't this beautiful?" she asks. "If it were sunset, it would be a beautiful sunset. Even so, it is a beautiful afternoon."

"You could have drowned yourself!" I shout. "You could have been dragged in by the undertow and never seen again! Have you no idea, now, Brigitte, what a fool you are?"

She shakes her head. "Oh, that would be impossible," she says. "I only went out to wish myself upon this beautiful sunset that is not there. I had no thoughts of drowning myself. You are so emotional, Roger. You must learn to be placid, like better directors and like me." She draws my hand upwards to her breast and I can feel it tensed against me in its watery pouch, the nipple itself pouting. "A lonely isolated beach giving way to a lonely, isolated ocean. How lovely that is."

I feel the fury upon me. "Your poetry is as execrable as your impulses, Brigitte. There is nothing isolated about this ocean; it is filled with death. Come back with me to shore."

She shakes her head, pushing my hand further against her breast so that with my unresistant forefinger I can probe the mysteries of her inner nipple itself, a feeling of porosity; a passageway to other rivers. "Stay with me," she says. "It's perfectly safe. Let's watch the sun come down together."

"It is cold out here. Can't you see I'm freezing?"

She turns to me, places her hands on my stomach, slipping the tentative shape of her fingers inside my trousers. "Don't worry about that. We can warm you up."

"I don't want to warm up, here! I want to get the hell back to the beach and get home and warm up! Do you want us to catch our death of pneumonia in this surf?"

Her hand becomes a cup, moving ever deeper, further into the pocket of my groin. "Hold me," she says.

And as she says this, as her hand comes all the way down to enfold my directorial scrotum, as her other hand comes up to drag behind my neck and bring me down for one of those absent, grazing, grinding kisses which are all Brigitte knows of oral love, I feel the idiot stirring within me and even then I know that I am lost; I am lost again, it is going to be the same cheat upon me that it has been all the other time, the cheat that begins in ephemera and vacillation and ends as a blanket hurled over me, a blanket to smother my sensibilities; a blanket to muddle fear and flight together and leave only the darkness of combination. I try to fight this mood even as I try to fight the erection that has darted between her whirling fingers but there is no hope. There is absolutely no hope at all. I cry, a cry like a bird, like a gull, like a sea-creature and bend into her, the full weight of me, the full consistency in her palm and my hands reach to the top of her dress to take it down. She whispers something pointless and idiotic—like everything which Brigitte has said to me these days—and rises on her toes to assist me and in a juvenile's eagerness, a juvenile's desperation I wrench it down to her thighs, trying to do it for all one would know, as if I had never seen her breasts or box before; carried back to that primal curiosity which is the beginning of destruction.

And she stands before me then, bared; the slight heaviness of her breasts drifting midway between her navel and the chestline, the fine, light markings around her chestnut genitals which are neither as bright as her hair nor dark as lies; the lips already visible from this angle; grotesquely, moistly parted, the waters lapping at them. She hurls her arms tighter around me and tries to draw me in, in and it seems impossible that this could be accomplished because my pants are bunched tightly around me, almost transparent with immersion. But somehow—I am never quite sure—this is done, the pants are lowered to my ankles. We are standing waist deep, thigh-to-thigh in the water and, somehow, she raises herself slowly against me, her thighs curving, her hole opening as she moves to my neck and coming out at a helpless, desperate seventy-five degrees it is impossible for me not to enter upon the gaping cave she has constructed for me; a cave full of moths, voices and light, a cave fit to die in and so I go into her, feeling her breasts bounce and jostle around the lines of my mouth; feeling her nipples erect with a flourish and then point into my mouth. It is easy to suck at them from this angle and I do so, hoping, absurdly, that there is no one on the beach watching us. The scandal would be terrific if Brigitte Bardot were seen to be fucking, even if her partner were her own, famous husband. I feel my orgasm begin to attack me with whimpers.

"Am I better?" she murmurs, biting at my earlobe with her teeth while she bounces for joy atop my rod. "Tell me, Roger, am I better?" For a woman whose body acts as if it were entering upon the last throes of completion, she is very calm, indeed.

"Better than who?" I moan, almost oblivious of the waters, oblivious of the particles of silt passing around us, oblivious of everything but her flesh, my need and that one still, deadly voice coming out unnecessarily from the center. "Better than what?"

"Better than those other girls you're doing it with? Am I, Roger? Tell me, am I?"

"I don't understand," I mutter, feeling myself rising, rising, now set for the explosion itself, poised on its rim and yet held back by that questing voice. "Who? Who?"

"Sophia and Elizabeth ... and all the others. Am I better? Tell me I'm better, Roger, or I'll stop. I'll move away."

I grind her to me, trying to hold her against that flight but I am weak in my necessity whereas she is strong in her demands; I can feel her flesh almost dissolving between my hands; her breasts shrinking like rapidly deflating balloons, her hole itself retreat and sharpen to a hair's edge in the waters. "No," I say, "no, no, no, don't do that. Stay with me. Stay with me." I am quite helpless, quite lost. Even the least of women can do this to a man—and may they be damned forever—when his need is past stopping's point.

"I will, I will. Tell me if I'm better or I'll go away." Her face swims, shrinks in my hands. I feel carried to the river bank of a kind of collapse.

"Yes," I grunt, "yes, yes, you're better; of course you're better, Brigitte, you're better than anyone. Better than anyone; better than best; better than all of them, better than any."

"Do you mean that?"

"Yes, yes of course I mean it."

"Better than Sophia?"

"Oh yes. Yes."

"Better than Elizabeth."

I am still trying to drive back into her, Brigitte's box a blunt edge against that insistence, her thighs clamped. "Yes, better than Elizabeth. Far, far better."

"Better than that American bitch, Jane, that is always on your mind? Better than that little cunt? Am I? Am I?"

"Yes, yes, of course you are."

"Bigger breasts, smoother flesh, better thighs, richer face, hotter comes, longer fucks, more come, more?"

"Yes, damn it, yes."

"Out of your mind? All of them? All out of your mind?"

"Yes!" I scream against the waves, "yes, damn it, all out of my mind," and she opens like a giant, uncoiled spring against me and the connection is restored but ever deeper this time; ever, ever deeper and like a mad dog unleashed my prick dives further and further into her; further and further toward the core, her nipples grazing my cheek, her hands energetically dragging me into her, my cheeks inflating then as I inhale her flesh and the slow lingering begins then, the premonitory twitches and jerks of finality and I launch into her like a starlet into her first picture, ballooning all the way up and up and so, almost unconscious, negligent of opportunity, I must have come that way, crouched to my ankles in the water, gasping on the water, the whole pendant self of her crouched over me as the rushing and the tearing came over, the sound of birds far removed and throughout it the beating of that gigantic pulse which I had put deeper and yet deeper into her most secret heart of hearts.

"Excuse me," a cracked voice said and there was an explosion of light against my eyes. "Is this row taken?"

I opened them; found something obscurely grey standing beside me, a small figure behind it. "Oh," the usher said. "I'm sorry. Were you sleeping?"

"No. I was just watching the movie. That's all. Thanks a whole lot. I appreciate it."

"Well, I'm sorry, young fellow. But the lady here wants to get a seat and we've filled up pretty fast. Do you mind letting her in?"

"Do I what?"

"Do you mind letting her in?"

I was barely conscious of the existence of legs below my belt. Somehow I shoved them in, poised against the back of my seat as something that might have been an old lady staggered by, grunting, and collapsed two seats away from me. The light went off.

"Thanks a lot," I said again. "The manager might like to hear about this. I'll just let him know."

"The manager doesn't pay me enough salary to make any difference. You go right ahead and get me fired; the trouble with you fellows is that you get so absorbed in this damned tripe that you think you're the only people in the theatre and then, where are we?"

"Well, I don't know. Where are we?"

"Right here," the usher said and went away, leaving me trapped in sweat and the sound of thin ticking. I was not even sure of his/her sex. Before me, the picture was still going on—it had something to do with Brigitte's romance with some kind of a guitar player—but I found it im-

possible to get with it for a few moments; stoked with my own fury and
with the vague memory of what had happened a few moments before
that. They were always vague memories, that was the point of it; after
it all happened, it was almost impossible to recall exactly what had happened—which, I suppose, was one of the blessings of my gift among
other things—but it was clear from the shakiness both within and without that it had probably been major, central, almost a prefiguration of
sorts. I tried to plunge myself into the screen but it didn't work, simply
wasn't working for me, so I nodded a few curses at the bundle of clothes
decamped on my right and threw the popcorn box which I had still been
clutching underneath the seat; went out to the lobby for another. They
had apparently changed employees during the film because a red-
headed girl, about nineteen, was behind the counter, surrounded by
weary old men who seemed to be interested in more than the candy and
popcorn she was trying to give out, but from the moment my eye
caught hers it was clear that even in this crowd, I was something special. We hated each other from that instant, that was all there was to
it. It would have been impossible for me not to have hated any red-
headed nineteen-year-old; not after what I had gone through was there
any coming to terms with the type.

"What do you want?" she said, breaking away from the men—who
weren't doing much buying anyway—and coming over to my side.

"Some popcorn."

"Aren't you a little too old for popcorn, baby? Maybe some crackerjacks
would be more your speed. Or a Mounds bar."

"I want some popcorn."

"It'll ruin your lunch. How you going to have a nice lunch with all that
junk inside you?"

"Damn it," I said, feeling the old, vague, desperate feeling; I was not,
in movie theatres, prepared to deal with anything of this sort although
elsewhere, there was nothing I knew better. "I asked for a box of popcorn. Now, do I get it or—"

"You get it," she said, picking up a box and going over to the machine.
Her breasts, in profile, weren't bad but obviously supported by the stiff
threat of bone, underneath. "Certainly you get it. You think I'd deny a
nice-looking young fellow like you a box of popcorn?" She drew it out,
thrust it down in front of me. "Twenty-five cents," she said, and chewed
some gum at me. "Or twenty-four if you pay very fast and get out."

The impulse, then, was not to slap her so much as it was to go directly
to a phone booth, call Barbara and order her down to the theatre. I could
order her down to the theatre and she would appear; her breasts small
in the sweater she wore but breasts nevertheless, her thighs tight and

small against her skirt but thighs all the same ready, at any time, to greet and receive me. I could bring Barbara before this girl and clutch her around the shoulders with one hand while I raised the fingers of the other to this redheaded bitch and said: *look here, now; I don't have to take any of this crap from you because I have a girl myself; I have a girl and here she is and here are her breasts and there's no way in the world that you can say that I don't know those breasts, haven't had them. So you just lay off me before I make some of that trouble you're begging for because this is my girl and that's all there is to it.* But I didn't do any of this at all, of course; I was not that kind of a man. What I did was to take the popcorn with one hand and give her the quarter with the other and then I got all hell out of there as fast as I could without seeming to be timing retreat; back into the doors, into the cool, inner spaces. The theatre was not as crowded as the usher had said; the majority of heads were clumped within four or five rows of one another in the center. I wanted no part of them at all, much less the old lady who had come past me. I went down to the very first row, past all of them, easing in toward the center; something that I very rarely did because it was extremely dangerous for the eyes; there was no doubt about it. The eyes could get into very serious trouble if you saw pictures from close up, to say nothing of the head and the interior of the brain. But it was too much; it was too much, it was all sweeping over me, the isolation and purity of the first row enveloped me and without even being quite sure of what I was seeing I was lost again; I was utterly consumed, a deep, cold sheet of silence coming over me as poised somewhere between popcorn and a final kind of testing, I watched what was trying to happen to me, happen.

I am virtually on the doorsill itself, poised for flight, when the voice stops me. It nails me with its assurance, its positiveness, its righteousness and leaves me stricken, suspended in that position, wholly unable to move. The voice knows exactly what it is saying. There is no way to get away from it.

"Listen, Marcello," the voice says, "I do believe we've had enough of this. Now it's time we had a talk and came to an understanding. I can't stand your acting like this anymore."

I turn slowly to face her, to face my wife, to face Sophia. It is unquestionably her; only a little worse for wear for all that she has lost the previous evening, and as I look at the fine, cold mask of her face closed tight over her cheekbones, I can see that I—a major, international movie star, one of the most famous, beloved, wealthy men trapped on the surfaces of this accursed planet—even I am in for some trouble. The face is unremitting. Meanwhile she crosses her arms; shows me, even in her anger, the more delicate, softer outlines of her upper arms coming from the black, sleeveless dress. Sophia makes herself up as carefully for a quarrel as for bed; maybe more so. This may be the key to all the difficulties in our marriage, although I am not sure that this is so.

"You go out and I'll lock the door," she says. "You'll have to sleep with one of your sluts all night and you'll never get back in. You'll have to see your slut with all her crust off, with her hole filled with your juices. You won't like that, Marcello. I know you; you really won't like that at all. So you might as well come back and we'll settle this. And don't try to look so debonair and astonished with me; it won't work with your Sophia."

I close the door, move back slowly into the room. Still pinned to my hand is the large valise filled with deodorants, unguents and contraceptives which I had told her was filled instead with the business and documents which would keep me late at the office tonight; once, so shortly before, it had clung to me with the buoyancy of transit but now it is a dead, sopping weight of consciousness; virtually an accusation. I place it carefully behind the door and straighten my cuffs. It is apparent that I will have to come to terms with the situation.

"Now, we're going to talk," Sophia says, "because don't think that I don't know what's been going on; haven't known from the first. I know where you went with that American bitch last night and I know exactly what you did. Pepe and I are old friends; he used to be my *sommelier* in Rome before he took a pension."

"Listen, Sophia," I say. "I wasn't doing anything at all that couldn't be done. Besides, she's a visitor in our country; I was trying to be courteous to a tourist. And in the third place, it's all done and gone; what I really wanted to do was to work on some business."

"Don't you tell me that, you bastard. I was almost going to let you leave and then lock you out but at the last moment, my old tenderness came back, the old Marcello-tenderness, just for a moment, and I said to myself: why not tell him to his face what he is? But do not press that tenderness; there will be vast difficulties if you do."

"Well, look, Sophia," I say, taking the few steps toward her and sliding my hands up to her shoulders. "That's all done and in the past and besides Pepe is a famous liar; he is known all over the province for the famous lies he tells. It was innocent; completely, completely innocent. Besides, why look upon the past; better we should think of the future we have. We are both young, beautiful, famous movie stars; playing in the best productions, symbolizing all the best of potentialities for millions; keeping all kinds of fanatics from doing something truly dangerous because of our presence, our activity and you wish to make trouble. Appearances are very important, Sophia; they must not be minimized.

What else have any of us got but appearances; why wreck everything?"

"Love, loyalty. Understanding, devotion. These are meaningless words to a man like you, aren't they?"

I sit down on the couch, pour myself a small aperitif from the instant-mix cocktail bottle on the table. "That's completely untrue," I say, raising the glass to her. "You happen to know that I'm completely devoted to you. Look at our joint appearances. Look at our international reputation. Look at the way we play so beautifully together, on and off the screen. Could any of this happen if I were not devoted to you?"

"Certainly," she says, folding her arms even more tightly and going to look out a window. "Certainly, since you are a man who emphasizes the importance of appearances, wouldn't you say? You would keep them up in all events, just so that our reputations would remain pure."

"It was just a figure of speech, Sophia. Why are we arguing like this? I was on the way to the office." Always, always, she can do this to me. For all that Mastroianni is; for all that he knows, all that he conceives and touches; he is like a child against the pure, hot rage of this Sophia. It would be enough to give a lesser man dread; for me—because I am Mastroianni—it only induces a kind of frustration; there is a simple inequity to all of this. Where would she be without me, this common, Italianate slut held in from disintegration only through her reputation and through the careful way in which, by demonstrating my public admiration for her, I have conserved her beauty? But I can say none of this to her. Always this defensiveness at the point of contact; always this withdrawal at the time of my need. It is one of my chief characteristics, having to do, perhaps, with all the decay and loss I have seen; all the mediocre pictures in which I have served only to lift them from abomination to a kind of provocativeness through the suspension of a single, grim mood. It is something to think about; in better times, worth consideration. But at the moment all that I do is to lock the door and, placing my valise on the couch, come back and look at her. She tenses, her body trying for an inch more of height and then, in one of those sudden changes which are so typical of Sophia—and so grating once the instants of passion are gone—she folds subtly within herself and turns away, shaking her head.

"Oh, Marcello, I can't stand this anymore," she says. "I feel as if everything, our whole relationship is coming apart."

"Be calm, be calm," I say and go over to the portable bar, make myself a careful drink and look at it for a few instants before I take it down in one choking swallow; feeling, as I do so, that I must truly personify all of the Continental decay in which I am becoming progressively immersed; a kind of dread and sickness compounded to a kind of exaltation which is tearing away at my appearance. "How would you like a drink as well, Sophia?"

"I don't want a drink! I drink only for social occasions! The trouble with you is that you drink too much."

"So I do," I say and pour myself another, smaller, drink; sit down on the couch now and cross my legs. It is obvious that I am going to be very late for my appointment; perhaps it is hopeless. "Let's discuss this like civilized people. What seems to be wrong?"

She turns toward me and I see that her face is creased with tears; another cheap, histrionic trick which has never failed to infuriate me because they are as meaningless as the winking induced by the lights of the *paparazzi*. "It's like you're not with me anymore, Marcello," she says. "You're always off in some kind of a fantasy world; when you're with me it's like you're with another woman and when you're not with me I *know* you're with another woman. I can't stand it; I simply can't stand it. And the rules of our Church forbid accommodation."

"It is true that I have had other things on my mind," I say. "Other interests; concerns and problems. I am an important businessman, you know; you cannot indefinitely sustain that first mood of clinging which we were granted at the beginning of our marriage."

"But it's getting worse and worse!" she cries, flicking the droplets of tears off her cheeks with a fine, graceful gesture; well-timed and meaningful as all of her surfaces—unlike her interior—always are. "Now I have the feeling that you are in dreams all the time."

"Ridiculous."

"Is it so ridiculous? At the beginning, there were just the two of us and we made love together every night; every night and during the days as well, we would close the shades against the sun and do it against the cries of children in the courtyard and there was a completeness. But now when you come to me it is with the reflection of another woman in your eyes. What did you do with that American bitch last night? That talentless harlot; what can she offer you that I can't?"

"We are merely old friends. We discussed old times together."

"You never saw her before in your life."

"Yes I did, a long time before I met you. There was nothing ominous about it at all."

"You just discussed old times."

"Yes."

"Where did you go?"

"The party was noisy, hot and crowded. We drove to a cool place and had drinks and considered the past."

"No," she says, shaking her head and going to the bar where she pours herself a drink of her own. "No, I won't listen to it anymore. I won't have any part of it. I am Sophia Loren and no man abandons me; not for his business, not for other women. He gives himself to me over and over again until his love crumbles to dust and my own body to powder but until that time there is nothing other than that passion. I will kill you if you do something like that again."

I sigh and take off my shoes. It is obvious that the question of alternatives is defeated; I am condemned to this scene over and over again until we have forced through to some kind of resolution. I want to be calm, calm—everything, after all, balances off in the long run—but I find this difficult for deep inside me, tearing at some absent wells of sensibility is a feeling of scuttling flight, a necessity to abandon, abandon … and yet how can I do this? It would do dreadful things to my cinematic reputation to say nothing of my sexual powers; a Mastroianni does not avoid conflict.

"I know what's going on," she says again. "And I simply won't have it. Our marriage is too important for me. Besides, we have to act together in all those movies. It's in the contract."

I put my glass on the table with a clatter, watching two dark ice cubes swirl absently at the bottom of a long crevice, and I look up at her. "Come here," I say. "There is nothing that the two of us together cannot resolve. Come to me."

She stands in the still-center of the room; her drink poised, the other hand reaching behind her back as if for equivocation or flight. A look of cunning floods her face from the neck up, an assumption of insight which throws all of her features into an unattractive cast of shrewdness. This too is a common habit; something which I can hardly bear. But I strive to be polite, to be courteous; to be controlled. At any moment, the *paparazzi* might vault in like flies, moving through the open spaces of the window to stand between us and catch the pictures which would surely torment the world. I have no right to visit such afflictions upon a public as removed from me as it is credulous and vulnerable.

"Come on," I say. "Put the drink down and come here. We can work this out sensibly, the two of us. Just as we have worked it out together so many other times, off and on the screen."

"I won't have any part of it. I know what you have on your mind. You stay right there and keep away from me!"

"Come here, Sophia."

"I will *not*. You are merely trying to drown me, drown yourself, destroy reality. I will stand right here."

I poise on the couch. "If you don't come here," I say, "I will be impelled to come and get you."

"You stay away from here!"

"And if I come to get you the touching and connection will be with far more violence than it would otherwise." I am trying for an attitude, you see. The question of dealing with Sophia always reposes in the selection of attitude. Yet I am not content with this, not transcendent with intimation as I usually am at such times; instead a small, sliding depression working within me on several levels seems to cancel out that possibility, leaving me drained. I wonder, in the last analysis, if I will be able to produce with her after all.

"Last time," I say.

She crashes the glass down on the bar and comes toward me quickly, changing her stride toward the center of the room like a racehorse and then moves ever more slowly toward the couch. Already coming through her face, spreading down to the barely-exposed field of her breasts is that look of dull sensuality which is her onset of sex; the planes of her face struggle against it but it is there and in it I see the beginnings of my tentative, equivocal, but necessary victory. I reach out toward her and she slides down against me on the couch, her body still held out against the possibility of touching but the softness of her skin denying this resistance; it is surely now, merely a matter of time. I lean my lips against her and inhale deeply, feeling the odor cast me past anger to some other kind of definition. She grazes a finger against my wrist.

"Oh, Marcello," she says. "This is impossible. There is no need for this kind of argument. Why can we not be happy together?"

"But we are. Very happy."

"Then why do you not show it? Why you always running away with those sluts, thinking about those sluts, instead of your Sophia, eh?" She is becoming kittenish, always a good sign in relation to what I am trying to do. "Your Sophia takes much better care of you than all those other bitches; your Sophia knows her Marcello."

"Of course. Of course."

"Your Sophia knows how to make it ripe and tight against you, how to open and close her limbs to make you shriek. Your Sophia knows the mystery of breasts; she lets you taste them like wine. Why you not happy with your little Sophia, baby?"

I put my hands on her shoulders, draw her slowly in toward me. When it happens it will happen with stunning swiftness; it must be this way in order to be effective but at the beginning, slowness is all; the drifting viscosity which will surrender to the grinding of bodies. "But I am," I say. "I'm very happy. You just don't understand your Marcello."

She draws a finger against my lips. "But I do; I do. I always understand my Marcello; I understand him better than anyone. He knows that. Why he not understand his little Sophia?"

"But he does. He does. Sophia is just bored and a little fearful. But she has no reason to be because Marcello will never leave her; never, never, never."

Perhaps this has been the wrong thing to say because with a slight moan she becomes rigid against me, her hands which had been stroking the back of my neck now ball up and I can feel the small beating there, almost as if astonished birds, trapped somewhere in the vicinity of the collar, were making their presence known. But it is no time for thought, no time for exploration or rationalization; it is a time to move forward because if I do not—if I allow myself to be entrapped somewhere in the frieze between preparation and recollection—we will, perhaps, be stretched out here forever, heedless of a time which will sweep and overtake us, carrying us back to the earliest manifestations of our loss. So I clutch at her more tightly, bring my other hand to bear and then, slowly, I grip at the zipper of her dress and pull it apart slowly much as I would part her legs for the first moist entrance. She presses harder against me, trying, somehow, to defeat this, but I am too strong, the conditions are too favorable and she cannot break it; there is little problem to parting her dress all the way down and letting it slide, while I force her arms' slow cooperation as they emerge, almost simultaneously, from the sleeves. Facing me only in an obscenity of a see-through brassiere; something which alternately highlights and conceals the familiar breasts she moves away from me now to confront me with a kind of equivocation, a look showing her poised as I was in that crevice of need, but then I embrace her and move her forward and manage to detach the brassiere without problem, allowing it to follow the dress to her waist. She is bare now to her slightly-thickening waist and I try to do with her breasts all the things that she would have me do; invoke old tricks and crochets to stimulate them, manipulate them with one hand while I play on them as wind instruments with my mouth, use the other hand to juggle and support them. She emits a small, Continental squeal and curves further against me, a declension of need and rising above her; as she moves prone on the couch I feel myself in a small cove of exaltation; a maestro, so to speak, of the breasts, an ignored but triumphant virtuoso of the nipple and areolae, working out interpretations in unusual and hidden ways, the core of an international reputation within this, and she moves further back, further back; her body almost liquid now, a white, heaving viscosity subsiding deeper and deeper into the couch. It must be very quick now, I understand that; preparation is one thing but accomplishment is distinctly another and so I move over her, parting my belt and dropping my pants with an exhilaration of ef-

fort and I make the entrance easily, easily. She mutters in gratitude. It
is going to be easy, now; with far luck I can move in and depart within
the minute, a few moments of after-conversation and then, having re-
galed her with all that is best and worst within me, drained out like a
clogged sewer pipe I can he on my business; seek subtler and more sat-
isfactory tangents. I flutter above her, moving belly to belly, wondering
vaguely how I was able to get inside her while her pants and skirt remain attached; it must have something to do with this extreme virtu-
osity of mine.

I flutter above her, then, like a butterfly, making the butterfly's
strokes, converting hidden pollen into sudden bloom and as I do so, eyes
winched shut and off in some access alley, I feel rising before me not the
usual image of a Sophia spread and pulsating which I have been able
to rouse with her at all times but instead another image; it is the image of Elizabeth herself, her eyes cold and distant, her body white and
as impenetrable as stone and as from a great, great height she is looking at me with an intensity which would contain sadness if it did not
have so much knowledge within it. I smash against that image again
and again, feeling my cock plunge in so deeply that if Sophia had a hole
for egress I would surely emerge through it and come into the muddled
spaces of the couch on the other side, trying with all my enfeebled worth
to puncture a hole within her; a clean, hard, bright spot where all ur-
gencies, all necessities will disappear but instead of diminution there
is rising, rising. She is quite lost against me now, her face shrouded
against the knowledge I have planted in her, her hips battering and
twisting against mine seeking a kind of adjustment, no matter how
equivocal, which will permit her her own orgasm. Always it has been
this way; at the moment of contact for me the auxiliary, terrible demands
from Sophia and I can feel a kind of rage twist and bend within me at
the pointlessness of this; she is trying to be more than a convenience.
So I wear myself through, my orgasm moving ahead of me, still untouched, and as I thrash and squeeze, pinching at her large nipples, as
I drive my teeth against her throat, I feel myself still scuttling after completion, a completion kept the necessary inches away from me, and then
as I hear that groan and sigh of near-despair which, for Sophia, always
indicates that she has reached her own moment of loss, I feel myself
thrust over and I begin to run out into her hidden parts, run out in great
spangles and rivulets and flashes and as I do so, the feeling of suspension vanishes and I plunge, plunge, far down upon her.

And in the plunging I no longer see Elizabeth nor Sophia herself; those
sad-eyed, sad-faced, struggling women are gone from me; instead, it is
the dark, clotted face of Brigitte herself I see, the child's face diminished

to a kind of obscenity because of what the sex has done to her eyes; the woman's body moving out in its own orbit, broken and forever separated from that child within. It is Brigitte I see; she is looking at me with a kind of infinite sadness, her face broken and drained by all but a kind of patience and as I see this—as I truly apprehend what is going on there—I feel a kind of depression and woe circuiting through me that I have never felt before; a sensation of stunned declension which drops, drops me from the height, and I fall from the high dark place testing; testing myself against the rivulets of despair that course all within and without me. My eyes shut tight I no longer seem to see Sophia, no longer see Brigitte whose image collapses painfully upon itself; no longer see anything of all these women, no part, no substance, being removed in all my sophistry to some remote cavern where darkness is all and aimless ghosts prowl the paths, chuckling and telling old stories to one another beneath the falling and odorous stalactites.

"You son of a bitch," I hear Sophia say from a far, far distance to me; "you son of a bitch, you left me hanging. You can't even fuck anymore. What good is this?"

But I say nothing, can say nothing, am locked in some investigative crouch near the tomb of the stalactites themselves, feeling and fondling their hard surface as the underground rain pours into my chamber.

I was somewhere out in the lobby. That was the funny thing; instead of being rooted in my chair, looking with unfocussed, swimming eyes at the screen I was already in the lobby, my coat poised over my shoulder, the whole of me apparently in a kind of flight. It had never happened before; it had never worked out that way: there was an easy working to the situational surfaces after all of this, a slow accommodation with the basis of the facts. But this time it hadn't happened that way; I was already in a full vault from the one space to the other and as I realized this—realized where I was, realized what I was doing; even apprehended, dimly, what might be happening to me—the first flight of panic set in. It came from some unreached abscess like the touch of an unknown girl's hand in the darkness; came with the delicacy and grace of a bird flitting across the screen of sky but for all of that it was real, it was there; it hit me with the cold fingers of loss and I felt it pour through me, working out then through my skin in a pulsing series of cold sweats. I had to get out; I had to get out of there. The point was that I didn't know exactly what had happened and I needed to get out; needed flight as I never had before, despite the fact that I had obviously gotten, somehow, to the lobby I found it difficult to move, my body frozen in position. A glance at the girl behind the candy counter brought the movement back. She was looking at me absently, a finger of a dangling hand raised in what might either have been reproof or a complex kind of approbation; her eyes distant and round in her skull as she took popcorn from one large machine and dumped it, all careless, into another. Our eyes caught for a moment and in that glance I think, then, that I must have seen everything, the totality of it the more because I was locked with a stranger and not with someone with whom I could pretend a relationship and thus dissemble; no, we were greeting each other in perfect isolation and the wall of her contempt slammed down then and with a cry I turned and ran from the theatre. I ran through the doors into the baking of the street itself, my eyes dazzled from the sun; I ran, I ran. Behind me came Sophia, came Elizabeth, came a whole procession of other wraiths, pleading, beckoning, cursing, but I wouldn't listen to them; I couldn't listen to them ... I didn't need to listen to them and I moved through the streets with the jerky purpose of an assassin, all fits and starts, guilt and twitches and got to my car and when I got there I slammed my door on all of them, leaving them to perish in the sun while, for a very, very long time I huddled over the wheel, all perfect withdrawal, trying to think of some way in which I could get through the weekend without going through the screen again.

IV

What I did was to go out to the track. The track is not the movies, has nothing whatsoever to do with the movies, has no relation to the movies at all but at a moment of stress, some time ago, I went out and lost $45.00 on three races and the feeling of perfect disaster and foolishment that swept over me was sufficient to obliterate the more complex histrionics that had sent me there. Perhaps it is all the same: the track, the movies, I have not thought about this deeply or often and, certainly, if they were exactly the same, the movies would not outweigh the track; I could go to them equally, parceling out favors, and might be tenanted equally by jockeys. But that moment the track seemed the solution; I had a long, long weekend yet to come—while the usual course of the weekends was to be far too short for everything that I had to put in them—and I had no idea of getting through it; no idea of how to get through it, in any event, in the same condition in which I had entered it; this was not a usual problem. It would have been easy enough to have called Barbara, of course: a bang was there any time I wanted it and there were other things as well, other intimations which might have been touched in the process to make it a truly interesting weekend, but

I didn't want it, no part of it at all. In the first place she wasn't that good-looking, and in the second place she could not possibly have any idea of what was really going on; to have told her would have been to have taken us to a very difficult and dangerous kind of alteration of circumstances in which anything, literally anything at all, might have happened; I couldn't afford it. I couldn't risk it. The basic point, I suppose, is that for one of the few times since it had started, the inside things were not all in their place but were all bucking and clamoring to become part of the outside and I couldn't bear that. I couldn't put up with that at all. In order to put up with it I would have had to admit that I was insane and I didn't want to be insane: not quite, not yet. There were better alternatives than insanity to living somewhere in the middle of the twentieth century in America; I wanted to find them. Insanity could be a safer bet, a kind of protection possibility lurking somewhere in the background, but it was nothing to try until you had tried the other alternatives first; I hadn't exhausted them. On the asphalt of the road, battling with cars side by side to find the exit road to the track I found myself surrounded by the floating, suspended faces of movie stars; stars I had known and not known, looking at me impenetrably, opening and closing their eyes in a wink which came close to collective obscenity. I fought my way through to the access road to the track, hearing the knocking and hammering of overheating in the car engine, wondering if the proper way to spend the weekend, ultimately, might not simply be to roll to a dead halt and spend the hours camped under the open hood, the smell of burning and futility wafting back over me with a stench so complete that it would make other thoughts impossible. But the car was in good condition; the car wouldn't overheat on me, the car was a 1956 Cadillac, exactly the same car that Paul Muni had driven himself to the lot every day that year, the dealer had guaranteed me a good deal on it and for the first time in history, a dealer had come through because even though I was not Paul Muni, the car ran. I parked it in a private lot, a little nearer to the track than the big public lot so that I would have a fast exit if I needed it and I gave the old woman who, along with a dangerous juvenescent who had the broad, flat eyes of a maniac was watching the cars as if they might explode, two dollars, and I walked all the way into the track itself, a gigantic, off-shaped candy box thrown up on the flats of a suburb; the sounds of slaughterhouse already vaguely in the air. I bought a tipsheet and a newspaper and had a beer when I got inside, which left me with something like thirty-five dollars to bet. The place was littered with filth of all kinds; it was fifteen minutes until the first race and already the air was heavy, heavy; heavy with some foreshadowing, perhaps, of everything which was to come, heavy with the smell of the 17% track cut-in which sooner or later would demolish everybody inside there if they only came and came again. Most of them looked as if they would. Most of them looked as if they had no other place to go.

I posted myself between two middle-aged men on one of the benches and looked through the tipsheet and paper without real interest; what I wanted was not a horse which would only win but a horse which, in beating the field by dozens and dozens of lengths would somehow, in the process of carrying my money home, bring home also a solution; a solution so vast, so enormous in all of its implications as to free me from whatever had brought me to this track in the first place; whatever muddling of doubts and gloom and flight and loss which had perpetrated themselves upon the paper I was holding in my hands, the muttering of the men to my right and left. The age of this crowd was old; old, they were not the people you saw in the movie houses or driving on the highways or working in most places, but rather the kind of people with whom you could find yourself riding back in the subways at some damned hour of the morning, people hunched over paper bags and newspapers with a quiet apprehension; people who had gone through all the events of the day and knew truly, then, that nothing that had happened to them was better than what had happened before or, for that matter, any worse; there was only a trundling in tubes from one kind of gloom to another with the occasional shriek and whining of breaks functioning as a reminder of mortality. The people in the subways when they ran out of reading matter would look idly out of the windows, staring at the grey walls as if, in full speed, they might clap over the train and squeeze it and finally bring a disaster so total, so totally immiscible that it would negate whatever else they were struggling with; would make the giving-up and the joining a pleasure rather than the worse. The people on the subways had huge flat eyes and would look at you now and then as if they thought you might have the answer and if they were sure you did they might come over to you, all seriousness, all deference, and tear your body open to find it. But these people at the track never looked up, when they stopped reading—which was often, because there was a fine, high, nice calculation of choices to everything—they would cup their hands over their eyes and put their elbows on the knees, tracing back to some kind of equivocation which might have its own answer; if they weren't doing that, they were looking up at the tote board overhanging the benches where all the possibilities, if not the answers, were given. There was a magic in the tote board and I could understand its purpose at last; when you looked at it, you knew where you stood if not where you were going; you knew exactly where you existed in relation to everything else that was going on within the contained sphere of the one race. The man whose horse was 10-1 was either better or worse than the plunger who was putting $100.00 on the 3-2 shot to finish third, but his relation to that other man—if he could meet him, if they were together, if they were being friendly in the crowd—was precise and it was defined; there was a basis upon which to go because the man with the 10-1 shot had the ability to thrust himself further outside the shell of immediate possibilities; could grasp visions that the other man could not and was therefore subtly expanded over him, at least for the terms of that one race. It was possible—it was more than possible—that when the 10-1 shot ran sixth while the 3-2 shot came in a galloping winner that the adventurer would have different thoughts for the next engagement and would join his more limited opponent; in this case there had been a metaphysical alteration. It was possible too that both horses would finish nowhere and both men would then have to make an intricate speculation upon personality, speed and its role in the universe; it was even possible that both might win or the adventurer alone might win which would mean that for the time contained in that one sphere, a kind of reality had been conquered and another one put in its place. But the fact was that, no matter who you were, you knew where you stood in relation to all of the others and in only a little while you would know where you stood in relation to the universe itself and that was good; that was definitely a reality. It was better than the other way because the other way you could contain nothing, you were split off and gone somewhere; gone, gone into miserable calculations, miserable obsessions. Yes, the races would have been much better than the movies if I had been constructed that way but the fact was that I was not; I was turned in another direction. It was my loss because I was not involved in simplicities and I never knew where I stood, not in relation to any of it. The easier way would have been the way I had been trying to take this afternoon but I was not geared for it; I had to launch myself inside rather than outside and in that tomb there was nothing but doubt; doubt forever.

I was not constructed for the enlargement and projection of possibilities; no, not at all. Everything had to come down to a hard center with me, one last spot where I could identify and touch the enemy-lover groping for me, but the terrain was difficult and the drive itself was limited by fear; so all that it came down to was old scatology, old myths, old jokes behind the curtains; I could see now that there was probably no solution in anything that I was doing because all that it would come down to, sooner or later, was a dirty joke. The further you voyaged inside the nearer you got to the central dirt, the more central facts, whereas if you went outside you came against other problems but they were the stones and mire of existence, a far easier manifestation than what was going on in the self. But there was no way to make sense of this; no way to equate the insight with need and I could sense, dimly, that I was probably in real trouble; that I was in the worst trouble of all because now I knew it: I knew beyond questioning exactly what was going on and maybe even what was gone wrong and yet I was going to do absolutely nothing about it except try to balance off the inside with the outside so that I could get back easier. It was frightening to the degree that I was able to be frightened; I had other things on my mind. More than that, it was simple: it edged in to a final explanation of everything that was going on; there must be some way—if I had been able to talk to anyone— that I could make it clear that the tote board and the movie star were the same thing and that I was the only difference; that the one or the other co-existed with the spirit forever, and that in the last analysis, after the gravestone had been hurled up and sanded down and engraved, it probably made no difference at all; voyagers and conservatives, seekers and followers, 10-1 and 3-2 shots alike huddled one by one under the sod, facing in the direction of the sky, everything else that had happened to them an abstraction. I folded up the tipsheet and newspaper and bought a program so that I would know who the tote board was saying was what and went to the windows to make a bet.

It was crowded in there; crowded already with a kind of apprehensive gloom, people piled back from the windows in lines that could not have been more dismal if they were on the way to a private and final solution and I looked up at the inner tote, suspended on high wires near the ceiling, to see that there were only two minutes until post time; it was getting close, one could see the despair on these faces accelerate to necessity as they moved slowly forward, patient because impatience meant possibly losing a bet but the knife-face of violence protruding through the flesh of all those faces because if they had a winner and got shut out they would most likely kill themselves; nothing breeds violence like internal violence. I was going to bet on the three horse, something called Carte Blanche, but as I watched the tote on line the odds went up, taking in one flash from 12-1 to 20-1 and this meant that very few people in the crowd had any faith in Carte Blanche; very few people believed that he was a good horse who was going to win today. I did not want that; I desperately wanted, for that moment, to be on the side of justice, truth and honor, huddled with my fellows on the back of a horse who we all agreed deserved to be the best and so I went instead to Cake Maker, the seven horse, a horse listed as 7-5 which meant that Cake Maker was definitely the favorite in this twelve-horse field. I bought two

two-dollar win tickets on Cake Maker and then found that I had just enough time to get to the $10.00 windows and take two tickets on him to show, which meant that $24.00 of faith and community were on the side of the legions of truth in the person of the favorite. Then it was time to go out to watch the race but the hall was crowded, still jammed with people, all of them moving slowly like stunned, scattered fish, in no particular direction, a few trying aimlessly for the exit doors to the infield, but being blocked by the drift of bodies at the door; a few, trapped in small pockets of space in the center of the crowd still looking aimlessly up at the tote board as if, behind its hard assertion, rested some larger mystery which might, in the blast of the public address system calling the race, explode to unleash from a height upon the crowd a nest of dwarves or elves or gremlins who would carry the good news all the way to the salt flats beyond the track and further than that. It was impossible to see the race or even to hear the call so I allowed the crowd to move me, by presses and surges, near a closed-circuit television set where, from a great distance, I was able to see the race as if spotlighted at the end of the tube; there appeared to be several horses running in a group and then one horse alone and then another, larger pack; I hoped that Cake Maker was in one of those groups although I didn't particularly care which one. Around me people were shouting and jostling; their faces had broken open and coming out from all corners of those faces was an emotion which might have been like grief if there had not been so much liability in it; it alternated between that and a child's anticipation. The set showed the horses getting near the wire and then the race was over and it blanked out. It was impossible to gather who might have won it; the numbers were not visible from this distance. I supposed that it was very important for me to care; there was no reason, after all, to be out at the track in the first place if I didn't care who won a race I was betting on. Not to care hinted of psychosis, of a whole fine network of breakdown which I might crash to and bounce upon if I didn't care. So I said to the short woman standing next to me—she was creasing her newspaper and alternately slapping it in her hand and placing it between her teeth—"Who won the race?"

"You didn't see? You didn't see?"

"I couldn't."

"I thought *you* could tell *me* who won the race. You can't see a damned thing in here."

"It's the angle," somebody else said. "They give you the wrong angle so that you can't see a thing, the crooked, cheating, lousy sons of bitches. I tell you—"

"The three," a tiny man said. He might have come up to my chest with difficulty, his small head bobbing wisely, viscously on the slump of his shoulders. "The three had it all the way at the wire."

"The three?" I said. "You mean Carte Blanche."

"I mean the three, I mean the three, who the hell knows what these names are but I tell you it was the three. Look at this, I had three tickets on the six horse to place and I don't even think he was running. I was going to bet the three but at the last minute I go off him like a fool right on to the favorite who I know stinks. I come out to the track saying to myself all the way: the three in the first, bet the three in the first all the way and I come here and I look at the boards and I look at the odds and I start thinking why the hell should I bet the three, he's a dog and now he wins for me, the rotten, lying, lousy sons of bitches put him over this time but if I had had him he would have still been running; you can bet your life on that. The dirty swine don't give you a break."

"The three won it?" I said. "The three?"

"I told you. You get away from me, sonny; you hear that? I don't want to talk to you anymore, you got something to tout you take it somewhere else. Just stay out of the old man's way, Johnny. The three, didn't I tell you the three, there it goes right up there, it's official."

The set had gone on again and now, since there was a close-up of the tote board I could see the figures. The three had won it. The PA system said that the race was official. More figures went up. The three paid $45.10, $12.80 and $7.80 to show. The seven was fourth.

"Didn't I tell you?" the little man said. "Didn't I tell you the three was an easy winner? Why don't they listen to me? Nobody listens to me; nothing I say gets paid any attention; what the hell is the point of any of it if nobody listens to you anyway? What's the point?"

"Oh, shut up, Harry," the woman said. "Shut up and leave the kid alone, will you? Can't you look at him? I bet he went off the three himself."

I got away from them, moving through the increasing, ever-darkening density of the crowds and got to a bench outside, found a small space and got in. The benches had space because everybody was either cashing their tickets or tearing them up or still hanging around at the base of the infield or the grandstand hoping impossibly for a disqualification or an alteration of the results, hoping that a voice, perhaps, would come out of the PA system and say:

LADIES AND GENTLEMEN, HOLD YOUR TICKETS PLEASE, THE RACE WHICH YOU HAVE JUST SEEN IS NOT A REPRESENTATION OF A PARTICULAR KIND OF REALITY WHICH YOU FELT YOU HAD TO HAVE: IT WAS A MYSTERY, A PRIVATE PROJECTION OF YOUR INMOST DESIRES IN WHICH THOSE WHO

WANTED TO WIN AT HEART DID WIN WHILE THE LOSERS—
THOSE BELOVED OF YOU WHO KEEP US GOING BECAUSE
YOU NEED AND NEED TO LOSE—WERE ALSO GRANTED THEIR
WISH BUT NOW WE SHALL MOVE AWAY FROM DREAMS,
DEPTHS AND POSSIBILITIES AND INTO THE CLEAR, FINAL
MOMENT OF RECKONING ITSELF; A MOMENT OF RECKONING
IN WHICH THE TRUE, THE REAL, THE MEANINGFUL RACE
SHALL BE RUN AND THE FAVORITE SHALL WIN BECAUSE FA-
VORITES ALWAYS DO WHEREAS THE LONGSHOTS, YEA EVEN
UNTO THE LEAST OF THEM, SHALL TRAIL THE FIELD BE-
CAUSE WE KNOW IN THIS LIFE—OH DON'T WE KNOW, LADIES
AND GENTLEMEN, DON'T WE KNOW ALL OF THIS REALLY
AND TRULY—THAT LONGSHOTS NEVER WIN. HOLD YOUR
TICKETS; HOLD YOUR TICKETS PLEASE BECAUSE THE JOCK-
EYS ARE GOING UP AND THE RACE SHALL BE RUN TRUE AND
FINAL OVER ITS DISTANCE AND HERE AT LAST FAIRNESS
AND EQUALITY SHALL TRIUMPH; THIS RACE WILL NOT BE A
PROJECTION OF YOUR NEEDS BUT A STATEMENT, ONLY, OF
THE WAY IT IS IN THE WORLD AND ALL THINGS WILL COME
OUT EVEN IN THE END. HOLD YOUR TICKETS LADY WRAITHS
AND GENTLEMEN ALL HOLD YOUR TICKETS, OH HOLD YOUR
TICKETS BECAUSE BEFORE YOU NOW IN THE STILL GREEN
OF THE PADDOCK WHERE EVEN THE BIRDS PAUSE IN THEIR
FLIGHT TO GIVE HOMAGE AND LOOK WITH PRIDE; HERE IN
THE STILL GREEN OF THE PADDOCK ONE BY ONE, LIGHT
AND PRANCING, WASHED WITH ALL THE COLORS OF THE
DAY, THE HORSES ARE COMING OUT.

But there was no such announcement; nothing like that had ever happened—although there was no saying that it never would—and I
looked at the tickets in my hand; pretty tickets of many colors and then
cast them in twinkling flight against the stones where they landed with
the patter of many birds. I went back to the program and the tipsheet
and the newspaper, balancing out the one thing against the other; the
two things against the third. I was twenty-four dollars behind; a day's
wages, that was, or the price of twelve pornographic books. I needed a
winner. I needed to get ahead.

It went the same way before the second race as it had gone for the first
except that it was darker and things seemed to be shut into a complex,
somehow more enclosed space; so much energy having already been
burned up, taken from its possessors and strewn to the infield gulls, who
seemed to be so well fed on it that they flew easily to the benches in the
back, the small contrived park, strewing themselves on all of us. We

could hardly have noticed. I could feel within me now pulsing the second and more important emotion of the racetrack; the sensation that was always the successor whether it came early or late and was, perhaps, the more satisfying of the two because it had roots and connections with reality that the feeling of mystery did not have and this was the sensation of rage, of loss, of entrapment; a feeling of irretrievable scattering. Not only energy had been burned up and forever lost in that first race but all kinds of possibilities as well; even if you got even—which, of course, you never, never did—you could never recapture the money you had lost and the hopes you had had but would only find a more equivocal kind of recovery; a recovery of a different sort, the darker recovery because it came out of the waste of age. One aged many years at a racetrack in the course of the afternoon because everyone was an adolescent when he came in and an old, old man when he came out; along the way were littered the catastrophes and removed successes of distant contemporaries because someone, after all, was collecting that $45.10, someone by the law of statistics had to; you didn't know what he looked like but he was there right at the payoff windows, dining on the ashes of your own futility, ashes phoenixed into reward by numerous unspoken disasters, a number of tickets in his hand, his large face beaming. One could see This Stranger, one could see and hate him the more because he had accomplished what he had only at your expense, but the hatred, like everything else at the racetrack, hit a bottom level of exhausted futility and then rebounded; you might be able to do to him the very next race what he was doing with you on this one. The Stranger was not the Enemy. The Enemy—if, at this stage of life, you were able to think of anything or anyone as The Enemy; perhaps the horror was that there was none and one would have to go looking in some other place entirely for the explanation of why everything had wound up this way—lurked within the tote board, dwelt at the heart of the giant machines figuring out the odds; the Enemy chuckled and nestled at the base root of the machinery himself and had no eyes and no ears and no sensations whatsoever; he was only dealing in percentages. So one could hate the enemy as well or more; hate him with twenty-four dollars' worth of intensity. I felt severed, elated, launched to some final plane of insight which would mark recovery. The second race was almost upon us; it was a second race feeling, no thinking of the senility and disuse of the fifth or sixth or seventh. No, before the second race you were twenty-four years old or so, a little battered, a little broken inside because now, having passed through juvenescence and its dreams you realized that you would probably never, after all, be able to fuck Sophia Loren; that if you got into the same bed with Sophia Loren even after fucking her you wouldn't know what to say to her, and you may not even have been able to come; the second was knowing that you were twenty-four and what was within reach was infinitely more desirable than what was not because at least you had access; the second was the superseding of the rage and pain of adolescence when if you drove yourself hard and harder against the wall of self, hard enough to break through the flesh and pour the waters into the density of an imagined receptacle, you could come to terms with the movement of the suns themselves against the canvas of space; it was the superseding of all that because by the second race you knew that the wall of self was impenetrable but, perhaps, you would be able to do things inside it; it was all a matter of testing, of resting, of coming to terms. I decided to go with the four horse, the second favorite, 3-1 on the board, a horse which had used to run in better races before something happened to it—senility? disuse? a seventh race of the spirit?—and it began to drift down to a lower and lower kind of horse; a kind of horse which, had it been a person, it would have felt itself demeaned: the second favorite, the four horse, was the horse for me because he had been in better places and had acquitted himself with dignity and honor but now he knew the truth and the truth was that it was better to come to terms with yourself as you were than to batter and batter and break. I bet six dollars on the four horse to win, finding the lines as congested as before but more knowledgeable somehow; there had been a subtle raising of the level of general consciousness between the first and second races and now people did not seem to be in such a hurry to bet; rather, they stood diffidently, almost queasily on the lines, holding their money in cupped hands as if it were a hat; their eyes saying, for the most part, that if the windows closed before they could get there it was perfectly all right with them because they knew the truth anyway; the truth was fine and clear and perfect regardless of their participation in it and they could come to accords with their world as long as it seemed capable of acknowledging the presence, if not the dire necessity, of that truth. I took the tickets away from the window cupping them to look at their colors against the changing flashes of the tote and then I went out to the infield—I had more time this time; time enough to get another beer and push myself through the rising urgency moving the other way—and found a spot on the rail near the stretch turn, feeling myself wrapped by the heat and the fluttering of the gulls, into another private space, and while there I watched the post parade and the call to the colors and the workouts of the horses themselves as, straining against the jockeys, they permitted themselves to be turned at the head of the stretch and to move slowly by, their frames flattened out against the sky and the black of the infield pool;

their eyes sad, serious, intent with knowledge. It was possible to sentimentalize the horses and to feel that they at the root knew more about everything than the rest of us; it was possible to do this if one were not very bright. One had to see the horses as objects, virtually nonexistent; all that mattered was the tote. I felt myself growing into maturity as I watched the odds on the four horse drop to 2-1 and then even money as he was installed as the favorite. I had placed myself far out beyond the rest, testing myself against the ultimate possibilities and I had won. I was correct. Most of the people believed as I did that the four horse was a good horse; that what he had seen and known could be applied to the present situation. I had the whole thing beaten. There was no need whatsoever to run the race.

But the race was run, of course; all races must be run—the final completion of the metaphor—and I watched the four horse take a long lead on the backstretch; as they came past me in the stretch turn I could see his fine, wide nostrils spread out against the air, sucking valorously as he tried to hold his lead and instead lost his action, his joints and limbs seeming to tumble in upon one another like a clown's collapse, a diminution as violent as the shrinking of the prick after completion and a damned bit quicker and the horse fell, fell gracelessly to the ground, the jockey bouncing harmlessly off him and landing easily on the turf, rising from his knees, a hand extended as if he had not just disgracefully lost the race but had, instead, won it right there and was now about to accept the victory token as well as some of his own winning bets. But after a while the triumph faded from the jockey's face and a kind of exhaustion seeped into the high, dark bones as the horse—the four horse—thrashed around the ground in an intricate kind of agony and a truck came out with two men riding its sidecar, one of them holding a shotgun, the other wearing dark glasses. Far, far down the track, a thin roar went up; probably the results had been posted on the tote and even those people around me in the stretch turn area turned their heads to see what was going on and then walked away mumbling, but I was still fixated, fascinated, upon the horse; he was rolling from side to side on the ground, his mouth open, something dark running out. It was hard to tell that a few moments ago he had been an even-money favorite against the field; a horse who had known better trails in his other times and even perhaps, had touched a kind of greatness; the qualified greatness of allowance races in any case; where the horses that weren't quite good enough to be the best but could beat almost anyone else played with themselves, before the big races themselves were run. Now, it was as if I had a kind of tunnel vision; everything to the left and right of me was blotted out and I was peering down a long, dark pipe at the horse;

the horse and I staring at each other against some wide space and I saw the pain come into his eyes; it was as if the pain was something special, very unique that he needed to communicate to me and in the intensity of that moment, I felt that the horse and I were alone, quite clearly alone and apart from everything else; communing with one another over the rail and through the sun, but then the two men walked over and the one with dark glasses lifted the horse's head the way a baby's chin might be chucked and stared at it and then began to pat his hands absently, alternately, down the horse's flank. A high, shrill scream cut into the air; a scream which could have been human except that nothing human screamed at the racetrack, and the horse struggled against the ground and tried to get up, its legs scrappling, the head flailing like a misshapen hand and then, somehow, it did achieve its feet with a whine of agony and, yes, it was quite clear, the left rear leg was broken, dangling at a precarious angle against the ground, the haunches seeming to shrivel around it. The man with dark glasses shook his head and made a pointing gesture at the man with the shotgun who had stood respectfully by the inner rail all through this, smoking a cigar and looking down the line at the tote.

"They're going to shoot that horse now," somebody next to me said. It was a plump woman with large, discolored patches of flesh running on her upper arms and palms and her eyes, turned toward me against the sun, showed a kind of utter apprehension of everything that was going on and would go on at this race track throughout the day; a sodden, ninth-race kind of post-senescence had settled upon her face; it was a face that looked as if it expected no surprises, none whatever, for quite a long time.

"I lost the double on that horse," she said. "You see?" She took a large wad of tickets out of her handbag and pushed them at me. "I had everything in the first race wheeled to that bastard; he was the day's best bet. If he runs even a little bit I'm hooked into a two hundred dollar double but no, that can't be, he's got to break himself around a turn. The son of a bitch can lie there and die as far as I'm concerned, But they're not going to do that; they'll shoot him."

"Well," I said, "they have to. He's in pain and he isn't much use anymore."

She shook her head. "They could save him," she said. "Pain is nothing and if you can keep them off their feet with drugs for the first couple of days in the cast, you can save them. But they don't want to save him. They want to shoot him. I'm glad. I'd shoot the bastard myself if I knew how to handle a gun."

The man with the gun walked over slowly, lightly, moving some-

where near the balls of his feet and crouched beside the horse, looking
at him, then reached out a hand to touch the mane. The horse whined
again and fell slowly back to one side, his flanks heaving. The man with
the gun shook his head and backed off.

"He deserves that and more," the woman said. She seemed to have
nothing more to say after that but handed me the tickets and walked
away, swinging her bag, the uneven texture of her skin making her look
like a cartoon character as she diminished in the distance. At the fact
of the shooting, a small crowd seemed to have gathered around the area;
it was a crowd just like the ones lining up at the last moment to bet except that they seemed a bit younger and their faces blunt rather than
shabby. Some of them took tickets out of their pockets and scattered
them on the ground, others slapped pencils against their cheeks and
seemed to be abstractedly figuring out the next race while they waited
for this one to end. The gunman moved back against the rail and centered his rifle while a larger truck came past the grandstand and
parked behind the horse in the line of fire, half-blocking the view. Some
in the crowd got down on their knees to see under the truck but I settled for putting a foot up on the rail and then half-vaulting myself; from
that perspective, I was able to see everything. The horse was demolished
with two bullets which seemed to hit its chest and neck and its body
seemed to turn to water, flowing out on the hard, bright dirt of the track
although there was no blood anywhere at all. The crowd seemed to sigh
and the man with the gun put it down to foot-level and, dragging it away
on the ground, went back into the smaller car. Meanwhile, someone in
the larger truck threw a canvas over the animal's body so that it was
now completely covered.

"Fixes the son of a bitch," someone said. "He'll never do that to me
again. Did it to me two races running but now he's finished."

"Caught him clean," someone else said. "Usually these things can get
messy. But he levelled him real nice."

"Level him nice, level him messy; the point is that this is one bastard
who's never going to put it to me again."

"You think so? They'll take him back to the barns and put a machine
into him and fix him up nice and he'll be right out to race in the third
tomorrow. And he'll be odds-on under his new name and you, you bastard, you'll bet on him and he'll go down the pipe and you'll say 'hey, I
think they oughta shoot that horse.' That's how it's going to work out."

"Doesn't it always?"

"Isn't that the way?"

"They're going to tow the son of a bitch away, now."

"Why couldn't he have broken it a furlong later; I would've sent roses to his funeral."

"He breaks it further than a furlong you wouldn't have enough money to send roses to his funeral. That horse wasn't going to win. He didn't have a chance. Not a chance."

"You say that?"

"Sure I say it. Didn't you see him stopping in the stretch turn anyway? He was beat."

"He was laying close in the backstretch. He hadn't even made his move yet. He was starting to make his move on the outside when he went down."

"Doesn't make no difference. That horse was finished."

"Maybe he broke it on the backstretch. Maybe he was running that way all the way through."

"Maybe you broke it on the backstretch too. Maybe you'll have a quarter left to go home. What do you like in the next race?"

"What's the difference? I liked this one in the second."

"So give me your choice. Maybe we can lay odds on he drops dead of heat stroke or something."

"They don't open the windows on bets like that."

"With you around they'd make an exception."

"It was really something when they shot that horse. Wasn't it something when they shot that horse? I never seen anything like that in my whole life. I was never out on one of those days before."

"All part of the game, baby. Just be happy they didn't shoot you. They got a special policy; they do all that with the big winners."

"Well, I don't have to worry about that."

"Yeah. Anyway, what you like in the third?"

I had about five dollars left. It would have been enough because I had gas in the car and a fair expectation of reaching home without disaster—and there was always plenty of money at home; I saw to that—but I was sick of it, then, sick of it with a ninth-race sickness; dwindled and shrunken and already far removed from all of it; I wanted to go home. Whatever I had had to solve out here was either solved or would never be—I couldn't tell the difference; there was no way at all of telling the difference; this was one of the main troubles with the track—and I wanted to go home, wanted to put myself in a small, enclosed space because I felt myself dimly, then, to be on the verge of other projects, other intuitions which, however related to whatever had happened to me this afternoon would end up so remote as to seem to have no connection whatsoever. There was no such thing as an uneventful day at the track; what happened was always meaningful and compartmented and the right metaphor for whatever had driven you there in the first

place but the best part of the knowledge you tried to gain was to know
when you had had it; when you had to go home and apply it in other
areas. I needed to go home, but the crowd was thick and angry at the
edges; a furious crowd, a raging crowd, a third race crowd standing out
there in the infield: losers all of them because if they were winners they
would either be inside cashing their tickets or at the bars having a drink,
but losers not without a fairly good idea of precisely what had done it
to them and what they could do about it. I felt hands slapping at me aimlessly, reaching out as if I was not only an obstruction but, perhaps, a
vessel of some information which, if only given to them, would negate
everything which had happened to them already and restore them,
clean and juvenescent, to the moments before the first race themselves
when, all equivocation and despair cast aside, they could make their bets
encased in a kind of quiet nobility because they had been given a Second Chance. But I had nothing to say to any of them; I barely had anything to say to myself. The PA system went on again and said that the
winner of the third race was Number 7, Beau Champion, a three-year-
old bay gelding by Swaps-Nashua's girl, the second horse was number
nine, March Militaire and the third horse was number one, Table
D'Hote and announced that the time of the next race would be 2:31 and
in the next race there would be no changes and then clicked off. In the
brief hush that followed, I could tell that they were waiting around me
for another kind of announcement from the system, this one would say:
ALSO, LADIES AND GENTLEMEN, THE EVEN MONEY FAVORITE
IN THIS RACE WAS DESTROYED AT THE STRETCH TURN DUE
TO A BROKEN LEFT LEG BUT THIS IS NOTHING FOR YOU FINE
PEOPLE TO WORRY ABOUT; HE WASN'T GOING TO WIN THE
RACE ANYWAY AND EVEN IF HE HAD IT WOULD HAVE MADE
NO DIFFERENCE AT ALL TO THOSE OF YOU WHO BET HIM BE-
CAUSE THERE ARE SEVEN RACES LEFT THIS AFTERNOON
AND ALL OF THEM ARE BOUND TO BE VERY DIFFICULT. SO
DON'T TAKE ANY OF THIS PERSONALLY, LADIES AND GEN-
TLEMEN, PARTICULARLY DO NOT TAKE THE FACT THAT THE
ANIMAL WAS DESTROYED PERSONALLY BECAUSE HE WAS
AN ANIMAL IN THE FIRST PLACE NOT ANY OF YOU AND IN THE
SECOND PLACE THE RACING ASSOCIATION DOES EVERY-
THING WITHIN ITS POWER TO MAKE YOUR DAYS PLEASANT
AND COMFORTABLE AND REWARDING AND UNTROU-
BLESOME BY DESTROYING ANY HORSES WHICH DAMAGE
THEMSELVES DURING THE RUNNING OF THE RACES. CRIP-
PLING, DISASTER, MISINFORMATION, THE BLASTING OF
HOPES: THESE HAVE NOTHING TO DO WITH YOUR BENIGN

RACING ASSOCIATION WHICH HAS RESOLVED TO BLAST THEM FROM THE FACE OF THE EARTH WITH RIFLE OR WITH EXACTAS: WE REALIZE THAT THERE IS ENOUGH TRAGEDY IN THE WORLD AS IS WITHOUT MORE FAILURE AND LOSS BEING HEAPED UPON YOU. THE WINDOWS ARE NOW OPEN FOR THE THIRD RACE AND REST ASSURED THAT IF YOUR HORSE DOES NOT PERFORM TO EXPECTATION BY REASON OF SHATTERING INJURY OR BROKEN BONE WE WILL SERVE TO MAKE AMENDS TO YOU PERSONALLY AND BEFORE YOUR VERY EYES WHEREAS IF HE PERFORMS POORLY BY REASON OF MYSTERY AND NOT FACT WE WILL RETURN HIM TO THE BARN TO RUN ANOTHER DAY, MORE SUCCESSFULLY. MYSTERIES ARE FRUITFUL, FACTS ARE NOT: WE OF YOUR RACING ASSOCIATION ARE GEARED TOWARD THE ACCULTURATION AND PROPITIATION OF MYSTERIES. ONTO THE SHROUDED GREEN, UNDER THE SUN ITSELF, SEE NOW, WATCH, FOR THE HORSES ARE COMING OUT.

But I was not listening to it; not even in the channels of the mind was I listening to it, I was trying to get out. I got through the undergrandstand once again, small pockets and tumors of people billowing around me and into one of the alleys which lead downstairs and outside of the track. The coolness came up over me then as I trotted down the stairs; a total and almost final coolness; all of the heat and energy being alternately drawn and dispersed within the acres of the track itself while the surrounding areas, having no kinesis, lacked heat as well. I got downstairs and outside the grandstand and handed my program, tipsheet and newspaper to a small man who thanked me and offered me a quarter and asked who had won the second. I told him I didn't know but the four horse had been destroyed.

"Really? What happened?"

"Broke his leg on the stretch turn."

"Be damned. Finished out of the money then, right?"

"Right."

"I'm a lucky son of a bitch, I swear. I was pushing myself like mad out of the office to get here in time to bet that race. I wanted to bet that horse. I thought he was a sure thing. I would have lost a hundred dollars on that horse."

"You are lucky."

"Just proves that you can never figure horse-racing, don't it?"

"That's what it proves."

And walked then past the umbrella of the ticket-takers window, past the stands where tipsheets were still being sold, where people were still

coming in from the subway, a first-race look upon them seeming shock-
ingly irrelevant against even the faces of the tipsheet sellers who now,
in the afternoon's first gloom, seemed to have already learned something. I got to my car, feeling the dreadful humidity of the flats pouring
in through me, soaking all of my garments together in a consistency
which felt like glue, trying to keep my mind perfectly blank because
again perhaps I had learned something and I wanted to keep that
knowledge intact to me. I got to my car and the wild-eyed juvenescent
asked how I had done and I told him I had lost, had lost everything, had
broken myself utterly, which was probably the right angle to take in any
event because he was a man whose tote board was all internal, and if
calculations seemed to drop to the proper odds for a course of action he
was considering he could have done it; he could have done anything at
all. The car started easily and I got out onto the roads, deciding to take
the back alleys and service accesses all the way home; no turnpikes or
highways for me. I tried not to think.

But not to think is not the cancellation of dreams and all the way back,
one by one in solemn procession, it was as if the faces were assaulting
me; the faces of my women moving in an infinitely removed, infinitely
sad aspect, looking at me wistfully, peering through the windshield.
Brigitte was there and Elizabeth too, and Sophia was still shouting to
me, telling me to grow up and stop living in fantasies; also there were
the faces of girls I had only glimpsed vaguely in other moods, girls with
pretty faces and bodies who, like cheerleaders on the opposite side of a
football stadium are never quite known; perceived only with sadness
and loss. They were all there considering me, looking at me quietly; now
and then one of them—usually it was Elizabeth—tried to say something
infinitely gentle and sad and wise but I couldn't hear them; I could only
hear Sophia, she was shouting obscenities now and only the wall which
cut me off from her kept me from screaming back. But the wall was still
up there, the wall was secure, the wall was impenetrable; it was this
more than anything else which had saved me, was saving me; would,
if I were lucky, always save me. So I tried to blot them out against the
heat-screen of the windshield, moving my car back home and I barely
knew who I was or what I was doing or where I would go after I came
home. I didn't know. I was in a new space; a new eave of possibilities; I
felt myself dimly, largely on the verge of massive changes but I didn't
know what they were nor did I want to think upon them. The track had
done its work; it had done its work well. I was not the same person who
had gone out there; barely accommodated with that person and yet, still,
the faces swam, drifted above me, lost in their lustre, the voices questing, trying to reach through the glass to me. I got home with all of them

and shut off the sights and murmurs as if they were a large, console television set or better yet a movie projector that I had pulled the plug on and parked the car and went upstairs. It was hot. It was very hot outside. I had lost thirty dollars and expenses and it was not even five o'-clock on a Saturday and yet, underneath me, I could feel that the time of drifting was over; the weekend was about to turn. The weekend was about to move over slowly on itself like a crumbling planet and turn into something else, perhaps a fragment of a sun. Everything was different; I felt virtually outside of myself climbing the stairs, a character in an intricate, ill-plotted home movie stumbling in cartoon gait, in cartoon time against the screen of consciousness. I went inside—it was stinking, stifling, hot—and opened some windows and there was a note for me under the door in an envelope marked to MARTIN MILLER. I opened it and, of course, it was from Poirier. He had forgotten to sign his name to it this time and the whole thing was childishly, ineptly typed, as if he had written it, somehow, at the bottom of a coal mine:

Dear Mr. Miller:

I've been thinking more about your situation today because I'm that kind of man. The ordinary Unit Supervisor would forget the whole thing and let nature take its course on Monday. But to me my investigators are like part of the family and I see to them like a father or a brother depending upon their age and stage of life. So I've been thinking about you a great deal and I have some advice for you which you're free to take or leave although of course I certainly hope you'll take it.

Far better than have you brought up on charges with all the unpleasantness and embarrassment of a hearing, I think that you should resign without prejudice, giving proper notice, and then everything can be dropped. As you know and as I've told you, if you are dismissed from this position you will never be able to get another civil service job because this will become part of your permanent record and will be forwarded to all government and city and state and even private agencies in the event that you apply for a job. This would hurt you very badly.

On the other hand, I've been around long enough to know that if you just went ahead, Monday, and put your resignation in and gave notice and said that you were leaving for personal reasons, then that would be the end of it because the last thing in the world that the Department is interested in doing is in persecuting someone or harassing him for the rest of his life. Everybody feels very sorry about what has happened to you Martin and what has happened here and would be just as happy to let the whole thing drop. Your resignation would end the entire problem and that would be the end of things as I say.

I thought I'd write you a note about this and leave it at your house for you to think about rather than to talk to you about it first thing Monday morning. In the first place, Mondays are very busy, difficult days around the Center and I'm too busy and too many things are exploding around me to be able to take time off and talk to one of my workers. And in the second place I thought that by giving you a chance, Martin, to sit down and think this over for the rest of the weekend, it might be better for you because it would allow you to come in Monday with all the facts in front of you and with a fresh mind and then you could do the thing that is right. So pardon the intrusion.

You may think it's pretty silly of me to care so much about a worker of mine that I would give up part of my weekend to do nothing but sit and think about his problems and then write him a letter explaining what I've been thinking and take the time to come over on the subway and leave that letter under his door but that's just the kind of person I am and the kind of person I try to be for my workers and if you can't understand that, well, then, there's no reason worrying about it at all and I very much hope, Martin, that you will come in first thing on Monday morning and decide to do the right thing.

Your supervisor,
JAMES POIRIER

I tore this one up too and put it into the wastebasket, thought about the beer for a moment and decided that I didn't need it; that nothing I had on my mind had anything whatever to do with beer. Whatever I had on my mind had to do with something else; something else much larger and subtler and complex than Barbara—but Barbara was the only person who came even near being a metaphor for it. As a matter of fact, Barbara was one of the very few people I knew. I went to the phone and dialed her number, listening to it ring several times and as it came to me that she might not be home; that she might actually be out, I felt a panic gnawing and rising in my stomach; the kind of panic to be felt by the jockey on a falling even-money shot with no bailout warning whatsoever and not a shred of insurance; a five-foot, nine-inch, 195-pound jockey without any future and with not much of a past in the bargain. I hadn't realized the urgency to be that great. But after a while the phone was answered and it was her voice and that, at least, was one thing that I didn't have to think about, not ever again. She said hello and I wondered if the whole thing had been a trap or ploy; she sitting by the phone grimly waiting for it to finish ringing six times so that if it was me and if I was needful, I would have suffered that much, without any penalty on her part. But I wasn't needful; I wasn't needful at all in that way. I had that much over her. She said hello again.

"This is Martin, Barbara."

"Oh, Martin. Hello. How are you?"

"Fair enough."

"That's good."

"Did you get home okay last night? No problems on the subway, were there?"

"Why should there have been problems on the subway? The subways are perfectly safe."

"I didn't say they weren't. I was just asking. I got another note from Poirier today."

"Oh? Did you see him?"

"I was at the track. He slipped it under my door. He wants me to quit; he says that if I quit they'll drop charges and that will be the end of the whole thing."

"Isn't that nice of him?"

"Isn't it? Otherwise—"

"How did you do at the track?"

"The track?"

"You said you went to the track. You mean the races. How did you do there?"

"Oh," I said. "I lost. I had a couple of bad experiences. It doesn't matter; I only go out there once in a while. I'm not really interested in racing, it's just what it can teach you."

"Oh."

"Barbara," I said, "you want to come over here? Maybe we could spend the rest of the afternoon and the evening together."

"Isn't that lovely? The rest of the afternoon and the evening. And what about tomorrow morning? Should we spend tomorrow morning together too? Is that on your mind?"

"No," I said. "It wasn't. But it could be."

"Oh it could be. Isn't that lovely? I should just sit around here and wait for you to call and let you tell me what's convenient for you and then just jump in the subway and come over. That's very nice. That's just lovely. It's something to look forward to."

She didn't do it well. At her level of attraction it would have been very difficult to have brought off, but I could admire her persistence, her tenacity; what might as well have been called her integrity. She was playing it as if she was far more attractive girl—as beautiful, say, as Brigitte Bardot or Sophia Loren, although not the exception that Elizabeth Taylor was—and I had to give her credit for that. She put a value on herself. It was nice to know, after an afternoon at the races, that there was such a thing as an intrinsic valuation and that this girl had it.

"Okay," I said. "I'm sorry. I really don't mean to sound that way. I had a very nice time last night and I just thought that we could see each other again, that's all."

"And what about me? What about my time last night? What does that count for in your scheme of things, anyway?"

"I wanted you to stay. You said you had to go home."

"I never did."

"You said—"

"Forget it. I don't know if I want to come over. You could come here and pick me up and we could go for dinner someplace, though. We don't have to go to anybody's apartment."

"But I want you to come over here. I want to see you."

"Why? So you can screw me and have some kind of a cheap meal at home and then screw me again? Is that it?"

Obviously her parents weren't home and there was no question of an extension phone. But the dispassion didn't work, not all the way; she touched off some dim, hidden layer of rage in me; a feeling that I was approaching rock-bottom after all, a feeling of declension. Like everybody else I was stone within; stone below, it was only a question then of finding it.

"Come off it, Barbara," I said. "Neither you nor I can afford to play that game. We're not that kind of people. You know it and I know it so just stop this."

"What do you mean, we're not that kind of people?"

"God damn it," I said, "you know exactly what I mean so don't try that coy crap with me. At our level we can't afford to play it; we have to take what we find and call it clover. Now yes or no, do you want to come over here? I'll be perfectly happy to drive over and pick you up; it's all the same to me, but give me an answer. And if you're going to play the game, then the hell with this and I'll find something else to do."

"I can see why you're up on charges," she said after a pause. "I can really see why, now."

"I'm not up on charges. They're threatening to bring me up on charges. They're full of crap. When they do it I'll believe it. They're giving me trouble because I go my own way, that's all. Not any other reason. Now, yes or no."

"I should hang up on you."

"I hope you don't, because we can't afford that; we can't spare each other Barbara."

"But I should hang up on you."

"It wouldn't solve anything," I said, and I knew she saw it too because she didn't hang up on me at all. I heard her breath, light, tentative, searching to pace itself to mine over the wires of the phone and I matched it, leaning back against the table, knowing now that if I waited her out it would probably, in whatever equivocal way, work out.

"Well, there's no need for you to pick me up. I can take the subway down to you again."

"I don't mind the drive."

"No, it's all right. But no messing around, Martin. I mean, we'll go out to dinner. All right."

"Well," I said, "all right. Dinner and a movie."

"A movie?"

"After dinner we'll take in a movie. We'll make it a real date."

"I don't care for the movies too much."

"Well, I do."

"Because you want them to be your profession. But I think they're all cheap lies, all of them. I'd rather go someplace and be with someone and just talk."

"There are good movies around."

"They're all the same. I prefer reality; I think that reality is much better. Don't you?"

"Well," I said. "It all depends in the first place on who you are. And it depends in the second place upon what kind of reality you have. And in the third place it all depends upon what kind of dreams you like to have. It's hard to make a flat statement."

"I'll be down in about twenty minutes."

"Okay."

"I'm not exactly dressed to go out anywhere now. I'll have to fix myself up a little."

"Anyway you come is fine with me, Barbara."

She giggled. It was ultimately disconcerting, even at that distance. "That's what you'd say until you saw me. Then you'd say something else. No, I'll look nice. And Martin?"

"Yeah."

"I'm sorry I got angry with you. But I don't like to feel as if I'm a convenience for you or something like that."

"You aren't. You know better than that."

"I'd like to feel that there's a relationship here."

"Oh there is. There is."

"Because without a relationship, what's the point of anything? I've been that other way too many times before."

"Me too."

"So I'll see you then."

"Yes," I said, "I'll see you," and I hung up, another evening in the bank and twenty minutes to kill. It was all the same; everything was as it had been on Friday but it was all irretrievably changed too; she could sense that as well but only I knew in what direction. I set up the projector, taking the Sabrina film out of it and substituting a Honey Bee special; Honey Bee showing it all to the camera the way you like it but I couldn't quite get with it; the old feeling wasn't there although Honey Bee was damned good; there was no question about it. A long time ago Honey Bee had had thirty-four-inch tits, tits not much different than Barbara's although they hung somewhat less, but then she had gone South and had some kind of a silicone operation and now she was something else again; they were forty-six inches and came straight out all the way and the pressure of the silicone was so enormous that the nipples seemed to have shrunk to tiny, almost absurd dots in the center. Honey Bee had given an interview to the editor of a men's magazine I had read and had said that she was happy to have almost any kind of operation in the cause of science; it wasn't the question of bigger tits that was so important to her as much as it was the question of blazing the way, through her example, to other, less fortunate girls, who needed the operation even worse, but were afraid of the risks. Anything was worthwhile if it was to please a man, Honey Bee had told this editor and, besides, there were no risks at all; her breasts felt better now than they ever had; they were fuller and firmer and tighter and seemed to draw more sensation and men seemed to like her better and she liked herself better so the operation was a definite plus in all ways, all the way around. All that a girl needed was a little guts, a little gumption, a little interest in having some pride in herself. This film showed Honey Bee before the operation, probably just before she had decided to be so courageous and to further the cause of science. For that reason and for others it excited me; it excited me a hell of a lot but I couldn't get inside it, I had a large, cold, dead feeling inside me in relation to the film, a feeling I had had too many times before to try to beat, so I just left things alone and didn't push it. But the feeling had really never been as pervasive as this. It was like some four horse of the soul had tumbled inside me, falling to the ridges of the rail in real trouble and he wasn't going to get up, not until they used the final prod of the gun.

I sat on the floor with my hands around my knees, rocking myself gently in the darkness of the drawn apartment and watched Honey Bee dance on the wall while I tried to figure out exactly how I wanted to approach Barbara this evening in terms of what I wanted to do. If I knew what I wanted to do. That was the difficult point, the really difficult part of the whole thing. I wasn't sure. And I wasn't sure that I would find out in time. Meanwhile, Honey Bee bobbed and skipped and jumped, her little nipples playing a tattoo of knowledge against the well-known surfaces of the wall adjoining my convertible couch.

V

By the time Barbara came in, the machine was out of sight, packed under the couch and the film, on a whim, had been chucked into the incinerator. There was no point in taking the same chance twice, that accounted for the projector being out of the way and the film itself, seen from the vantage point of my post-racing insights, was an absolute disaster; mean and perverse and juvenescent; it had nothing whatsoever to do with other realities. And Honey Bee was probably a bad fuck in the bargain; behind all that silicone was no doubt a body of iron and bridgework, set for stroking only in anger, a tight, mean cunt laced by steel. It was all a question of seeing those basic things; I was almost proud of myself. Perhaps if I had told all of this to the man in the pornographic bookstore, I would have had a beneficent effect upon his business.

She was wearing the sleeveless-sweater, toreador-pants outfit which is pretty much the standard uniform for a certain kind of girl during the summers or whatever weather passes as an excuse for summer, her arms coming out impressively white against the dead black of the sweater, her breasts, cleverly encased by what was probably the best brassiere in her wardrobe, looking firm and high, almost jaunty as they preceded her to whatever destiny. I felt a dense moment of pity for her, looking at her standing in the doorway, because it simply made no sense: I had seen her breasts, suckled them, bounced and jiggled their drooping surfaces and under those circumstances it seemed almost impudent for her to encase them in the lie that her uniform represented, a lack of respect for the simple fundamentals of memory, but I was able to edge beyond that to see that she wanted me to lie to myself as she lied to herself; that she was looking for a naïveté and hopefulness in me to equal her own and that while she wanted me to dream of large, upthrusting, phallic breasts as I looked at her; well, then, no less did she hope to see those breasts herself when the sweater next came off; the sweater was the medium through which the real possibilities could be entertained and contained, as did the tote board, all of the energy which she could bring to bear. I almost wanted to fondle her then and tell her that it was all right; Elizabeth Taylor's breasts sagged too, and not only when she was lying in bed; most movie stars had breasts which sagged; the only women whose breasts didn't sag either had no breasts at all or were so filled with silicone that they were unable to separate within themselves the sensations of sex from those of pain; sex and pain were muted together in them at the moment of contact and all of America, the America of our heart and dreams, had been founded upon women whose breasts sagged, sometimes drastically, sometimes to navel-depth or more. I wanted to tell her that there was no reason for dissembling; that only in the last twenty years or so had the country gone slightly insane and focussed upon a breast straight rather than curved, arched out rather than in gentle descendance; I could have put an arm around her and stroked her and told her all of this and perhaps she might have understood and felt better. But if I had done that, I might have disarranged her brassiere or given her the fear that I would and that would negate the whole point of trying to tell her anything; trying to tell her that Brigitte Bardot's breasts literally swam on her rib cage when I poised over her for first and final entrance. So all that I did was to take her hand and smile at her gently and tell her that I was glad; I was glad she was there, it was good to see her, it had been a rough afternoon, she had no idea how nice it was to see her.

"Well," she said, "well, yes." She sat down on the couch with an appropriatory air and patted it a couple of times, then looked up at me to see what I thought of that. "No," she said. "That wasn't on my mind. I just thought I'd have a drink."

"What kind of drink?"

"Anything you want to make. It doesn't make any difference. I just don't know if I can stand living with my parents anymore. I don't know if I can take that nonsense."

"So be like me. Be liberated. Move out."

"It isn't so easy for a girl. Where I come from if you're not living with your parents and your parents are alive and you're not married, you're a whore, pure and simple."

"Who says you're a whore?"

"I was making an analogy. It's all part of the background, Martin. Besides, I'm in no hurry to get married."

I wasn't quite sure where that came from but I had a fair idea. She sat on the couch and crossed her legs, giving me a fair approximation of how her breasts might look if she stretched out naked on her back in bed, cupping them wildly between her palms and squeezing their life away, urging them into some small, abstract, sucking mouth. She looked at me sidelong as she did so—a knowledge coming into her eyes which was meant to approximate that in my own except that I was not responding, I was not responding at all; I was in some dim place far removed from her—and said, "well, aren't you going to offer me a drink?"

"Sure. Anything you want."

"I mean, you can drink where I come from. There's nothing evil in that. As long as you do it with plenty of company and you don't get absolutely bombed it's perfectly ladylike. My father gave me my first beer when I was thirteen, just so I wouldn't pick up the habit out of the house. They really can be liberal in small ways. I'll have a scotch."

"All right."

"With no ice, no water, nothing, you understand me? Just a scotch and that's it."

She was trying to drive herself into a mood, a mood where any one of a number of things could happen which would thrust the two of us out of some kind of concord to a new space altogether but I didn't know if I wanted it or not. My own mood lay upon me heavy, deadly, an eighth or ninth-race feeling full of small flashes of memory and precognition combined so that I seemed to dwell only tentatively in the present, being tied forward and back more persuasively. But it didn't matter; I told myself that again, nothing mattered; I didn't even know who this girl was or why she was over here and in such circumstances, how could anything connect at all. I made her the scotch with plenty of clinking of glasses and sloshing to let her know that I took her request seriously and then, so there wouldn't be any questions I went to the kitchen and got another of the cans of beers. Within my groin was a slow, turgid feeling, a feeling of dark rising against a canvas of disuse but I said: *oh, no, you're not going to get away that easy; there are other things which have to be settled here*, and the idiot need, smoothed by sense, subsided. I handed her the glass and she sat back, sipping slowly, doing something subtle with her left hand against her bosom so that her breast seemed to come out even further, protruding against the sweater. It would have been vaguely obscene if it had not been otherwise touched with burlesque; Sophia and Brigitte would never have been caught in such a position because the breasts were in perfect relationship to the rest of the body and remained there throughout. But Sophia and Elizabeth, of course, were exceptional women; for someone not at all in their class you had to give this one marks for trying. She was trying. I got the beer down and could tell from the first pressure of the cold fluid against my stomach that it was no longer a drinking day, that alcohol and my mood were not mixing and that to drink heavily would probably be to risk some kind of internal disaster. So I palmed taking the next drink and put the can down on the table. It occurred to me that I had no idea of what to say to her.

"I see your projector is gone."

"Projector? Oh yes. I put it away. I told you, I was just looking at some rushes."

"What kind of rushes were they? What film? What kind of an interviewing procedure is that?"

I wanted, then, almost to tell her the truth. I wanted to say: *Barbara, I was not looking at rushes of a film; I was looking at an eight millimeter clip of a British slut with enormous breasts and she's bare-ass before the camera and her breasts are loose and swinging free and when I watch the film I can get so absorbed that it's no longer me the viewer watching the bitch-slut on the screen but instead it's like I'm right inside the screen itself, right up there with her; everything so vivid I can touch and I'm out of the room entirely; up there on the screen instead and it's been this way for a long, long time, Barbara and I find it infinitely more satisfying than almost anything else in the world and all I want to do is to keep on doing it but there are always people like you around who make it difficult because you think it's better the other way and since you're in the majority I don't have much of a case. That's what I was doing, Barbara, if you want to know the truth: that's the way it's been for a long, long time and all I wanted it to do was to continue on this way because when you balance everything out in the long or short run it's probably the only answer to the problems of living—because, you see, I cannot, I simply cannot induce myself to believe in tote boards—but I'm running into problems, Barbara; I'm running into increasing problems and that's why I put the projector away. There's no way in the world that you can understand this or even begin to come to terms with it; there is no way short of putting myself against you and driving my exhausted cock on its gremlins' journey that I can possibly get you to listen, much less apprehend, what is truly going on here but that is the fact of the matter, the totality of the case and now you know and it doesn't make any difference to you except in terms of a kind of horror—I horrify you now, don't I, Barbara—and if you want to learn the truth, I've been doing this since I'm sixteen years old and I don't see how anybody could not be doing it. Do you understand that, Barbara?* But I didn't say any of this to her, of course, because it would have thrown the entire relationship, the entire set into another area altogether and I couldn't do it, I couldn't take that risk; I had other things on my mind. What they were I had no idea, but for the first time, I could feel them somewhere beyond the rim of consciousness, pushing turgidly at me like a handicapper's pencil, trying to burst through the membranous wall of skull and into the tent of consciousness itself, but I wasn't ready; I wasn't ready for any of it yet. So all that I said was, "Poirier left me another note today."

"You told me that."

"Oh, did I? Well, he left me another note. The poor bastard typed it out and probably took the subway and slipped it under my door while I was out. I can see it in his shirt pocket in the underground; it's trembling like mad and he puts a hand up to steady it and everybody looks at him as if it's cocaine and all that he wants to do is to shout at them: *you can't do this to me, I'm a Case Unit Supervisor in the Department of Welfare, I'm no pusher or nut.* It could depress the hell out of you if you thought about it long enough."

"He's only trying to help you, you know."

"I don't need his help."

She looked up at me through the scotch glass. "You're going to be fired you know, Martin. There's no way you can really stop it. Do you want to be fired?"

"I don't care."

"Don't you? What would you do?"

"I told you."

"Well, aside from that. That's a very hard industry to work in. Aside from that, Martin, what would you do?"

"I'd keep busy. I'd collect unemployment insurance. Maybe I'd write a novel. I've always wanted to write a novel."

"You really think you'd be happy that way, Martin? Do you really think that that's the answer?"

"Anything's the answer as long as you can come to terms with it; that's what I say."

She looked at me through the scotch glass, holding her lips, nose and eyes behind it so that in that vaguely distorted focus they seemed to shift and blur, seemed to find themselves suspended far above me. "I don't think your thinking is very straight, Martin," she said. "I'll tell you that frankly. Who do you think breaks into the movies?"

"Whores. Sluts. Idiots. Parasites with manners and luck. Big time novelists. Teenage girls from Memphis with nice asses. All kinds of people break into the movies."

"But they've either accomplished something or they have connections, Martin. Do you have connections?"

"You're saying I haven't accomplished anything?"

"Have you?"

"I know some people in the studios."

"Really? Enough people in the right places to get you a job? Do you really think you can get in cold, Martin?"

"Everybody does at the beginning. Somebody has to."

"And why do you want to go into the movies anyway? It isn't very much fun if you're not successful and most of the jobs, I imagine, are as bor-

ing as being in the Department of Welfare, maybe worse, because
you're near people all the time who *are* having fun and yet you're this
little clerk who has to go home every night and watch the television. Do
you think that's anything to look forward to?"

"You've got to start someplace. Everybody has to start from the beginning to get anywhere at all."

"But I don't think you want it, Martin. I don't even think you want to
get into the movies because if you did you would have gone out to California years ago and just started hanging around instead of working
in the Welfare Department. So I don't believe you." She smiled, a smile
that added depth and years to her features rather than the other way
as most smiles do and stretched on the couch, giving me another angle
of the breasts. It was a most interesting angle and performance, considering what she had had to say about the movies. I wouldn't have
minded taking up the point with her but in the next motion she had
half-curled her knees up to her stomach and sat and the moment had
passed. "I think I will have another drink, anyway," she said. "What the
hell. A smaller one but very straight."

"Whatever you want."

"I don't see any reason not to drink. Besides, you're going to take me
out and we're going to have a big dinner, right?"

"Of course."

She put a finger under her chin. "On the other hand, you may be out
of a job next week and then we'd want you to save your money. So perhaps I could go out and pick up a few things."

"No," I said. "That's perfectly all right. I want to take you out; I'll be
happy to take you out. We'll go in just a little while, now."

"Oh, I'm in no hurry. I'm getting high on your scotch. I really feel a little drunk."

Well, that was more than I could say. I made her another drink, deliberately, coldly, pouring in more than two ounces of scotch and gave
it to her. She didn't even react; took the tumbler with two hands and
sipped at it not at all tentatively, then took a large swallow and cough-
ing slightly put it down.

"I was straightening you out on Hollywood, wasn't I? Listen, Martin,
you've got to stop this business. I'm getting a little drunk so I'm probably talking too freely but I think your basic problem is that you've got
to grow up. In many ways you act like a little boy."

"You didn't say that last night. That wasn't at all what you had on your
mind, then."

But I wasn't going to get at her that way. She was beyond me, completely beyond me. They always are; Sophias of the soul, all of them,

making for their purposes whatever will suit, denying that which does-
n't. It is impossible to embarrass them or fluster them or touch them
with the merest connection if they do not know they want to be reached;
that is the whole secret. The vulnerability is a myth and a deceit; it exists only as another kind conceit in the engagement that goes on and
on and leads to nothing, absolutely nothing whatsoever. I could feel myself taking a darker, more violent turn and for reasons that I could not
begin to understand I found, suddenly, that I wanted to go to bed with
her; wanted to go to bed with her, perhaps, more urgently than I ever
had; strip the armor and the deceit from her and, making her breasts
fall to their natural level, in the same way I would make her sensibility retreat to that pocket where it belongs, all snideness, all doubt cast
away forever. But she must have seen this in me—they see everything
within you; there is no way you can beat them—and retreated subtly
on the couch, holding the glass before her. I had absolutely no doubt that
if I came to her in the wrong moment she would drench me with
scotch.

"We were talking about Hollywood. Hollywood is a lie and a fictitious
lie at that, Martin, because it doesn't have anything at all to do with the
things that people all over the country are doing right now; it merely
gives them something that they can feel reduced by; something which
makes them feel every minute of every day: well, whatever is happening to me can't be too important and I can't be too important a person
myself because this is not a movie and I am not a movie star. Except it
is. Except they are. Everybody's in the movies. That's what the foreign
people are trying to teach us, but we can't listen to them because we're
so full up of the other sickness. But they're trying and a few of us are
learning anyway. Maybe we'll all grow up some day."

"But you're wrong," I said. "You just have it all wrong; the whole lot
of you do. They aren't lies, they're reality. They're as close to reality as
most of us can come because most people aren't strong enough or good
enough or brave enough or big enough to discover reality so they don't
exist for most of their lives, like Poirier. But the reality is there if you
can only come out of yourself and try to touch it and if you're good
enough, they'll show you the way. I tell you, the only real things in the
world are happening up on the movie screen and as far as the foreign
films are concerned, their women are better looking than ours and have
larger breasts and if they aren't larger, they're better formed and they
show more of them. Where is all the sex coming from unless it's from
the foreign films? We had to learn it second hand. They know the same
reality Hollywood does."

The business about breasts must have bothered her because, even with the scotch glass, she brought her hand up there, stroked herself and seemed to be half-concealing, then she sighed—as if accepting for the thousandth time the shape and meaning of her breasts, the dull, familiar tone of her nipples—and dropped it and went back to the glass. "That's not fair, Martin," she said. "And it's ridiculous as well. Everybody knows that the movies are full of lies. The trouble with your supervisor, Poirier, is that he's seen too many movies, not the other way. And he's just given up."

"You're wrong."

"And the trouble with you, probably, is that you've seen too many movies too; you're just full of them. Sometimes you can even act as if you're in a movie and it's just ridiculous. Now that's what I think but I'm a little drunk and not responsible and now I feel that I have to go to the bathroom if you'll excuse me."

She got up, went there. As she clicked the door closed I wondered idly if she was going in there to insert her diaphragm but I knew that was ridiculous; she had once told me that she wore it almost all the time so that if something ever did happen it would be without embarrassment; she couldn't stand making a ritual of sex, it should be spontaneous. But, listening to the flushing sound of the toilet—was it to cover the slight groans I understood some of them made during insertion?—I wondered if, perhaps, she had come over with no intention in the world of going to bed with me but had changed her mind. I decided that it really didn't matter either way; something perverse in me drifted out in that sauce and tried to listen to the spang of urine in the bowl but there were no other sounds until the faucets began to mutter and I gave it up. When she came out, it was with an expression subtly different from the one with which she had gone in; her face and bare arms seemed to be lightly, delicately suffused with the kind of sexuality which women cannot conceal when they want to go to bed. I found myself slightly excited at this pitiful gift she was bearing back on me. She came over to my chair and leaned over and stroked my hair.

"Poor Martin," she said. "I really didn't mean to upset you. It's just that I like you a lot and I don't want to see you all confused and getting yourself into trouble because you don't understand what you're involved with. I didn't mean to upset you. Poor Martin."

Poor Martin, poor Martin. I reached up a finger and drew it against her breast, pressing in slightly, circling the place where the nipple might have been. She didn't stop me. She tensed slightly and leaned over and kissed my hair, leaving a small trail of moisture behind as her lips worked their way over my skull.

"Just calm down and try to understand things," she said. "That's all I ask of you. Is that so much? If I've learned a few things, a stupid girl like me, why can't you?"

"I've learned. I've learned everything I need to know. I learned it a long time ago."

"No you didn't, Martin. Nobody ever knows all they need to know. Except in the movies. In the movies they know everything." Her voice broke subtly, became richer. "And we're not in the movies. It's a shame, Martin, but we just aren't in the movies."

I tried, then. It has to be said that I tried. If I did not really try then there can be no understanding and without understanding there is death, decay, waste, a slow, unmarked procession to the graveyard where in the mutuality of excavation nothing matters; nothing at all. Whatever had been congealing within me, whatever had been indefinably there broke free and it broke free in a fine, high assault; a kind of desperation, a need to drive myself into her, but more than driving myself into her, to come out the other end in some high, detailed place where, perhaps, there might be a glimpse behind manners. I wanted to get beyond manners. I wanted to rage and beat and meld against her, then, that stifling urgency coming from the hidden parts of myself and as I found myself getting up from the chair, found my 1 hands digging at last, hard, as hard as I wanted, even harder than that, into the resistant flesh of her upper arms, it was not in need of tearing but of accommodation and she came against me and I put my arms around her and then, in that first thrust of our pact, we agreed that we were going to do it, we were going to do it right now, and if our reasons were entirely different, not to say everything that lay behind them—because I wanted to be in the movies and Barbara, Barbara believed that her life was better—that this was only another one of the infinite number of small suicides, losses and murders which have possessed the act from the beginning. I got her clothes off almost by wrenching at them and she gave small shouts and began to tear at my own clothing and somehow, in an agony of stumbling and apologies and embarrassments as we moved briefly apart from one another, we were both naked and I put my hand on her hand and she put her other hand on my genitals, squeezing them softly until they rose in greeting and I led her to the couch, dodging litter on the floor and the depression of the scotch glass as I put her down that way, all the way on the couch and I got on top of her. I felt the slipping, sliding, tearing of entrance. She ran her hands against my mouth and then brought it down to her breasts. I covered her breasts—her small, sloping, hanging breasts—with my mouth and went at them as no other man, inside or outside of the movies, had ever gone at any woman's breasts before; ever, ever.

I wanted to break through; I wanted to tear through, then; if breaking and tearing were to be done I wanted that. I wanted to see her face, her face only as I rose above her in the shriek and pounding of orgasm; wanted to subside upon her sweating, dusty flesh in the totality of the afterknowledge knowing that it was this woman who had made me come and not a procession of abstract others, all laughing at me. I wanted to keep the other faces off the rim of consciousness; the voices and faces that were always there at this time of mockery and as I fought them down, almost physically, moving my head back and forth on her breasts, chewing to keep the mysteries away, I felt that I was succeeding, for no Elizabeth, Brigitte or Sophia came my way; the screen of the inner eye was dark, everything was outside and I was entering upon it. I realized then in some vast, pointless crevice that if I was able to succeed, if I was able to keep them away, I would probably be converted on the instant to a new level of function; something between, say, what I understood and what Poirier knew and that somewhere in that accommodation, in that grey, endless canyon, I would have to make my life as best it suited; I understood that what would happen then would be both better and worse than everything which had been before but mostly it would be different and I was willing; I was willing to do it, I put myself against the thrashing of her limbs, my teeth still tearing into her nipple, the fingers of the other hand rising to grope and grasp and tug at her other breast and I told myself that if it were going to be that way I could probably live with it to whatever equivocal end. Because I was tired, tired; that was the thing, I was tired of all of it: the tote board had winked into me an apprehension of just how tired of mysteries I was and now I wanted but peace, a kind of reality into which I could snuggle myself and be lost; lost, I wanted to be lost in this girl as I never had been with Sophia and Elizabeth and I pounded against her in a restless child's eagerness, forcing her breasts to protrude as far from her chest with my teeth as the sweater and brassiere had made them in another way and she moaned something and said "hey, hey, hey, now; you're hurting me, take it easy," and I let the breast slide back although there was no anger in her voice, not even a kind of remonstrance but only a sound of witness; she was witnessing me. She was watching me. I was performing for her. Bound off in some abstract place, then, clowning for her delight, I muttered and bucked, trying to get the last few inches in against her dry interior and as I did so I could feel her opening under me and her murky wetness spilled it; spilled out against me with such force that I could feel myself sliding back, back. And still, driving in to make the connection again I kept the faces off, the screen still dark, the sounds behind some thick, gauze curtain and I began the sliding, equivocal journey toward coupling, moving the last few miles and as I did so, then, the whispers began.

They began on the offstage of the consciousness, dry, subtle, almost imperceptible and then, as I increased my speed and moans, trying to throw them off that way by putting myself in an isolate pocket they came in nearer and nearer, working to the midpoint and then the forefront of the cerebrum and the voices were the soft, urgent voices of women. They were calling to me; they were calling to me through all the spaces of my need and what they were saying was: *Martin, Martin, what are you doing; you can't do this to us, Martin, it isn't right; it isn't fair, think of us, what's going to happen to us if you go away.* They had never called me Martin before; I had always been an anonymous abstraction and I thought that they had not even known my name but apparently they had; they had all known it from the beginning, the dirty bitches always knew exactly who you were and what you were doing and they treated you as if they didn't just so that they could keep you in a perpetual interrelation of doubt that was the key to the whole thing. They knew who you were every step of the way, that was all there was to it. I could feel Barbara's arms going around me and she forced my head down to her breasts roughly, muttering something like, "I don't care; I said I don't care, Martin, do them, do me, do me good," and I felt an absent flash of pity for a woman who had all her feeling apparently centered in her breasts rather than in her cunt and her breasts were so small to boot; it must have been a continual humiliation, this sexual act, if everything came down to what could be aroused in what were her least essential points, but I wasn't thinking of Barbara, not really. I was trying to think of her; trying crudely, desperately, to make the joining but I was slipping, sliding, moving further away and now the faces themselves drifted over and I saw them poised in the solemnity and beauty with which a girl must raise her head for the first kiss; the eyes dark and shadows, the mouths slightly broken but yet resolute with a complex kind of grief.

Elizabeth was there and Sophia of course and Brigitte and Jane was there too but she and Brigitte were not shouting at one another as I might have expected but instead were joining hands, holding their hands together in a gesture of simple elegance and comity looking down at me. And the others were there too: Grace, whom I had not seen in many years and Anna, who had been fun in her own way but whom I had dropped a long time ago because being with her continually was just too sick; Simone was there looking like a young girl in the slow cast of loss over her face and Hope was there and Ann and even Jayne and Marilyn whom I had lost so tragically; Jayne and Marilyn who in their

girlish, vulnerable way had been, perhaps, the best I had ever had, only
to be cruelly yanked out of my consciousness by events so terrible that
it was impossible for me to comprehend them: events worse than plun-
der, worse than assassination, and behind them were others also; others whom I could not recognize because I had not seen them for so long
or because they had aged so in their loss; girls I had tumbled with once
and never again: anonymous starlets, high-paid prostitutes, vagrant
models, all of them were there. They came in an army, behind the major grouping there were hundreds or maybe thousands of all the girls
I had possessed in the pain of my nights and dreams and they were all
looking at me the same way and they were reaching toward me, their
eyes full and rounded in that graceful gesture and I couldn't leave them;
I simply couldn't leave them. There was no way in the world that I could
leave even the least of them; the least flat-fitted model whom I had
banged when I was twelve or thirteen years old between the covers of
a magazine because if I left them I forsook myself as well and I was the
only thing I knew. I was the only thing I knew, the only thing I had; the
rest was apostasy or recreation; only in that huddling could I understand what I was and what I was meant to be. Without that history I
had no existence; without those dreams, touches and terrors, I had no
possibilities. And so, I felt myself rising, rising to a high place, my hand
raised in greeting, a light gesture of warmth and I tried to tell them with
my eyes and that hand—because they couldn't hear me, I knew that
there was no way at all that they could hear me—that I loved them,
loved them all, that I would never leave them but would stay with them
forever tenanting in the tombs of my soul, each night a dawn, each dawn
a blending. I tried to tell them that, giving them an absurd V for Victory sign and all the time of course I was riding Barbara, riding the flat
plane of her body like a jockey but she was a failing horse; she was a
horse collapsing around the stretch turn, she tumbled out from under
me all glass and shattering and I could only hear her cries from a far
distance. "I'm near, I'm near," she was saying, "I'm near, Martin, do you
hear me; you've got me hot, I'm almost on the edge, keep on pumping,"
and I kept on pumping but only my cock was in it, not the brain; perhaps the cock wasn't in it either but only a distended tube carrying out
the wastes which had accumulated while I had been making love to the
gallery beyond. But I thrashed and dug at her, feeling from that distance
her hands digging into my shoulders and as all the lights of consciousness went out—they were waving at me *goodbye, goodbye, we will be
back; we will be back*—I felt myself in a dull, constricted tunnel pounding and heaving at her and I came; I finally came, I came with a feeling of rushing pain as if my bowels and not my balls had opened up and

put everything that I had to put into her in a series of brief, flopping strokes and she gasped and uncoiled and threw her head back. "Martin, Martin," she said and came at me going off into some private spaces of her own, her face under the hard lights and in this posture seemingly twisted by a kind of torment but the cries she made were not of the damned but the ascended and I felt her fluid swimming at me, rushing at me with such force that I could barely stay in her; I was wet, sopping wet, a small matchstick placed within a huge bottle of oil but I held it stubbornly and she finished with a couple of gasping thuds and it was over; the horror was over, I was definitely able to tell by looking at her face and watching her respiration that it was over. I had done it. She lay loosely, slackly underneath me, the fingers of one hand dangling, reaching for the scotch. Her nipples had now inverted, turned almost inside, giving an intricate look of concavity to her breasts. She heaved once with her hips and spilled me out and I moved aside from her, taking my weight off her, put my shoulders against the hardness of the couch which spoke also of a kind of resolution and then I went for some cigarettes and when she brushed them away had one myself while she finished the scotch.

"That was all right," she said after a long, long time. "That was really all right. I guess I never made it before. I thought I had made it but I guess I didn't. I guess you can tell that way."

"Good, good."

"Men make it all the time; they have no idea of what it's like for a woman. How could they understand?" Her breath was still irregular, I put a hand on her chest to pat her in the space between her breasts. Her body felt like metal. It didn't matter. I felt for her, perhaps, such pain as I had never felt for another human being because she didn't know; she simply didn't know what was going on. She would have to be protected against that by someone but I did not want it to be me. I was already away; away, I had other things on my mind.

"Not all the time," I said.

"What's that?"

"Men don't make it all the time. They make it most of the time. But every now and then ..."

She smiled at me and held my hand. "In Hollywood they *do* make it all the time though, don't they, Martin?"

"In Hollywood."

"Well, anything can be Hollywood."

"Not anything."

"That's my whole point. You can have Hollywood right here. Everybody makes his own Hollywood. Or can make it. Do you think you know what

I'm saying?"

"I guess so."

"That was very nice. I liked that very much. I guess I'll have a cigarette, now. I didn't mean to push you away before. I was still—enjoying
it if you know what I mean."

I gave her a cigarette and lit it, then watched as she put it out after
one puff. "I don't even need it. I don't need to smoke now."

"I'm glad."

"Sometimes you don't need to. I could just lie here for hours and hours."

That was not what I had in mind. What I had in mind was something
subtle and complex; I was not quite sure, even then, of what it was but
I suspected that it had nothing whatsoever to do with her. I wanted her
out. I wanted her out desperately. And yet there was no way of gaining
that.

"A penny."

"What's that?"

"For your thoughts. What are you thinking?"

"Oh, not much. Or a lot of things." I was stricken by an idea, then. "I
was thinking that I was hungry."

"Ha. That's a man. From one thing to the next thing, no pause in between. Well, how hungry are you? Let's figure out what we're going to
eat and we'll pick it up."

"Oh no," I said. "Oh, no. I want to take you out to eat. I said that's what
I wanted to do and that's the way it is. So we'll get dressed and just get
out of here."

"But we can eat in. We can save money. No telling what we'll need the
money for some other time."

"I wouldn't hear of it. I want to take you out. We can go to a nice place
in the neighborhood I know," I said, "and then I can take you to a movie."

"To a movie?"

"Why not? I can show you my side of the argument. You've shown me
yours, let me show mine."

Her eyes fell and she began to grope at the cigarette pack which was
lying beside the couch. "You didn't like my side of the story? Is that what
you mean?"

"I don't mean such a thing at all. I liked it very much. Now the loyal
opposition should have a chance to take the floor. That's all I meant.
Nothing else."

She let the pack fall and sighed. "Oh, I don't want to go out yet. I could
just lie and lie. Why don't you hold me?"

"I'm hungry," I said. I tried to keep all rage, passion, urgency out of my
voice. The important thing was to be mild. Once they saw urgency, they

always went the other way. All of them. It was one of the basic laws governing how they functioned.

"Oh, all right," she said. She swung up on the bed gracelessly, her thin legs taking the shadows through the window; the largest of them passing briefly over her vagina and then upwards. "All right, all right. We'll go out to dinner and get you fed. Dutch treat."

"No," I said.

"Well, then, Dutch treat for the movie. If you want to go to the movie. And I'm insistent about that."

"Fair enough," I said. "Fair enough." It was just. It was poetically just. I got up slowly and went for my clothes, fumbling through them to see that everything was in place, one toe kicking the hard metal of the projector which had been shoved underneath the bed.

VI

I almost told her all of it, anyway. That was the thing. Somewhere between the cocktails we had in the restaurant—it was a small, gloomy, vaguely German place over on the East Side but it was quiet and cool and empty which were benefits—and the main course which took a long, long time to come, I almost leaned across the table, putting my drink down with a crash and said *listen here, Barbara, listen here; I really think that you deserve to understand exactly who you're dealing with here.* I almost said to her then: *it is important that I start at the absolute beginning to give you some idea of precisely who you are dealing with so that illusions will be dispelled and in a comity of insight we can proceed from there* but I did not. It was close but I did not do it.

What we did was to talk about the Welfare Department: the pointlessness, the drift of the organization; the way it seemed to be, in all ways, truly symptomatic of everything which was gone wrong with the American twentieth-century; the utter cutting-off, on both sides, of both employees and recipients from any consequences of their acts or, for that matter, of any sense of identity. You had no identity and this was, perhaps, what caused all the trouble. I said to her that Poirier's problem was that in his thrashings-about for an identity he had decided to select that of case unit supervisor and Barbara said I was all wrong; that the problem was not so much a seeking of identity as a question of coming to terms with a very grim, very terrible situation and people, in trying to do so, kind of lost their minds. It would happen to anyone; the people who worked in the Department of Welfare would all have been much better off if they had been elsewhere, while anybody who was elsewhere would have been just as crazy as the employees if he had wound up there.

I tried to point out that she was missing a vital insight: that the people who worked there were working there because that was part of their problem; that the department took in a kind of individual who already had a predisposition toward functioning in a certain way; that the Department of Welfare, ultimately, was staffed by people who loved their work because they needed nothing so much as something to hate, just as the people in the infield at the racetracks needed the tote board to tell them what or who they were. People, then, sought their destiny and what they did was an enactment of that wish; the Department of Welfare was inflicting that upon its employees certainly, but all up and down the line of America, all within and without the industries, the same thing was going on. So the sickness could not be confined, could not be attributed merely to its base; it was linked back to the condition of its inhabitants and the inhabitants were linked back to the nature of the Republic and somewhere in the very dead-center of this the truth might be known if anyone cared but no one did care, they were too busy dropping notes off under people's doors or riding the subways in the darkness and heat of July when they could be out doing something else or they were too busy bringing other people up on charges in order to reinforce the system; no one cared. I could have taught them but I didn't care either. That was the truth of the matter: I cared less than all of them precisely because I saw more. But there was no way of communicating this to Barbara, much less to Poirier. There was no way of breaking through to them, asking them to understand that everything that they were was the function of what they wanted to be and that beyond the possibility of Acts of God or great historical convulsions or the accident of mortality this was true of almost everyone in the country; he wound up being exactly what he had wanted to be from the first. Perhaps if I had been able to make this clear to her there would have been a beginning, some tentative beginning of the communality of insight which the people outside the tote boards said was "catching it right" but I didn't care. I didn't care anymore.

It was, in short, pointless dinner conversation; the kind of conversation which goes on almost inevitably between a man and a woman who have just fucked and whose function is to stretch out the moments between the first fuck and the anticipated one, the real one to follow. It was rooted deeply in the need of her part to deny that any such thing as fucking could possibly have occurred to a girl as reputable as she and on my part it came out of some more complex emotion; a need, perhaps, to voyage beyond the simple disaster of what had happened between us in our

rooms to some other kind of epiphany. But it was purposeless, purposeless. We went through cocktails, two cocktails, appetizer, sauer-
braten and dessert like that, talking about the Welfare Department and
a little bit about our relation to it—because everybody had to have a relation to everything; without relation there was no identity and without identity there was only chaos; a kind of dark chaos which only I
among the millions had evaded because of my better insight, but my
sensibility wasn't in it, much less my heart, because now, past all of this
there was only the desire to tell the truth. I wanted to tell her the truth
very badly. I needed to tell her the truth. And yet there was no way in
which it could have been uttered in that restaurant without becoming
something else, lies perhaps, evasions certainly, in any event a cancellation of what I found myself slowly reaching toward through the haze of
cocktails and the afterpain in my cock and groin.

I could have told her—if only I could have told her—that it had begun
a long time ago; that I had been doing it since I was thirteen years old,
first in loss and then in doubt but that now, finally, I was not doing it
those ways but rather in affirmation: that what it came down to, simply enough, was that the stars had more reality than this girl herself
and that what I did with them mattered infinitely more than anything
which could pass from my turgid genitals and into her. I could have
given her bits of sociology, pieces of old data wrung from the senti-
mentality of scholarship; I could have told her, then, that a broken home,
a loveless childhood, a wandering existence must always find either a
kind of affirmation or a most definite kind of death and I had found the
former and forsaken the latter as the most important of all that most
tentative series of choices which I had been compelled to make; which
all of us had been compelled to make. I could have told her that not very
long ago, a decade, or maybe less than that—and a decade meant nothing to the bleak, spinning universe—I had come to the understanding
that I would either have to find a certain justification for what was going on or I would die and although death, in the stretch of years, was
an abstraction it was also something so final that life, perhaps, was all
that we could know anyway; life was perhaps an absolute as timeless
as death if you could only see that way. I wanted to tell her that I had
made my choice then, for life, and it was a question of how I could best
find it and I had found it within the pathway of my own skull, the best
place, the only place, the place where all beginning had begun, and that
within that I had found a balance and a righteousness where I could find
them no place else. I could have told this foolish girl with the bare arms
and with the breast still pointlessly, mechanically upthrust toward her
neckline, the breasts that had no significance whatsoever because she

was simply incapable of acknowledging what they were—as I had ac-
knowledged what I was—and proceeding to make the point with one finger and a good deal of intensity that I was perfectly content with what
I was doing; that there was absolutely nothing wrong with what I was
doing; that all the trouble—if trouble there were—came not from me but
from what the world would have made of what I had become and so
from that peripety—because I was a sane man, sane enough to enter-
tain not only peripeties but epiphanies themselves, those tiny orgasms
of the psyche—had come a kind of accommodation and everything
that I had built up around me. I could have told her all of that just, as
in so many embraces, I had whispered the same to Sophia, Brigitte, Elizabeth, Ann, Jane, Marilyn, Jayne, Angela, Judith, Rhonda. They had understood—even, at the very beginning, Sophia had understood the best
of all—and she, perhaps could have been led to understand this as well;
if I only had been able to make her understand then there might be a
beginning to our relationship and even a kind of outcome waiting for
us at its termination but I couldn't say any of it to her. I couldn't say any
of it to her at all. Because if I had said it to her I would have been mad
and I wasn't mad; not in the least mad, I was sane, sane, sane, locked
in coldness, locked at last in the finality of what I had glimpsed in my
room pumping her. So I only talked then about the Welfare Department
and replied to what she said with intelligences of my own and that is
the way we made it through dinner. For her, I must have been a very
proper escort; locked into that small, equivocal security in the restaurant we must have, for her, created a small, real exile of need and cunning, possibility and inference, because, toward the end of the dinner she
took to stroking my hand and bidding me hello with her lips and I let
her; I let her because none of it made any difference. I could do it with
this girl. I could handle it with her. Because there was no alternative
and because now I saw how it would all end before me; the path
slammed down in my mind by my gallery as I had fucked her was clear
and final and all doubt was lost. Nothing was a mystery anymore except what was happening inside and that would be settled inside, inside. Everything would come to its final asking, eventually.

"Well," she said, when I paid the check. "That was very nice. I enjoyed
that."

"A movie," I said. "Now we'll go to a movie."

"You really like the movies, don't you, Martin? You really can't get over
that urge to go to a movie, can you?"

"Is there any need to? You said you'd give the enemy equal time, remember that?"

"I don't think you're the enemy."

"I didn't mean it that way. What do you want to see? You have any preference?"

"Not really."

"Foreign or American?"

"I guess foreign."

"I guess not. There's a retrospective over at the Bijou right in the neighborhood here. They're showing PILLOW TALK with Rock Hudson and Doris Day."

"That was awful, wasn't it?"

"It was a big hit in its year."

"Well, that doesn't make it good. Most big hits are awful. What do you want to see Doris Day for anyway? She's about forty-five years old, isn't she? And awful looking."

"It's a comedy. It's a light comedy."

She went for the pack of cigarettes again, lit one with such a flourish and urgency that I thought she wouldn't be satisfied; would dive for another. But she only smoked it with a drawing kind of intensity; the same intensity that I had shown against her nipples. "Oh, what the hell," she said. "If you want to see it, we'll see it. It's not going to prove a thing to me, though. I'll probably absolutely hate it and make the rest of the evening miserable for you." She smiled.

"I can risk it."

"You really like to see Hollywood films, don't you? Hollywood is something special for you."

"No, I see a lot of foreign films too," I said. "There's nothing wrong with foreign films; they can be great sometimes. It all depends." I stood, feeling the table sway under me as I put my palms flatly against it; she rose with me, putting out the cigarette in the ashtray. I put down a tip and paid the clerk at the register—he eyed me with the numb Saturday-hostility with which, transmuted, I would doubtless greet my clients Monday—and we went out into the hot spaces of the street touching, hands together. She ran a finger through my palm, put her head against my shoulder, then withdrew it as two dangerous-looking youths passed murmuring obscenities to one another, then put it back again. I let it rest there. I had nothing to lose. It didn't matter.

"Right down the block," I said.

"I see it. It's kind of an old theatre, isn't it?"

"There are newer."

"Sometimes I think a movie theatre is the most depressing place in the world. More depressing even than a bar-and-grill. They must be the worst places going."

"It all depends," I said. "It all depends." I put an arm around her and guided her to the window. The price signs were up, the old lady behind the window was slumped down, there was nobody anywhere around us. I paid while she stood in that half-elusive, half-protected slump which girls always seem to assume while waiting for their escorts to pay their way in—and then put the arm around her and guided her through the doors, into the blasts of air piling out of the house. I was affectionate, careful, graceful. It was the first time I had ever taken a girl to the movies. I gave the doorman our tickets and got us into the lobby—the creased, blotched lobby of a theatre on a decline so slow and yet so tumultuous that nothing short of a bombing would stop it before the walls themselves began to fester and clambered in against one another—and asked her if she wanted anything. She said she would have a candy bar and I bought her one; then, after thinking it over, decided to have some popcorn because it was important to do everything as if I were alone; if not, it would be fraudulent, it would come to nothing. We went inside—once again the place was almost empty; I had had my usual luck—and went into a middle aisle and she sat against me. The short subject was on, something dealing with Oregon and the sawing down of trees in that pointless state and I let her subside against me, her head a slight, almost inconsequential pressure against my shoulder, her hand chastely dipping toward but not cupping my genitals as she slipped it back and forth on my thigh, then dropped it to my knee. I could hear the paper of the candy bar crackle and a chewing sound.

"So what?" she said.

"The feature hasn't started yet."

"What's the difference? Feature, short, they're all the same. There have to be better places in the world to spend an evening."

"You're just afraid," I said to her then. "You're just afraid to be in the movies. You're afraid because you might find out that they're better than the life you're leading and then you'd have to take a good, long look at this life you're leading and you wouldn't be able to stand it. That's all. Why don't you give it a chance?"

She took her hand off my knee, I could see it reach like a bird in the darkness toward her face. "You're wrong," she said, "and there's no need to say that. No need at all."

"There are people around us who want to see the picture. Let's not talk; it bothers them."

"Nobody's around us. We're all alone here. Why did you say that? It isn't fair, it isn't right."

"But it's true, Barbara," I said, gently. "It's true and you know it's true and now the short subject is off and we're going to watch the movie. So just relax and let the movie come on."

"I like my life. I like being with you. I don't mind anything that's happening to me. What's wrong with life anyway? How do you have the right to say that Martin?"

"Because it's the truth and because you never listen to me so I have to tell you. Hush, now, we'll miss the picture."

"That's a terrible thing to say."

"No it isn't. It's the truth and the truth is never terrible. We're here tonight, Barbara; the two of us are together tonight because it's true and because for you at least there's no one better to be with. Now fact's facts, so face them."

I could feel her hands clawing at me now. "No," she said. "No, no, no, don't say that to me."

"I won't say anything to you. I want to watch the picture." The curtains swung closed, lights going on greenish behind them for an instant and then they cut open again. The titles started. "I said that I wanted to watch this picture."

"I should leave."

"No you shouldn't. And you won't. Just stay."

"I could get up and walk out on you, Martin; I tell you, I could get up and leave you. I don't need this. I don't need to sit and listen to this. I should get away from you."

"Don't do it," I said. "You won't do it anyway because I'm your last hope. But believe me, Barbara, even if you did, I would hardly know the difference. Not here. Not now. Just sit and watch the picture."

And then, not knowing whether she has heard this or not; not knowing whether she has stayed or not, I watch the colors of the screen brighten and, poised with a piece of popcorn in my hand like an arrow I feel myself once again being drawn, being drawn utterly, and everything outside in the totality of its discovered abstraction vanishes for I am here, I am back, I have returned. There is nothing but space and tension and I can feel the waters drawing, drawing; drawing me back to that first and most ultimate of all resolutions.

I am poised above Doris Day; the muscles in my arms have gone slightly to fat and are having trouble supporting me comfortably but I am a heavy man and must struggle to keep my weight off her, otherwise I will give her pain. She is lying underneath me, naked to the bone on the chaise longue, her face drawn and yet open, her eyes shuttered against my necessity and I am working upon her, muttering the proper words of encouragement and solace as I try to find myself into her dry, dwindled material. Doris Day is not young anymore; she is forty-five years old or perhaps forty-six, her breasts, even from this angle, sag badly and her voice is the high bleat of the woman who knows that what she is losing is, this one time around, not something which she will be able to pick up in a discount sale on the morrow or work out in a quarrel with some man; no, what she is losing this time around is nothing but the real thing itself, but I do not care, it whips me into a perverse excitement heightened by the obscenities she is whispering to me: obscenities uttered by Doris Day who has never, to public knowledge, let a filthy word cross her stream-of-consciousness. "You disgusting bastard," she is saying, "you dirty, filthy, son-of-a-bitch, you put it right in there and you *fuck* me because if you don't I'm going to die, I'm going to fall all to pieces right on this couch. Fuck me, *fuck me*, you cocksucking bastard," and strangely enough, the couch looks exactly like my own at home although considerably more embattled of course because I am quite a large man and Doris is not a thin woman at all; the richness of her slightly mottled thighs themselves accounting for several pounds of weight.

It is strange: oh, God, it is strange to be fucking Doris Day right off in her air-cooled, bachelor-girl apartment because usually it takes several moments or hours until the scenes I play out find their resolution in screwing but it is not mine to wonder why; particularly with such fortune stretched out underneath me, pleading, whistling slightly through her repaired—and beautifully Anglo-Saxonate nose— humming with biting lips, guiding me with fingers and winks to the orifice itself. Now, as I thunder into her, all pressure and tearing, I feel that I have reached a true state of ascension; something profound and almost noble has happened to me because I am not only fucking Doris Day but, perhaps, in the fucking I am fucking America itself; her body a continent, her veins a map, her arms direction signals guiding me home. To the mighty heart of the land itself I plow: it is slightly wrinkled, slightly dry, but pounds nonetheless for its age, is none the less willing for all of its losses and I can feel myself making the easy, oozing penetration; fucking America like this it is very much as if I have driven into a large, expensive, profligate motel, her body a lush carpet underneath me, her cunt a television set, her driving thighs a pair of air-conditioners hastening me to relaxation. What ease, what grace, what relaxation I feel! It is too much even for the likes of Rock Hudson. But nevertheless, courtly to the end, I hold back my groans and sobs until I have completed the insertion and then I begin to pound her, make batter upon the large cake of her body, perish in the oven of her American heat and as her arms wind around me, as her mouth opens to scream cries and obscenities that only America could understand; as all of this happens to me it occurs to me that, perhaps, I have finally vaulted to the last level and plunging deeply, deeply, into the steaming night of her, I think of girls, strange driven girls, lying in all the bedrooms of the nation, standing by its highways, gesturing to me with mouths absent of understanding and I would if I could lift myself out to deliver to them all of myself for love; all of myself into them, but Doris is demanding and tedious and so I return to her thinking only then, as the last shroud comes over me and the spurtings of the ocean on either end, that there are any number of men who might envy me if they only had some understanding of what I was doing, but if I had understanding of what they were doing, I might pity them. It is very strange and complex and my orgasm is like a giant bird, torn wing to wing by rifle fire, falling, falling, in the hot, drenched sun of that damned Southwestern city.

THE END

The Jewel and the Madonnas
By Barry N. Malzberg

That last line remains, 53 years later, the best I have ever written, certainly the best climactic line. Martin Miller is figuratively copulating with Doris Day, "Her body a roadway or continent, her veins a map, her breasts mountains"; to be with her in this way, he knows, is to be with America itself, the ruined, ravaged, damaged beautiful continent and as he works his uneasy way with those mountains he is soaring, plunging... "It is strange and complex, complex and strange and my orgasm is a great bird, torn wing to wing by rifle fire, falling, falling, in the hot drenched sun of that damned Southwestern City." The USA edition not being immediately to hand I am translating a translation from the French edition. Eric Kahane, Maurice's brother, was responsible for that translation; unlike his notorious brother he had retained the familial name which Maurice had had changed for him when the Nazis penetrated France. Torn wing to wing by rifle fire. Falling. Falling.

I typed that paragraph in the bedroom of a three-room garden apartment at 216 West 78th Street. It was early July, just past the rocketry of Independence Day and the sense of the fire, the situation of the incendiary Republic must have been on what passed for my mind that sinister Saturday morning. My wife was at the trademark research office to which she had returned about a year ago; I was child care in that morning and Stephanie Jill, on the threshold of her second birthday was on my knee, a bouncing indolence when, in this all too domestic situation, that line came on like Saki's cobra. *This novel is not what I expected it to be,* I thought, anticipating what Maurice Girodias would say to me nine days later after I had conveyed the novel to the Gramercy Park apartment which was serving as his first outpost for Olympia Press USA. "You give me such beautiful promise, the ladies are described well, the sex is hot, you even seem to have found out what color Brigitte's *bush* is and then, suddenly, you give me angst, despair, depression, misery, disappointment, horse racing, horse racing death! I will publish this novel because it is a masterpiece and you give me no choice but I will lose all my money." He sighed, a pornographer entrapped by a sense of duty, just like the hapless author behind him. "I have an idea," Maurice had said three weeks earlier. "It is a great idea for a novel and I offer it to you. There is this clerk, see, or maybe he works in a movie box office, he loves actresses, he loves sex, he loves the movies and he imagines himself fucking the stars of those movies. That imagining is so vivid that he is actually doing it as it happens."

"We do not use imaginary actresses," he continued, "But the actual stars. We do not use pseudonyms, we use their real names. I tell you, this novel will be a scandal! It will create great excitement! It will be legendary! Every man in your country wants to fuck star actresses! This novel will be a scandal and a great success."

"And what happens to the protagonist, the box office guy?" I asked, already imagining Martin Miller as a Department of Welfare Social Investigator with a complaining, restless not-quite-girlfriend. "What happens to him?"

"What do I care what happens to him?" Maurice thought for a moment. "He becomes Joe E. Levine or something. You owe me this novel," he added. "This first novel of yours, it is brilliant but nobody wants this kind of literary play. I will publish it because it is exceptional but it will sell nothing. I do this for you, now you do something for me. I want you to write this novel. I will give you the same advance. We will call it *Screen*."

"There may be a lawsuit," I said cautiously. "Or lawsuits. You say you want a scandal."

"A lawsuit? I would love it. We will write in the contract that if one of them sues I will pay all costs."

I learned a few months later that Maurice's inspired idea, what he took to be the narrative conceit of a lifetime was one which he had been offering to every writer who passed his field of vision, everyone who his Ophelia and Traveler's Companion had been publishing in pink or green editions; the new hardcover line was supposed to be classier, of course, which is why he had taken on my Nabokovian *Oracle of the Thousand Hands* but now that Maurice, like a high-priced allowance horse, was being slotted back into the lower claiming ranks, he wanted something both more or less than veins like a map, a corpus like America itself. Which means that his reaction to the manuscript (and no doubt that blazing final paragraph) was almost as sour as it had been to *Oracle of the Thousand Hands*. Still: "I publish this, it is a masterpiece but I lose all my money."

He did indeed lose all his money but the hapless Martin Miller and his adventures were not the cause; the work was actually sublicensed in five or six countries and became something of an underground (far underground) hit; sales in this country were abominable (Barney Rossett, as an emblem of the entire literary establishment in this country was out to destroy him) but Lehmann-Haupt did review the novel in the *New York Times* of 4/7/69 ("has some wit and style") while making it clear in the nature of mainstream reviewers to this day *he* did not, of course, find the narrative at all, ahem, stimulating. (*I Am Curious Yellow* in movie theatres at about that time got the same reaction from the television critics..."Just a dirty movie and I of course am untouched by such cheap pandering.") Algis Budrys of all people gave that and *Oracle* a brief paragraph in his *Galaxy* review column, noting that the novel served the desire of the adolescent he had been to go riding with John Wayne and make out with Maureen O'Hara. He expanded upon that when we sat next to one another at the 1969 Nebula Banquet..."Reading this was like reading my story. You got hold of something really powerful there." *Screen* apparently was for him what *Portnoy* had been to Jewish boys of a certain age, it provided that strange kind of double-vision afforded the certain ager when he finds himself reading about a long-denied version of himself.

So the novel got around, if not quite in the fashion Maurice had envisioned and certainly not in a way which would have served his hopes. For all the cold fact of its three figure total sale as one of the first seven novels of the new Olympia "upscale" line, for all the cold fact that police had invaded a warehouse in which copies of the British edition were awaiting distribution, confiscating the entire shipment (entrants in which were peddled at very high prices in that country's collectors' market for years thereafter), despite all of it or perhaps because of none, the novel over these 50 years has in the aggregate paid me more than all but one other, that being the collaborative *Running of Beasts* with Bill Pronzini. *Beyond Apollo* has paid me less. Among readers of science fiction its existence is pretty well known although only a few have read it and this will be the first reissue for the domestic market in over half a century.

This is probably the point in this essay at which I should, as I once suggested to Robert Silverberg when he hit a rough spot in *Tower of Glass* to "literary it up" and that would be relatively easy; I literaried it up pretty good for the other essay, the other novel in this volume, and *Everything Happened To Susan* for all its *mise en scene* certainly presents less possibility than *Screen*, here, after all and as I have noted in my Afterword to the Stark House *Best of Manhunt* is a work like *Manhunt's* set of works which point to the access of the buried life and death of the Republic; here is the spectacle of our lives desperately re-imagined, re-worked into film; film has taught us everything we know about how to express everything we know and Martin Miller in his industrious banality is getting far closer to that dreadful reality than any pundit of our politics (except for Norman Mailer and maybe Hunter Thompson) has gotten in this half century; here is the yearning and the desperation, the focus and the loss of focus, the penetration and clumsy switchback of our doomed and shuffling polity. Here are the veins, the mountains, the steaming or desiccated ruin of the country gussied up at rallies and seminars like Doris Day's hair when she met Rock Hudson, here if we could still find her would be the aged Brigitte or Sophia, here would be the surviving Martin Miller himself, still staring at the screen as he pounds away at the Jewel. Here is the entire mess of unfocused and desperate desire, still gleaming at hopeless remove as we scramble through the dark. Here is Maurice Girodias with his big plans; here is Malzberg with his only slightly smaller plans, here is Stephanie Jill squinting somehow at her birthday a half century later, the candles flickering like fireworks in the clamped and descending night. Maurice wanted a scandal. He got one all right. Wrong place, wrong time. Dead in 1990 after having just given a television interview.

February 2020: New Jersey

CINEMA
(THE MASOCHIST)
....
BARRY N. MALZBERG

CHAPTER I

Susan permits the man to enter her, feels him squirm and inflate inside, the rising pressure, and then, as if from a great distance, the sting of his discharge. "Oh boy," he gasps unprofessionally, obviously out of the role, and then he remembers his lines: "Screw you, lady," he says, disengaging with a grimace, "that's just to show you you don't mean nothing to me. I don't get involved with women." He staggers to his feet, breathing heavily, a strange and absent look on his face, twitching under the lights. Then, "I don't believe this," he says. "I just can't believe any of this."

"Cut!" the director screams, "cut, you screw-up!"

Susan groans, knowing there will be a retake, and thinks about the pain of entrance. She is not quite sure how long they have been working, but she is sore all over …

CHAPTER II

Susan has answered an advertisement in a weekly sex newspaper calling for young actresses or models, one hundred dollars a day, honest work, no fooling around. No other details were offered. The answering service which took her call told her to report to an address on the upper West Side the following morning where she was subjected to an interview, which necessitated her undressing. Ten or fifteen girls had shown up but only three or four passed. Susan realized the advertiser was in the pornographic film business when she saw the script and was told she would have to pretty much work on her actor's instinct to improvise dialogue.

CHAPTER III

The man conducting the interviews said his name was Phil and that he really had nothing to do with the owners, and did not, in fact, know who these owners were. "You got to face the facts," Phil told her after she had put her clothes on and finished the biographical details, "there's a big market for this kind of stuff, and, it can be done with taste and style. Potentially, skin flicks are a very good thing; we can reach all kinds of people who would otherwise have nothing to do with their messages and we can teach them something, if we only learn to sneak it in. What we want is a more intellectual kind of production: a little taste and skill along with the heavy stuff. There's got to be plenty of plot to make it redeeming. But you don't have to worry about nothing when you go to work for us; if you go good, there might even be legitimate opportunities for you. This is a growth situation." Phil had added that he had absolutely no personal interest in the actors or actresses, a lot of these damn fly-by-nights were just using blue films as an excuse for sex or worse but he, Phil, was all business and had no intention of asking Susan for a date. On the other hand, if she wanted to have a cup of coffee with him after the session that was perfectly all right. He would like to get to know her a little better and discuss several interesting things. Right after the filming, he would look forward to it ...

CHAPTER IV

In the script, Susan is playing a young girl who has come to New York to look for a legitimate break in show business but has instead been forced into the making of pornographic films to support herself. The girl she is playing has had some kind of unhappy affair with a naive man who thought her forward and accused her of making indecent advances to him out of the sacred bond of wedlock. Resultantly, she suffers from a deep sense of shame and now seeks to degrade herself. All of the characters in this film are seeking degradation. In the course of the role, then, she is to have intercourse three or four times, as well as much petting, and one incident of sado-masochism with a tall man holding a whip. "He won't really hurt you but you've got to *scream,*" the director said, and when the whip comes down on her naked back, she feels cold terror moving through her and she screams so loudly that the whip-man backs off, trembling. "What's this?" he says. "Why are you taking it so personally," and the director says *cut this,* and that is another sequence that must be reshot.

CHAPTER V

Susan also came to New York several months ago to look for a legitimate break in show business, but, the fact is, she has very little talent and no luck and thus she has been forced into the making of pornographic films to support herself. Presently she is living with an unpublished writer named Timothy West who feels he is on the edge of a major breakthrough in style and technique but, at the present time, is an assistant supervisor for the New York City Department of Welfare at a salary of twelve thousand dollars per year. "You have no idea how doomed the welfare system in this country is," Timothy has told her, "but you can make a very good living at it, and you can hardly call it work."

He'd met Susan at a singles bar five or six weeks before and had little difficulty in talking her into living with him after their first night together since she was two months overdue in her rent and her landlord was quite hostile. "I don't know what to say, Susan," he'd said to her when she'd explained to him that, on the following day, she was going to report for an interview for what she suspected was a role in a stag movie. "On the one hand, I think we've reached a point in our relationship where I very definitely don't feel personally threatened by this kind of thing but, on the other, I don't know if it's the kind of thing you should be in, for your sake.

"Of course the dirty movie is more or less a metaphor for the total corruption of human relationships which we've seen in the Assassination Age, the utter collapse of real feeling and connection but then again, maybe a new ethic will come out of these ashes, one built upon an acceptance of the body and all that it entails. It has to be your decision, doesn't it? Whatever you do, I'm sure that it will be for the best." And then he had suggested that, since they both had to get up early in the morning, they postpone having sex for just this one night so that they could be well rested and build up even more anticipation for the next night.

"Of course," he had said, clenching and unclenching his hands, a fine line of sweat appearing above his upper lip as he flexed his shoulders over his typewriter and shook his head, rereading a difficult paragraph, "of course, if you feel that this is a defense-mechanism of some sort and that I'm really *avoiding* sex or if you really want it, then, well, just say the word and we'll go to it. I have a great deal of desire, it's just that I think we shouldn't take sex as a matter of course. God, I can't seem to make the metaphors in this scene work. If only I could do it, I could send it to the *Hudson Review* but for them the point of view has to be basically urbane." She had to say no, that it was perfectly fine with her, that they certainly could let the sex go for this one night. Timothy said the trouble with the short-story market is that it seemed to be almost all gone even though the short story was the basic American form, but, if you could get something into one of the prestigious quarterlies which still carried them, editors and publishers all over New York would come to your door extending contracts and checks for your first novel.

CHAPTER VI

The actor with whom she has had most of her scenes had ejaculated early on, of course, and since then they have been simulating. It is very late in the day, however, and even simulation is becoming painful for him; the director has had to conceive certain camera angles to hide his genitals. "I don't want you to think there's anything wrong with me," the actor whispers to her as he wedges against her thighs, seizes her breasts, begins to work on them for the twentieth time that day (she has long since lost all sensitivity there), "but I just had a real heavy session last night, not expecting today would be anything like this and there just isn't too much left in me. Do you want to go out and have a cup of coffee afterward? I feel that we should establish some kind of relationship." He says all of this as he is slobbering over her breasts, which causes some of the words to be mumbled so that she catches only half. She says thank you very much but she already has an appointment with someone. Amazingly, he has a sudden erection; it prods her enormously as the director gives an *ah*! of satisfaction, and the actor says he understands perfectly ...

CHAPTER VII

There are five or six actors in the film Susan is making; she has no clear impression of any of them other than the boy she is with. From time to time, the script calls for group scenes but, for reasons best known to the director or the scriptwriter, she is to engage in sexual acts only with this one boy. The others pair off. While she is on the floor, underneath the heavy lights, she can hear the sounds of stroking and gasping around her; she has a sense of beams of light cutting through the scene and imagines that a panoramic technique is being invoked. Then too the light will cut off suddenly for seconds or minutes while she supposes the focus of the film swings to the other pairs of actors. In addition to what is directly involved in the film, there seem to be a whole series of films being made in this enormous loft. Down at its perimeter there are other groups of people, more cameras; in the exact center of the area, a more ambitious documentary seems to be in preparation with domestic animals posed around a couple on the floor and almost concealing them. This particular operation is a very large one, but perhaps a number of film companies are saving on expenses by using one common, huge space. Susan tries not to think about any of this too much. At the beginning of the shooting session she decided that a narrowing of perspective is the solution, a focusing of her responses to the immediate situation in which she is involved and leaving the larger implications of what life is all about to others.

Early in her dramatic career, in a class called Intermediate Acting, she had been told by the university instructor that she seemed to do her best work when she was in a limited, concrete situation, and she had never forgotten this. "Try not to think of abstractions," the instructor warned her, "most actors find these very confusing." Susan has resultantly not thought of abstractions in many years although the instructor had turned out to be a compulsive adulterer who had had relations with most of the girls in his class and, in a fit of insanity, had married one of them as the only way of getting into bed with her.

CHAPTER VIII

Susan, now twenty-three, had not had intercourse until the age of seventeen, having come from a closely knit suburban family in northern Ohio where most of the opportunities offered her had been in the back seats of cars parked dangerously near the road. She had felt that there must be something more to life and its Ultimate Act than headlights, insects, and the whimpering of the male as he jammed a knee against the steering post trying to lean over the seat. She had been deflowered in a fraternity house during her freshman year at college, however, and had not had any problems with sex since. In her junior year she decided to limit her sexual activities to those boys with whom she had established a relationship of some sort and this cut down on the frequency, if not on the intensity, of her couplings. She had never had an orgasm but had not found anything objectionable so far in sex.

After college she lived with three men before Timothy. Two of them had been vaguely artistic; the other had wanted to marry her after they had established a comfortable, continuing relationship of many years' duration. Aside from one demented coupling with her roommate in their sophomore year of college (her roommate had offered to show her that orgasm was always the same no matter who the partner), Susan's sex life had been thoroughly unremarkable up until this point. It was in no way a preparation for this branch of show business.

CHAPTER IX

They are told that the final scene will now be filmed. Susan was not sure; she has lost some fundamental sense of time. A large, sullen German Shepherd is brought into the working area and Susan is told that she will have to copulate with him, preferably in a rear-entry position as this is where he is most experienced. The point of the last scene, the director explains to give her motivation, is to illustrate the utter degradation of the character's life and the depths to which indiscriminate sex can lead even a respectable person.

The dog is half-dragged in on a long chain, the assistants concentrating on doing something with its rear legs. The beast eyes

Susan with suspicion and the director says that there will be no trouble with the animal; it is the most docile and well-trained of all the dogs with whom he has worked and is so slightly built that Susan will not even feel entry. There have been troubles, he says vaguely, with certain dogs or actors in the past but not since they began using the kennel. For the first time, Susan protests, not because of the animal but because of what she calls an artistic revulsion; she asks if it would be possible to skip this scene or to assign it to someone else because she does not feel capable of doing it with conviction. The director repeats that the whole point of the film is to show the brutality and degradation of the character as she falls into fucking at random. The director is an old man, at least in relation to the principals in the room—forty-five or so with glasses that glint under the spotlights. And he has what seems to be a foreign accent but there is such a precision in his speech and gesture that Susan is unable to take him personally. He seems mostly to be another piece of equipment in the room, moving her in and out of position. The whole film has led up to this scene, the director goes on, to eliminate it would be to deny the movie its artistic integrity. He has been in this business for too long already and anyway time is important, too important for this nonsensical argumentation. The boy with whom she has been copulating giggles and tells Susan that there is nothing to worry about; he is rather experienced in this business and says he recognizes this dog and he has always behaved like a professional. Susan asks again if it would be possible to have another actress do the scene and the director replies that unless she completes her assignment, her pay will be withheld. For that matter, everyone's pay will be withheld unless the movie is wrapped up now. The other actors circle around the director, but, instead of showing anger toward him, they give her baleful looks. "You can't be a college girl all your life," one of them says, which seems to Susan to be a harsh and unnecessarily cruel remark inasmuch as she has been out of college for two years.

She sighs and says that she will do her best. She will try to go through with the performance. Then she allows herself to be placed in the appropriate position and closes her eyes, trying to imagine how the character she is playing would react to the situation. Remembering her theatrical training she forces herself deep into the role, thinking of herself as an inexperienced, rather stupid girl who, in a search for humiliation gravitates toward German Shepherds. She conceives herself to be in the back seat of a car, perhaps a 1961 Ford Falcon, moving on the stiff pins underneath the cushions as the driver looms over her, still looking for the gearshift. In less time than she might have thought, it is over and she decides that it has not been that bad.

CHAPTER X

The partial manuscript of Timothy's novel-in-progress has been submitted to seven hardcover houses, three paperback firms and, for serial use, to seventeen magazines. None of the responses have been particularly encouraging although one of the quarterlies did return his manuscript with an offer of a reduced subscription to writers that would have enabled him to receive the next five years of their review for only a fraction of what he would have had to pay at his local newsstand. Timothy tore up the subscription blank and form letter, muttering something about the exploitation of writers but this was a mystery to Susan, who remarked that in making its offer the review was certainly acknowledging that he was a writer and this was a part of the recognition for which he had been struggling. Timothy became savage when she said this and called her a stupid cunt, but, later on, after they had made up with a brutal fuck, he said that he could see her point and that no outsider could ever understand the agony of the writer, which was a very private and terrible thing.

CHAPTER XI

Timothy lives in a walk-up apartment on the fourth floor of a building on the lower East Side of Manhattan; this building adjoins an all-night fruit stand and a bus terminal. Even in the early morning hours, Susan can look outside and see, through the fumes of buses accelerating their engines, the figures of old women leaning over the fruit stand, probing goods, their shopping bags over their arms. The clash of gears and the high shrieks of the women as the buses roar past them blowing clouds of pollutants, give her the feeling that for the first time in her life she is communicating with something real and basic. Timothy, however, has said that he cannot stand the location much longer and will have to look for something else in a quieter area, perhaps in the upper West Side where the streets are abandoned by midnight.

CHAPTER XII

After the filming she has coffee with Phil in a small, dismal restaurant near the loft. Phil seems to be on excellent terms with the manager and the staff because they are given the one decent booth in the place. "You did very good," Phil says, looking between his watch and the kitchen doors, peering around the screens, "very good; I hear excellent reports about your work. I think that you very definitely have a future in this place if you want it. Very few people can come in like you, cold off the street, and act worth a damn. But you showed heart and real conviction. For you this is not just a way to turn a few bucks; you're a pro. I can always tell the difference."

"But I don't know if I want to do it any more," Susan says. "I did need the money very badly, but it just isn't the kind of thing that I think I could do again although I have nothing against it on moral grounds." In her handbag, over her arm, she has the check for the day's work, seventy-five dollars instead of a hundred because casting, and direction fees have been deducted as well as a small amount per capita for the use of the loft. This is not what she had been promised but, it is not a bad sum for eight hour's work and it is, although she will never admit this to Phil, the first money she has made as a professional actress. "I have to go home soon, you know," she says. "This man I'm living with … I'm living with a man you know … I have to make dinner for him. We have an agreement to share the household tasks and this is my week."

"Oh don't be concerned about that," Phil says with a shake of his bald head, looking at her intently, "I get the drift; I don't mean to put the make on you or anything like that at all. It's strictly business; I never get involved with the help. That's the first thing you've got to learn in show business. This other stuff never, the make isn't on my mind; I'm a married man and I just wanted to talk. Not that you aren't very attractive, you understand."

"I appreciate that."

"I just wanted to talk about a project," Phil says. "They've got something coming up, what you might call an epic, and I'd like to see you try out for it if you'd be interested in some serious work. They couldn't pay a hundred a day on this one because that's only the rate for one-shots and specials. It would have to be maybe half of that—like fifty, say, but it would be steady and you'd have yourself a secure income."

Susan thinks abstractedly about the epic. "What kind of movie is this? Is it a straight part?"

"Something like that," Phil says. "The sex emphasis would only be there to keep the viewer's attention but actually it's a very serious idea. You want to go up to my place with me and maybe discuss a little bit what this project will be?"

"I don't—"

"Yeah, I know about dinner and so on but the thing is I don't like to do business in public places because you never know who might be listening in. But if we can go to my apartment where I know it's confidential, I'll be able to fill you in very quickly. Of course it's up to you to say yes or no about that, but, unless I have a chance to talk to you very soon, I have no way of knowing if you'll be right for the part, and there are lots of others I could ask. You saw them all around you. Kids coming into that loft are desperate for work; they'd grab any part. I don't really have much to do with the production but I'm like a liaison in case you want to know my basis of authority."

He extends his hand. He is a heavy, short man, not unlike her father physically although her father has what Susan has come to think of as a suburban veneer or maybe only a kind of resignation which has turned him expressionless. Phil has vigor or at least a certain attitude of positiveness and hope which she finds rather attractive by contrast, not that she ever had much use for him because he had felt that she was wasting time in a dramatics major and should have done something practical like teaching which would have made her very much like her mother. She and her mother have nothing to do with one another at present. Her mother would hardly be sitting across a table from the New York producer who is now patting her gently across the table, his eyes fixed upon her with concentration. She feels the touch, cold as guilt, harsh as memory, and her fingers curl against his palm. She realizes she is being suggestive, that not to follow through would be unfair to him. "All right," she says. "I'll go to your apartment and discuss it if you really want me to."

Susan imagines herself in bed with him. This is one of her oldest traits; she can always picture herself having sex with any man, no matter how repellent he may be. In her mind she lies spent against his necessity, the feel of him rushing into her again and again and finds that, despite what has happened to her already today, she can apprehend him as she never could Timothy … or even the German Shepherd.

CHAPTER XIII

Susan lies underneath Phil in his bachelor apartment. It was very simple really; he wanted to discuss business but, first he must have a drink and, as long as he is having a drink, she might as well too and then the shades in the apartment were drawn and they went into the bedroom and Phil began to tell her how really attractive she was and Susan felt the old mixture of reluctance and fascination coming over her. The tensions of sex emerged from the contradictions between the two of them and it became very easy, in fact inevitable to undress. She took off all of her clothes and lay beside him. In the dark she could hardly see him and imagined his body as it came down to drape her, as the flesh of many lovers. A multitude of scenes pass through her mind, recollections from college through Timothy. Then somewhere in the middle she has a twitch of feeling, a small explosion and an uncoiling. "That was good," Phil says, getting off her, instantly talkative, instantly efficient, "that was very good; you're really very good." And, putting on the lights, he begins to dress hurriedly, tossing Susan's clothes over to her at the same time to indicate that she should dress as well. He seems to be one of those men who make a complete distinction between sex and their ordinary lives, no flow between them. But she can hardly credit herself with being very experienced. Being sexually experienced for a girl is not something to be aimed for, or at least Susan still believes this. Phil, dressing, seems to move further and further from her and in the act of dressing herself she suppresses all knowledge of what had happened between them. It had been as mechanical and limited as a transaction in a store; a little bit of seed had passed from one of them to the other but that was no reason to get personally involved. Vaguely, she wonders if everybody in the pornographic films business approaches sex in this fashion or whether her relationship with Phil has been unusual. It hardly seems worth being concerned about, in the fading light of the room with her clothes back on, sitting comfortably in one of the easy chairs flanking the bed, a cigarette in her hand while Phil puts the final touches to his appearance and sits down facing her. "This really isn't where I live." he says. "I wouldn't want you to think that I live this way because it wouldn't be fair to you. I just use this place for business. I don't want to have you think that I make a habit of going to bed with girls either: I'm strictly business, strictly, but I found you very attractive and just lost control of myself."

Susan wonders if this lapse of control to which Phil refers is really true and wonders what he would be like if he was really detached sexually; she decides not to follow this line of thought through. She is not experienced, she is willing to admit this (sexual experience being the kind of thing which girls from her background cannot concede to) and she may, just possibly, be in a little bit over her head. "It's all right," she says, trying to sound matter of fact and holding her cigarette uncomfortably. "It doesn't matter at all. You don't have to apologize for anything."

"I'm not apologizing. Where did you get the idea I was apologizing?"

"I don't know. I don't mean anything by it. Please," Susan says, beginning to feel really uneasy: what would Timothy say?, "you were going to tell me about the picture."

"Oh yes," Phil says, "the picture. I have to fill you in on that, don't I?

I don't really know that much about it; I'm just kind of a liaison man for them and really don't know what they have in mind most of the time." He looks vaguely at his fingernails, shrugs, examines the ceiling. He seems to have lost all interest in her, at least for the moment. His eyes perfectly blank and dull as he stares at the smoke coming from her cigarette and says, "Why don't you drop by early tomorrow morning and I'll discuss it in the office? I really don't have the time now; I got another appointment. If you want the job you can have it, that's what I said, but after the day you've had you must be tired. I know I am." He stands heavily, ponderously, even with a gesture not unlike her father's, and goes to the window, pulling aside a curtain to look at some unknown aspect of New York for a few minutes and then wanders back to the center of the room. "If that's okay," he says.

"All right," Susan says. She stands, finds her balance slightly uneven; wonders if there is a slope to this room as there is supposed to be in all buildings in New York, but decides that it is only the aftermath of compound sex; she has, after all, had intercourse or simulated intercourse at least ten times today, the last instance being a social relationship and she has the right to feel tired. "Do you want me to come down tomorrow?"

"I guess so," Phil says vaguely. He is informed by vagueness, everything about him is vague; even his figure seems to have a blurred outline in the half-light of the room. He paces abstractedly and goes to the door. "I got a lot of things to think about so if you don't mind, maybe I'll run along right now. You don't have to leave this second. I'll see you in the morning."

"I'm going," Susan says, "I'm going," but, before she can even rise to follow, Phil is gone, the door swinging vacantly behind him; she sees its absent sway on the hinge, hears the diminution of his footsteps, hears the clatter of traffic outside.

She has had a full day in New York. She has participated in the making of a pornographic film, she has had intercourse with the agent of the film's producers, she has been offered a leading role in a forthcoming production by the same company, she has come to terms with herself in, perhaps, ways that she was not accustomed. At the end of all of this she stands in a hotel room fully dressed somewhere between retention and flight; she has a delicate feeling of being poised at some critical instant and she senses that if she could only investigate this feeling, if she could allow it to come over her fully, she might find out something about herself that she never knew before. Even as she understands this a spotlight whips through the window, traversing toward the other side of the street and she decides that she had better go. Timothy is waiting for her (or she hopes Timothy is waiting for her) and, at the end of all of this, perhaps in sleep, will come another accommodation. She leaves the room slowly, quite a pretty girl really, only a certain high tension moving from her cheekbones to her eyes indicating that anything at all has touched her. She senses that if she were to tell the men in the street who stare at her what she had been doing that day, they would be amazed but, then, they might be perfectly matter of fact. People in New York accept all sorts of things as matter of fact.

CHAPTER XIV

At home she finds Timothy asleep over his typewriter, a half-page of his novel still in the machine. He is incredibly dedicated to his work but his job in the Welfare Department gets him down; constant demands are being made upon his compassion and sense of balance, he says, and he finds it impossible to maintain toward his work the kind of polished detachment intrinsic to the creation of great art. Nevertheless he cannot leave the Welfare Department, having tenure and needing the income too badly to be able to take time off to finish his book or look for another job. His face looks astonished in repose; his pores open, his nerves twitch under the mask of impassivity, and he groans heavily, adjusting himself more comfortably in the chair, allowing his head to sink fully into his cupped hands. Susan pats him on the neck and reads what is in the typewriter which seems to have to do with the reaction of a welfare investigator to a particularly aggressive client. "I CAN'T STAND THIS ANY MORE," MR. MORALES SCREAMED, the page reads, "MY WIFE AND CHILDREN ARE STARVING FOR LACK OF BREAD AND YOU STAND THERE IN YOUR BUSINESS SUIT AND TELL ME ABOUT RULES AND REGULATIONS. I TELL YOU THAT THIS IS NO TIME FOR RULES AND REGULATIONS. EVERYTHING IS BURNING. THE WORLD IS BURNING. THE FIRE IS COMING UPON ALL OF US, EVEN UPON WELFARE INVESTIGATORS, AND YOUR OLD SIMPLE RIGIDITIES WILL NO LONGER HOLD US BACK." HENDERSON FELT THE WAVES OF TERROR MOVING UP HIS PORCINE BACK, WAVES OF TERROR INTERMINGLED WITH COMPASSION BECAUSE HE COULD PLACE HIMSELF IN THE MIND AND HEART OF THE MAN MORALES, THIS SIMPLE DISPLACED PERSON, TORN FREE FROM HIS HISTORY, WHO COULD EXPRESS HIS LOVE NOW ONLY THROUGH HATRED, THROUGH THE VENTINGS OF HIS TERRIBLE FEELINGS. HENDERSON COULD FEEL A TWITCH OF

COMPASSION BUT THEN, WHEN MORALES REVEALED HIS KNIFE, THIS COMPASSION TURNED TO ASHES AND HE WAS AFRAID, TERRIBLY AFRAID. IN THE NEXT ROOM HE KNEW THAT THE TEN MORALES CHILDREN HUDDLED, EARS TO THE THIN WALL LISTENING FOR THE SOUNDS OF DESTRUCTION, AND WHAT HAPPENED THEN SEEMED TO OCCUR UNDER THE EYES OF MANY WITNESSES, WITNESSES UNREACHABLE THROUGH PLASTER. "WE ARE BURNING," MORALES SHOUTED, "BURNING FOR YOUR SINS," AND HE ADVANCED UPON HENDERSON WITH THE KNIFE. THE CLEANNESS OF THE FEAR JOLTED HENDERSON, HE ... and at this point the page, 261, ends. It is the first part of Timothy's novel which Susan has read since the time, some weeks ago at the beginning of their relationship, he handed her the opening chapter, saying this was what he was doing and perhaps she would like to see it, not that he particularly cared what she thought because no serious writer could bend and sway to another's opinion. Susan had found that first chapter, which seemed to be about Henderson's initial sexual experience in Bedford-Stuyvesant with a fat welfare client many years older than himself, vague and somewhat confusing, but it did have color (as did this section) and it convinced her that Timothy was certainly a novelist. Now she turns away from the typewriter already disinterested, already feeling herself turned inward toward abstraction, having very little to do with any of this, just for the moment a visitor in the room, someone extrinsic to the entire situation. Timothy could be a stranger, this apartment a museum preserved frozen in time, for all her responses; she wanders idly off to the kitchen and, deciding to let him sleep for the time being, makes herself a cup of coffee and allows the events of the day to work through her. The mail is in, scattered on the kitchen table, and among the envelopes is a letter from an old college girlfriend, forwarded from her last address. She is interested in reading the letter but her curiosity is mixed with a good deal of trepidation and she decides to let it wait for a moment. Just for a moment; she hears Timothy groaning and stirring in the other room and knows that he will come in shortly in a foul mood and she will have to tell him what her day has been like. She already knows the composition of his; it has come out of the typewriter.

CHAPTER XV

For a while the sheer magnitude of pornography on the newsstands of New York had dazzled Susan; she passed newsstands and magazine stores with the slightly averted and astonished eyes that she had once turned on the boxes of sanitary napkins displayed in local drugstores; later she had gotten used to the pornography along with the rest of New York and finally, in fear and caution, had actually begun to buy the newspapers, only to get a lead, she told herself, on the kind of environment she lived in. The models who posed for the pictures were easy enough to understand; they looked like almost anyone who you might see in the street who had elected to pose nude in sexual positions for the money, but the advertisements were a different matter altogether, and, in the reading of the personal ads, Susan's comprehension began to buckle. There was simply no attitude with which to properly handle them. Pleas for partners were published by fetishists, lesbians, homosexuals, heterosexuals, urinary-oriented males and females, coprophiliacs, and animal-lovers. They were placed by leather devotees, young men interested in massage, and people seeking various kinds of anal intercourse. They were written by stocking fetishists, ear fetishists, breast-feeding fetishists, and old men only interested in conversation and companionship. Women were looking for mixed sex and mixed groups were looking for women. Old men sought young boys and young boys sought older women. It was the need, the desperation, the insistence of the advertisements and above all the mad sense of certainty that their needs were somehow justified and justifiable which informed all of them left Susan feeling slack and empty. She had read about such people. She supposed that at one time or other she had seen them, but the idea that they actually existed, that they were as serious as she and were willing to publicize the fact was something with which she could not deal. It would be easy to believe that the ads were not real and that they were being printed by the owners of the newspapers themselves as a kind of satire. But the advertisements had a mad patterning and consistency which no publishers could possibly simulate and they repeated—she began to become familiar with certain quirks of phraseology—shades of meaning which were peculiar to the authors. The same blurbs would recur over a span of weeks. Not long before she met Timothy, when she was very much in between all kinds of things, she had had to struggle against an urge to make contact with some of the advertisers, simply to see if they existed and then, at the moment of actual connection, to flee but she had resisted this impulse. It was cheap and she also feared getting into very dangerous waters. The people who published these advertisements were a fraternity, a conspiracy in fact; they were humorless, passionate, and devoted and they would not suffer outsiders easily. Besides, Susan was simply not prepared to deal with the kind of people who found water sports interesting. It had taken her long enough to find out what water sports *were* (one of the personals columns in the newspapers had filled her in finally) and that was as far as she wanted to go with the matter.

But there was that feeling of something lacking and it complicated everything. Reading the advertisements, Susan, past her initial shock, had begun to feel a sense of regret, even loss, probing through the delicate parts of her, fine tendrils which almost touched the quivering, dirty pages of the newspaper: here at least were people possessed of certainty. They had their lacks, they had their losses, but one thing was clear: they knew exactly what they needed to make themselves complete and they could put it into words, send their prayer through newsprint out into the world. It would be very simple if you only knew of one thing in the world which would ease your needs; coprophilia or Greek culture would be a small price to pay for the knowledge that dreams could be made flesh through simple connection. Susan had not had that certainty for a long time; ever since she had turned against her father for failing to understand her many years ago, she had given up the belief in easy answers. Of course this had nothing to do with the newspapers which made everything very easy indeed. She toyed for a while with the idea of placing her own advertisement under a box number: YOUNG ATTRACTIVE GIRL, NYMPHOMANIACAL, DESPERATELY SEEKS SEXUAL INTERCOURSE, PARTICULARLY WITH INEXPERIENCED OR UGLY MEN, just to see what kind of replies she would get. The responses would be very interesting and amusing and she could discuss them with her friends but finally she decided against it. In the first place, very few women seemed to advertise in the sex newspapers and, in the second, the monomania and desperation of the kind of man who placed advertisements made her feel that she would be getting in beyond her depth, even to release so much as a box number. So she had begun to lose interest in the sex newspapers which, shocking and amusing at first, turned out to be the same old stuff, week in and week out. The advertisers became familiar to say nothing of the editorial content and meanwhile her money had seriously begun to run out and she could not bear the idea of having gone through everything she had to become a receptionist-typist in New York City. So she had begun to read the advertisements with something else in view, maybe a job, maybe a real contact, and the movie thing, when she had seen it, had been not unlike hundreds of similar ads that she had passed over. But this time it was different because she really wanted to get work related in some way to the field of her talent and she had had a bad fight with Timothy the previous evening—a raw, ugly one having to do with the kind of neighborhood in which he was living which could not, like some of the other arguments, be sealed with sex. So she had gone for an interview and was eventually selected to star in a pornographic film. It was simple, really. She wondered if people who enlisted in the Army and wound up in really serious trouble in the war zone had found it as easy and inevitable to get into the situation as she had. There was nothing consequential to it at all. The most complicated or unspeakable acts could occur in broad daylight, in expressionless buildings, surrounded by people leading unknowing routine lives. She knows that she must think about this as well as the compromises Phil's offer will lead her to in her artistic career but there is time enough for that later.

CHAPTER XVI

Not too much later Timothy awakens and comes into the kitchen, finds her sitting solemnly, stirring a cup of coffee and asks her about her day. Did she actually get some work? His demeanor seems to shift between trepidation and excitement; he wants to know what has happened to her but, on the other hand, is afraid to find out. She says that it was nothing much—mostly nude posing and posturing and that there was no physical contact with any of the other actors, all of whom were unattractive. Timothy nods and shrugs, shakes his head, and says that he will not discuss it anymore. Even though they are living together, they are entitled to lead their separate lives, at least up until a point of real commitment, and therefore she has the right to her privacy. He says that he has had a terrible day at the office. There is a new state investigation beginning in the area of Manhattan covered by his welfare center and all of the unit supervisors must submit complete reports to the auditing committee describing the efforts at rehabilitation made for clients and telling what percentage within the last six months have been fully restored to a normal way of life. Timothy says that he is not quite sure what the state means by "rehabilitated" but supposes that, if they are using the word in the financial sense, they want to know how many clients are actually off relief which, he says, is too small a percentage to make the very nervous administrative head happy. The administrative head, therefore, in a full meeting with the supervisors, has instructed them to interpret "rehabilitation" as meaning those welfare clients who have been led to a higher and deeper and more fundamental understanding of their lives due to the efforts of caseworkers, which would be a very large percentage indeed. "Under the new social casework procedures, over eighty-five percent of our client-load is showing some genuine capacity for enlightenment as well as a high deceleration of the level of decompensation in terms of unnatural mores," the administrator has said and Timothy had spent the remainder of the day putting together charts and statistical studies indicating that four hundred and fifteen of the five hundred and twelve families carried by his case unit have shown a high deceleration of the level of decompensation. "I can't stand it any more," he says to her, pouring a cup of coffee and running a hand absently down her shoulder, "I simply can't stand it any more, it's too insane," and then his fingers become insistent, the cup of coffee is forgotten, falling with a clatter to the table, and he presses his groin against her. "Let's do it," he says, "let's make love," always showing at the moment of insistence a delicacy in his language and bearing which Susan finds amusing; he seems incapable of using the word *fuck* in talking about sex although in other contexts he uses it all the time. "Let's put ourselves together," he says stammering and she sees as always the core of vulnerability in him, the thing which has always excited her about Timothy. Never has she seen a man so needful who does more outside the context of sex to deny that need. "Oh God," he says, "I want you so much," and moves toward her, puts himself against her. She can feel him arching, rising. All of this takes place outside a core of fundamental detachment in her because Susan has already had quite a bit of sex today. "Please," she says, pushing gently against him and trying to disengage herself, "please, not now, I'm tired," but Timothy will have none of that. "Why," he says, "what's wrong? Have you had sex already today, is that why you don't want it?" There is nothing she can say to that at all. Having sex with him now is a matter of pride, a matter of showing him that she has not been touched, not been used, and so she permits herself to come against him. Her clothes are falling away from her; she is sore inside; she feels now as if her body is closing down heavily against the pain in her center but she must show him that she can react, can participate, and so, falling onto the kitchen floor, she allows him to work on her. As always he is quick, forceful (unlike the characters in his novel who always take a great deal of time to have sex and then think about it endlessly afterwards), grinding himself into her and she feels the spurt of his come surrounded by his groans, closing her eyes, turning inward, shutting it all off from herself. She has proven herself to Timothy, she thinks as he lies heavily on top of her, has proven that she can meet him on his own ground and then it occurs to her, almost for the first time, that she is not sure that she even cares enough for Timothy to make this proving valuable to her. In fact she is not sure that she cares for Timothy at all, but, in its strangeness and complexity, this becomes a thought with which she is utterly unable to deal and so she lets it pass, sliding from various levels of consciousness, down the roof, into the eaves, through the sidings, into the basement, and sleep overcomes her like rainfall.

CHAPTER XVII

The next morning she sees Phil again. He is very detached; it is as if nothing at all has passed between them. The film, as he explains it to her, is a massive documentary; the most important pornographic film to date, not that it is dirty at all but rather that it will merely use pornography to involve an audience in some very serious insights into the quality of their lives. The film, Phil tells her, will be a sexual history of the world from the time of the Garden of Eden to the present; major and minor historical figures will be portrayed along with hundreds of the common people, people whose names are now unknown, and startling insights will be gained into the present condition of the world through this view. Some of the characters will be as famous as Abraham Lincoln or Saul of Tarsus; others as obscure as the eighteenth-century Italian composer Clementi or the nineteenth-century American poet Brett Harte. The sweep and scope of the film, Phil says, will be enormous; it will encompass some seven thousand years of recorded history within a period of eleven or twelve playing hours. The overall theme of the movie is that sexuality is the driving force of mankind and that all of the disasters and cataclysms of modern day Americans can be seen as the outcome of sexual frustrations. Through a frank look at the sexual lives of these historical figures, Phil says, the film will function as a purgative to the audience which will come to see that if Abraham Lincoln had wanted sex, sex could not have been that bad. "You have a nation that is terrified of sex, terrified of relationships, terrified of human connection," Phil says, "and the audience that comes to this type of deal is the most terrified of all. Let's face facts, most of them are using it as a substitute for the prostitutes they don't even have the guts to get. They come into these theatres and are filled with fear and then their fantasies are exploited in a private way. I'm a very realistic man; I've done a lot of thinking about this as you can see and I ain't got no illusions about the audience, but I do believe that you can do something with them. You can say this about them, at least they're *there*. They are willing to take a chance on themselves which is more than you can say about the million others who would love to see dirties but don't have the guts so the dirties got to be dressed up for them. We're going to do James Knox Polk in this one; we're going to do Hitler; we're going to have Napoleon and the three Wise Men and Marie Antoinette and Clara Bow and Amelia Earhart and Jean Harlow and Shakespeare and almost anyone you can think of, as long as they're dead because there's no point in crossing with the slander laws. But otherwise there are no holds barred. There's even going to be some stuff in there about the Kennedys, because you've got to lay it on the line, but, of course, you watch your step with those people. The director is a guy from Europe, did a few films over there. This is his first in the States and he's going to get the biggest budget they ever put up for such a film. If it works out the way we think it's going, it's a career break. This isn't only a sex film, you see, this is a major statement."

"It seems to me," Susan says, adjusting her hands over her lap and trying to look sexually inaccessible, "that you're going to have hundreds of people in this film. How big can any part be? Not that I would mind getting one, of course." She adds this hastily, with a ragged sense of timing; knowing that an edge of anxiety may be penetrating but unable to catch it. She wants a part in this film desperately; Timothy and she ended the evening with a serious fight in which he accused her of being a dilettante with no serious interest in acting who was perfectly willing to continue calling herself an actress because "it's a profession where if you're not *doing* anything, you can just say that you're out of work. While a serious writer has to keep on working all the time." She had not liked this at all; it had, in fact been very painful and she had resolved that she was going to be able to go back to him this evening and say that she had a serious role in a big production. A substantial part. Weeks of employment. "But I don't really know how good the parts can be," she adds rather lamely and then drops the whole line of approach, seeing the glint recede from Phil's eyes, his forehead moving parallel now to the floor. He has not really listened to a word she has said.

"You don't understand," he says after a pause. "That's why it's such a desirable thing to get, that's why people are begging for a shot in this picture. There's going to be a lot of doubling up here; only five or six actors are really going to play all the big parts; the same guy playing Beethoven, for instance, is going to be Benjamin Harrison and then William Jennings Bryan; the girl that plays Eve will play all the sensual, seductive parts like Dolly Madison or Tallulah Bankhead and so on. There's a terrific need for versatility and artistic range if you follow what I mean. And that's really part of the hidden meaning of the picture too; the point is that people are always the same when you come right down to the sexual basis of reality and all the differences are just external. I've done a lot of thinking about this; I think that they've got hold of something really important here and personally I'm a little excited to be affiliated with it." Despite his claims of elation, Phil's eyes are dull; his gestures seem strangely out of kilter. "Filming is going to begin tomorrow," he says. "That's when the whole thing starts."

"Tomorrow? You're starting this tomorrow and you're still interviewing for parts?"

"I'm not starting this tomorrow," Phil says. "They're starting it tomorrow; I told you, I just work for them. I'm only an employee; I have nothing to do with the way things go on; I just try to tend shop. The reason that they're still interviewing is that they want to go right down to the wire and make sure that they have absolutely the right people. They need a strong cast, there's no question about it. Of course, once they get going, they work pretty fast. It's all a question of overhead; the business works on a tight margin."

"Do I get a part?"

"They're going to shoot it in the same place you were working yesterday. They're going to clear out all the other productions and just run this one straight through in the whole area. It'll take about a week to get the whole thing down."

"Just a week? You said it was a long-term production."

"You don't understand," Phil says, his eyes darkening and his hands coming together in a subtle wringing gesture. "Most of these films are made in a *day*. A week is a terrific project in this business. I never *knew* a film that took a week. Of course there's never been a production quite like this in the whole history of the business; so that's an important point too."

"I'll take it," Susan says. "I'd like to go to work." She has resolved to be businesslike, determined; she will let no personal factors intrude between her and the job and, if this is the way in which Phil wants things to be done, she will cooperate. She looks at him with what she hopes is great positiveness and detachment and says, "You want me to come down tomorrow morning and get started?"

"I'm not sure yet. I don't want you to take this personally but you showed a certain, uh, reluctance, in the sex scenes. You aren't really experienced in this kind of thing, I can tell. Of course that isn't too bad; the less experience you have, the more conviction with which you can play. But you didn't flow with the action; I heard complaints that you were working against the action and making problems for the others. Of course," Phil says vaguely, "you got to admit that that's a point too; an absence of professionalism in this kind of film can sometimes be just the ticket. You got to take all these things into account. I been in the business for them a long time and you learn that there ain't no easy answers; you got to swing with it and take the long view. They can offer you fifty dollars a day if you want a part in the picture."

"You're going to give me a job?"

"For fifty dollars a day."

"But I thought— "

"I told you it would be less, sweetheart. It's nothing personal but when you get away from the one-shot deals and into extended work there's a tighter budget and you got to bring these things into scale. It's not that I wouldn't like to offer you more but they're businessmen; they got to operate on a margin and anyway you're dealing with a very ambitious film here. It's much more expensive than anything they've ever done before. And it could be a career break. Let me tell you something if you promise not to get too excited and to keep it a secret; this may break right out of the sex houses. The director has some very exciting ideas and this is a film which might eclipse the circuit altogether and even become a road show. Of course I can't make no promises but this could be an important step— "

"All right," Susan says. "I'll take the job. I'll do it."

"There's going to be some pretty wild stuff here, you know, the director has ideas about what he wants to put in and altogether you'll have to keep an, uh, open mind," Phil says and fades off into inarticulately; at the moment out of words he looks at her bleakly across the expanse of desk, his palms open, his forehead parallel to the surfaces. He seems to have lost his faculty of speech for the time being or maybe it is merely forgetfulness; in any event, a small series of shudders and tremors seem to pass through him and he reassembles himself slowly. Susan wonders if he is a sick man, if it is a characteristic of people in this business to be highly neurotic, or whether he merely feels guilty about the sexual relationship which he has imposed upon her. She feels like reaching out to him, touching him gently, almost maternally, and telling him that it is all right, she expects nothing further from him, there is no reason for him to feel guilty, but then she understands that this would probably be very silly because sex does not seem to be what is on his mind now. "I guess they could make it fifty-five a day," he says. "But for fifty-five a day you might have to get into some pretty weird stuff. I tell you frankly, this director has a lot of ideas which he wants to try and they may strike you as a little bit strange. Fifty-five would be the top rate and for that they would expect real cooperation. Your back would be to the camera most of the time though. You'll notice there are very few full faces in this kind of stuff; that's for the protection of the actors because you never know who'll end up where in fifty years. Fifty-five a day and that's the top. You get five days guaranteed at that rate; if there's any more filming after that, it drops to forty-five. That has to be to protect against a cost-overload but it shouldn't go more than five days."

"You said a week."

"A week, a working week, five days, what's the difference. Anyway," Phil says, "anyway, that's the situation." He stands ponderously, seems to weave in front of her, then turns and looks out a window. "If you don't want to take it there are plenty others so you got to tell me now."

"I'll take it," Susan says. "I'll be down tomorrow morning and start work."

"All right," Phil says. "I'll arrange for you to be on the payroll steady then. You doing anything tonight?"

"What's that?"

He turns, leans over the desk, puts his palms down flatly and says, "I asked if you're doing anything tonight, that's all."

"Well," Susan says, feeling her balance beginning to go; she has not figured this man out right at all, she has missed the situation as well. This is the way he conducts his life, his attitude has had nothing at all to do with what happened between them. "Well, I told you, I was living with this man; I mean we had nothing special planned tonight but I have to go *home*—"

"I don't understand it," Phil says, shaking his head. "All these fragmentary relationships. Everybody's always shacked up together; in my time you didn't have to live with someone to have sex with them. It wasn't that big a deal. Listen, you don't have to explain your whole lifestyle to me, just give me a straight answer. You want to go out tonight and have a few drinks?"

"I couldn't. I just couldn't."

"Because if you can't, that's all right too. Business is entirely separate. You don't have to think that I'm forcing you or anything because I already offered you the job, right? So you know there's no monkey business. Listen," Phil says, "I'm a married man, right? You should know that about me right away. I'm a perfectly happy married man but you've got no idea of the tensions or pressures which build up in a marriage; sometimes you need a little something else just for a sense of relief. So it doesn't mean anything serious whether or not you go out with me. I'll meet you here about five?"

"I told you," Susan says rather frantically. "I told you, I just can't have that kind of involvement. It's nothing personal, I think that you're very nice but—"

"All right," Phil says. His eyes recede, his form seems to diminish subtly, he retracts to an edge of the chair. "It was only an idea. It has nothing to do with you at all."

"All right," Susan says.

"Because I know how your whole generation is and you start taking things seriously when it isn't anything like that at all. I don't want any messing around on the project. You got a big responsibility there and this thing has got to come off on schedule and on the money."

"Yes," Susan says. "Yes." She has the feeling that, somehow, her life will terminate sitting in front of Phil, that time is overtaking her, that everything is moving away from her slowly and her last moments will be spent in this chair. She forces herself to shift, then gets up; a peculiar disorientation comes over her; she thinks she might faint but she stands in front of him, slightly disconcerted but in control. "I'll just be going along," she says. Vaguely, she recalls some phrases from prior unsuccessful job interviews. "I appreciate your time. It's been very interesting. Thank you very much for talking to me. It's very nice of you to see me." Saying this, listening to herself as if from some distance, she moves toward the door, poises against it for a moment trying to frame some line that will enable her to depart from Phil in perfect grace. Then she sees that he is no longer looking at her; that, indeed, his eyes have fastened with a moist glaze to the telephone. It occurs to her that as far as Phil is concerned she has already left the premises. He sits there in stasis, one arm poised toward the phone, his shoulders in mid-shrug, no movements across his face. Susan opens the door and leaves. Halfway down the hall she hears horrid sounds coming from the vicinity of Phil's office, sounds which seem like metal striking against rotating machinery, high shrieks but at the dead-center of all these sounds she believes that she hears a human voice. It is many octaves higher than Phil's but then again one never knows. She resolves not to think much more about this and leaves the building hurriedly, moving into the midday crowds that circulate through Times Square. She wonders what any of them might think if they knew what she had been through and what she was going to do but, she decides that they are, in one sense or another, very possibly in the same business and she drops the whole issue, spending the rest of the morning investigating strange stores that sell nothing but ties for a dollar forty-nine, others which are going out of business momentarily and making clearance sales, and book markets where the majority of Timothy's competitors for the diminishing hardcover market can be observed on sale for a dollar ninety-eight, seventy-nine cents, and thirty-nine flat, depending upon their value and relevance to the current social situation.

CHAPTER XVIII

That night she receives a phone call from a man with a strange accent who says that he is the director of the film in which she will appear. He has obtained her number from Phil since he wants to talk to all of the cast before they assemble. "What I am particularly interested to know," he says, "is your knowledge of American history; we are going to be concentrating in the modern era and also upon some of the major political events and I would like the actors to come to this with a certain familiarity. I would like to suggest that you do some reading immediately; you will want to read Theodore White's books on the making of presidents and you should read Samuel Eliot Morison's history of the American people. All of these are out in paperback. Also I would like you to do some reading in the formal American comedy and drama just for background of course; any standard text will do. Do you have any particular familiarity with this era?" Susan says that she has a reading knowledge of some American history. She is, after all, a college graduate, and, for some reason, the man on the phone begins to stutter with rage, becomes even less coherent. "They think, these goddamned people, that just because this is a dirty film we will sacrifice all style and scholarship but this is never to be! We will reconstruct art in the face of the void. Enough of exploitation which even within a rigid format can become a framework of artifice and beauty," he says. He has been at work on the script all day and on the phone all night. "This script is absolutely miserable; we will have to improvise," he says. "It seems to have been written by an unintelligent monkey with certain vague perversities in the way of human behavior but we will prove to this monkey that his conceits cannot possibly keep us harnessed," the director says and then begins to cough. He says that he is sorry but he cannot seem to get over the cigarette habit which appeals to all the latent self-destructiveness in his European temperament and reminds her that he would like to see her reading the recommended books at the earliest possible opportunity. Then he adds that he will of course see her tomorrow morning and hangs up. Susan replaces the phone carefully and goes back to the living room where Timothy, leaning over the typewriter, looks at her incuriously and asks if she is carrying on some kind of relationship behind his back. She starts to explain and then realizes that he is not listening. She only goes to him and rubs his shoulders absently for a time, scanning the row of paperbacks on shelves over his head to see if there is anything useful there. She sees a couple of titles by Norman Mailer and Gore Vidal but suspects that this is nothing like what the director had in mind.

CHAPTER XIX

Later that night, after they have violent and perverse sex, Susan falls from Timothy and onto her own side of the bed, falls into sleep that way and has a dream. In the dream the film has opened in first-run theaters throughout the world and is an enormous critical success. Her own performance is praised as being of great delicacy and range, showing not only artistic control but that kind of rare sensitivity and fragility which are almost never combined in newer actresses. She seems to be attending some kind of show business party; virtually every celebrity of whom she has heard is there and seems to be interested in talking to her but she, in a formal, strapless evening gown, is unable to socialize because she is pinned off in a corner by Phil who seems to be talking intensely to her. She cannot understand a word he is saying; he is talking in a strange language, Portuguese perhaps, from the context of which every now and then a familiar word or phrase emerges disconnected, floating like a bird above a swamp. "No percentage," Phil is saying to her before going off into another flood of Portuguese or "you understand integrity is the key," and she moves to respond, trying to forestall him with the touch of a hand or even a breast but he will not be stopped. Over his shoulder she can see the faces of people anxious to meet with her and offer her promising opportunities for her career: a famous Hollywood producer is there, three female actresses who she has always admired, the senior senator from the state of New York, and her father as well, with a conciliatory and beckoning expression on his face, motioning for her to come toward him and grant forgiveness. She attempts to move toward them, pick up the strands of her career but she cannot pass Phil; his short, blunt body is in the way and, as she moves to pass him forcibly, she confronts him fully through the eyes, understands, in one glance, that he is in some kind of unspeakable pain and that as much as she wants to she simply cannot hurt him in this way. Perhaps it is not Portuguese which he is speaking at all but a kind of neologistic language which is the product of severe brain damage. Perhaps he is trying to communicate with her in the only way he knows how and she is the only person who can understand him. "Good God grant," Phil says and whisks his fingers down the underside of her bare arm, across her hand and then caresses her under the chin, "God grant good," he says and now moves toward her purposefully, his language still somehow incomprehensible but more demanding: he wants something—she can tell this now—there is some unspeakable need at the heart of his purpose and, as her father, the senior senator from New York, the three female actresses, and the Hollywood producer look on, Phil tears his clothes open with a cry and plunges himself into her (she is suddenly and inexplicably naked), begins to fuck her with wild churning motions accompanied by expostulations of Portuguese. The whole thing is very embarrassing to her. He is insistent; there is very little that she can do to put him off; she can feel his turgid prick within her already beginning to spring veins of ascension, and, as his sperm breaks free, he begins to speak once more in his strange language. She understands it perfectly this time. Crying out of his despair and rage and need, Phil has found the perfect language of necessity which she had misinterpreted all the time, and, as the senior senator checks his watch, shakes his head, whispers something to the actresses and the producer and leads them out of the hall, the force of his come moves like a hand into her and she wakes from the dream screaming, completely disoriented, completely frightening Timothy who had gone to bed in the hope that he would be able to get up at four that morning to work fresh on a desperately important epiphany in his novel.

CHAPTER XX

The fraternity room in which Susan had been deflowered had been plastered with pictures of naked women from the more popular men's magazines; not only the walls but the ceiling were covered with photographs of breasts and thighs and the occupant of the room, whoever it was (it was not the boy who was working on her) had, out of some demented cunning, removed the faces from the pictures and cut up the breasts and thighs in such a way that in perfect dismemberment they glinted from all sides of the room. Susan had found herself being laid directly under enlarged pictures of two enormous breasts; the breasts were not similar and had obviously been taken from two separate women. She had been able to inspect them with unusual intensity, even abstraction, while far inside of her, in some area which seemed sealed off, massive burrowings were going on, burrowings surrounded by seizure; the boy reared over her, snorted and disappeared again as if on a mission of excavation from which he would appear sporadically to make quick reports; Susan ran absent fingers over the back of his head, feeling the harshness of his hair and tried to keep her mind on other things, things like the breasts which swum above her angle of vision, appearing under the stress of the moment to take on not only mythic dimensions but a kind of movement. This abstraction was difficult, the boy being so insistent, and so Susan closed her eyes against the breasts, closed her eyes against the aspect of all the walls and worked into herself instead; far beneath her the deep sound of his orgasm began (she knew exactly what it was; she had always known what it would feel like when finally they came) and she, beginning to split apart in his fury, had a sudden sensation. She was no longer herself but had been dismembered, cut to pieces so to speak, and these pieces— her breasts, her thighs, angles of her mouth, her eyes, her cunt—were being hung to dry along the various ropes of his memory: many years later those parts would have frozen into artifact, totally separate from the girl she had been they would still dangle from the ropes of recollection within him and now and then he would probe, inspect, stroll through those alleyways or courtyards and look at the parts of her that would be displayed within. It was something to think about. It was really something to think about; that that was what she was coming to. She wondered if the girls who had their pictures taken for the centerfold had any similar apprehension; if, at the very instant that the camera caught their picture, they could feel themselves being split apart into the many small pieces which they would become. She had learned in an anthropology course recently that savages feared the camera because they thought it could entrap the spirit: similarly, she found that she feared what the boy was doing to her because, through this wedge driven above her thighs, pieces of her were being taken away forever. But she got over all of that just as soon as she learned that it was characteristic for virgins to have a lousy time the first time out. At least this was what the boy told her shortly afterward and she found out that every bit of it was true. Two or three years later, in fact, and just for the hell of it she allowed one of her dates to send a nude picture of her to one of the men's magazines saying in a letter that she would like to pose but nothing came of that. Susan was then in the process of finding out that sex could be used for purposes other than merely its own sake so the way she had first had intercourse really wasn't that significant after all…. despite the meanings she had put onto it when she was actually involved. On the other hand, she was only twenty-three and like everything else so far, she feared the episode might only come back to haunt her someday.

CHAPTER XXI

Later in the night it seems that Timothy has some kind of nightmare because he begins to talk loudly in his sleep and Susan, who has given up any hope of rest and is sitting quietly drinking coffee, can hear every word distinctly. "The lousy dirty stinking sons of bitches," Timothy says with perfect clarity and a certain conviction which seems less declamatory than merely pedagogical, "they're out to get me, every single one. I tell you; I can't stand this anymore." He sits up in the bed, closed eyelids masking an intent stare toward the ceiling and, using a finger, he points in the direction of a window. "I'll tell you who you are," he says and Susan leans forward; she is always interested in learning something, even at four in the morning she will take knowledge where she can get it. "I'm going to tell you right here who you are, I'm going to nail you to the wall," Timothy says in a voice now faintly musical; Susan attends closely, she does not want to miss any of this. Timothy motions with a forefinger; it pushes the air trembling; it turns and cuts through areas of light. "You, Mrs. Morales," Timothy says, "you, Stella Smith, you Ramon Perez. You George Washington Williams III and you Mrs. Mendoza. All of you, all of you," he says and hurls himself down on the bed, perhaps to sleep again. There is no further information that night and eventually Susan returns to sleep, sinking this time into an effortless doze where she receives, in 1981, the Academy Award for best supporting actress. The citation notes her struggles against early adversity but does not give details, which is fine with her. A man sitting next to her might be her father but she does not dare to turn to take a full look; there is always a chance that he might merely be some leading member of the academy.

CHAPTER XXII

In the morning, Susan reports once again to the loft. It is very much the way it was the first and only time she has been there except that areas have now been cleared and she is confronted by a huge, unbroken aspect which sweeps the full length and width of the building uncluttered by furniture or equipment. On the perimeter along all four sides of the loft are batteries of cameras, strobe lights, sound equipment and technicians, dwarfish men who seem to swing through the jumble of machinery with the greatest of ease and reach positions of adjustment from which they perch to look at the actors with expressions of gloom. There are twelve of them altogether, Susan counts, including the director who is seated uncomfortably in a heavy chair in the center of a chalk-marked circle; the actors are clustered around them, and, feeling ill at ease for being one of the last ones to arrive, Susan goes to the rear of the clump and sits down rather gracelessly, folding her skirt around her knees. She has decided to come to this first session in a skirt and sweater, elaborately made up and carefully coiffured although she is not sure exactly why she is doing this; it can only be a waste of time. The actors, some of whom she recognizes from the other day, look at her without interest and return their gaze to the director who seems to be in the middle of an impassioned speech. She can barely make out a word that he is saying although he pauses now and then to make gestures *expressivo* in the air and fasten his gaze intently upon individual actors. The boy with whom she had scenes yesterday is seated next to her and he gives her a wink, moves closer, runs a hand up her arm in a protective fashion which Susan decides she does not like. "Hello," he says. "I was hoping you'd be here."

"No," Susan says, "nothing like that at all. Really, I won't discuss that." This does not make too much sense to her but it connects to something in his eyes. He lowers them, shrugs, drops his arm, and continues to stare at the director who is now in a high-pitched full mumble. "Artistic integrity," the director is saying. "We must apply ourselves with unusual dedication. This is no ordinary enterprise. Crucial matters are being undergone here if you can understand that."

"When do we start?" a girl in the near row asks. Her voice wavers on the word *start;* the others begin to mumble and she shrinks below Susan's eye-level. "Well, I only wanted to *know.*"

"Familiarization lecture," the director says. "Matters of primacy, acculturation. We are taking a group of strangers, hardly amateurs, and trying to weld them together into a cohesive group which can produce at least a simulacre of art. I should have known it was hopeless, however. Was trying a little backgrounding."

"I'm sorry," the girl says. "I just thought—"

"No thought. Actors must be schooled against all thought. Was speaking of the sociopathic elements of the script, those which will contraindicate to a certain extent rationalized interpretation; but there is no patience here for a rigorous format. Corrupt country, absolutely corrupt," the director who has now become quite comprehensible says; his accent having slid away from him and left him in a ponderous drawl; he stands unsteadily and, raising his fist, seems at the point of making some serious declaration, which will, perhaps, accomplish the task of familiarization satisfactorily, but he is interrupted by one of the technicians, a red-headed dwarf with a long cane and piercing eyes who scuttles over to him, whispers something meaningful in his ear and then departs, giving the actors a rather horrid wave behind his back, an absent twitch or two of the fingers charged with significances which Susan can hardly bear. All of her senses seem keyed up this morning; maybe it is the active night's sleep she has had; maybe it is knowing that at last she is going to begin to act seriously. "I understand," the director says, "that the equipment is now prepared and that, therefore, we can go to work. Because of extrinsic factors we must shape our efforts and our schedule to the limits of the technicians; rates are quite high and overtime cannot be tolerated. Unfortunately, in our consumer culture, there is no time for rigorous application or scholarship but this is, possibly, for the very best, inasmuch as I think that all of you are idiots. You will, please, disrobe at once.

"I do not think you heard me," he says as the actors remain frozen in their postures, Susan particularly beginning to feel a certain chill at the edges. "It is that kind of film; it is necessary that your clothing be removed throughout. All of you are experienced. All of you have been informed. You will move in and out of various scenes. Some of you will be acting in three or four consecutively, then will be sitting out as many, but the flux of the film is remarkable and essentially you are a company, a disciplined company rather than a passel of actors. You must be on call all the time. It is far faster and easier for all of you to disrobe and remain that way. The loft is not chilly. Of course, if any of you object," the director says and pauses—he really has no speech trouble at all now—his voice is distinct, even the drawl has left his rhetoric, now he sounds like Phil (for whom Susan has been looking but does not appear to be present) making a serious point. "I will not have this," the director says, "I will not have any question about this issue," and now the actors do begin to undress; by twos and threes they get to their feet and stand uncomfortably, the men already yanking at their belts, the girls fumbling for their brassieres or those without brassieres already pulling off the sleeves of their sweaters. Susan feels her breasts come free, feels the gaze of the actor and director upon her, hopes that she is not, at this particular stage of her life, becoming some kind of a moralist because this is certainly not the time or the circumstances for anything of that sort.

CHAPTER XXIII

She remembers something that Phil had told her in the bed just before they had gotten down to serious business, something that she had possibly put out of her mind before. He had leaned over her, immense, naked, an expression of rage combating shyness in his face, and had said, running his hands over her, "You know what the purpose of these movies is? It's very simple really and I'm surprised that no one has ever figured it out yet, at least to print. We got to give the guys and girls who watch this the idea that the whole world is a dirty movie because this gives them hope, you understand; they don't feel so alone and helpless if we can make them believe that this is exactly the way it happens. You see, you're dealing with a kind of person, maybe, who has had such troubles with sex that he can hardly believe it exists; oh he knows that something's going on between people but so little is happening for him that he begins to worry if the whole thing is a myth, something invented by the world to keep him frustrated and angry. They can get very dangerous to themselves and others if they stop believing in sex; so what we got to do is to restore it to them in some way that they think it is believable. That's why we look for a kind of actress who isn't so experienced, who doesn't look like she's been around over the lot; that way the whole thing is more credible and the audience can picture themselves more easily. In the forties they had whores doing this stuff but that hasn't worked for a long time. You're really built, you know that? Even more than I thought from a distance; I could hardly believe that you were so built," and he began to make noises which she or at least he took for passion; bent over her, began to nuzzle and fondle. As he went over the top, a glazed, frantic expression appeared in his shielded face and Susan saw his vulnerability so clearly that just for an instant she thought there was connection but then, as almost always with men the sensitivity went away and there was only greed, insistence, and the juncture of his loins throwing into her a knowledge so hot that all she could do was absorb it.

CHAPTER XXIV

As they stand naked, in embarrassed, uncomfortable positions, a technician passes among them with a stack of scripts. He hands her one with the name SUSAN crayoned on a piece of paper clipped to it and she takes it, feeling the weight of the pages, looking at the title page. She finds that many of the pages are blank; presumably those in which there are scenes in which she is not participating. Turning at random she finds on page 80 a long scene between a character called Madame Curie and her husband Pierre. Foul words leap out from the page at her and she begins to read avidly but before she can even see what kind of role has been given her, the director claps his hands and climbs a parapet from which he addresses them with his hands held as a megaphone.

"These are your scripts," he says. "You will study them. You will note that they are not complete; the master copy is only in the possession of myself and a few other people. In order to get the best performances out of you, it has been decided that your knowledge of the script will be limited to your own parts, this means that you will be able to reduce your focus to the necessary. You are to study these scripts all the time; when you are not actually involved in scenes you will be preparing. Later on, a full summary of the plot will be given you but at this time that would only interfere with your conception of the individual roles."

"Where are we supposed to be when we're not on the set?" the actor next to her asks. He gives Susan a wicked nudge, his eyes fixed on the director. "Off to the sides?"

"Exactly. You will be constantly called upon to participate and must be near the set."

"I don't think that that's dignified," the actor says. "I mean to say that doesn't seem to be right. We're entitled to separate dressing facilities and a place to relax; we can't have people staring at us all the time."

"I'm afraid you don't understand," the director says. "That is wholly untenable. We are working with certain rigorous limits here."

"But it's not fair," the actor says. He nudges Susan again; possibly he is pleading for help. "We can't just come in and act; we're entitled to some privacy. Isn't that right? Doesn't anybody here agree with that?"

"I agree with that," Susan says. The actor gives a sigh, pokes her again, and the director looks at her with an even, steady glaze in his eyes, making Susan feel suddenly very foolish and dangerously exposed. "Well, I *could* agree with that," she says. "Maybe we should just not worry about it too much; after all, the important thing is just to get the film going, isn't it?"

"The hell with it," the actor mumbles. He moves apart from her slightly, taking a determined stance, his hands on his hips. "Look here," he says positively. "We're entitled to some dignity and respect. If we can't get private dressing facilities, I'm going to refuse to participate."

"That's perfectly all right," the director says. One of the technicians comes over, mumbles something in his left ear, gives him an absent caress of the left shoulder and walks hurriedly away. "You can leave right now," the director says with even more assurance. "There are plenty of replacements available. Your roles are quite expendable."

"Just because we're doing this kind of work doesn't mean that we're not entitled to a little dignity!" the actor says in a harsh, pleading voice. The edge of his assurance has been broken; now fear seems to be tumbling out. "All right," he says, giving Susan a look of fury. "I won't object any more. If that's the way it has to be—"

"I'm afraid you don't understand," the director says. "You've made your point very well. You may leave—"

"Now listen—"

"I don't have the time. You people are utterly replaceable. We are not getting involved in negotiations. You will please put on your clothes and leave the set at once."

"You don't understand," the actor says, his assurance now completely gone. "I've had dramatic training. I'm a professional. In Seattle in 1968—"

"Please leave," the director says. Technicians once again come from behind the equipment, now gather, three of them, in a wee mass around the actor, staring at him through piercing eyes, hands identically on their hips. The actor gives a shrug, stoops, and begins to assemble his clothing. "Is anyone going to come with me?" he asks. "Am I the only one who had the guts to stand up—"

"I'm sorry," one of the technicians says in a lisp. "You are no longer permitted on the set. Please leave."

The actor turns toward Susan and says, "We at least know each other. There's some contact here, isn't there? Don't you think—"

"I'm sorry," Susan says and turns to him fully, trying to explain; it is important to her that she make the boy understand why she cannot leave but before she has a chance to find the words or even the way in which she will approach him, the three small technicians fall upon the actor like a net, grab his arms and legs, and begin to drag him off to the side, one of them cunningly using a foot to kick his clothing toward the wall. The actor struggles soundlessly, all arms and legs and stop-motion, and passes out of the line of sight and behind one of the cameras. Susan feels a shudder inside herself; she must admit that she has been somewhat moved. After all, the actor and she have had a kind of relationship. She wonders if the others are staring at her because she did not show loyalty to him. However, when she peeks from the edges of peripheral vision, she sees that all of the actors are standing in frozen positions, staring at the ceiling or floor, many of them with their hands clasped, a few quietly chewing gum. They look like well-behaved prisoners aligned for a public official's visit. Susan decides to try to stop taking things so personally; it is, after all and as Phil has said, a business and perhaps she had better detach herself.

"You see," the director says, "the actor is merely a tool. We cannot tolerate any behavior which takes him out of that role and, if necessary, I will take similar action with any of you. This is a serious production."

Somewhere offstage Susan can hear struggles and remonstrations, but this does not matter to her anymore.

CHAPTER XXV

The first scene goes very quickly and well and Susan decides that this kind of movie is not so difficult after all. She appears in it playing the role of the widow of Warren Gamaliel Harding as she is informed of his rather sudden death while on a vacation trip in 1924. A quick scan of the scene assures her that she will be able to act this role with conviction and, once under the lights, she feels nothing at all except the desire to fulfill its implications as set down on the printed page.

A heavyset, middle-aged actor, also nude, plays the role of the political assistant delegated to give her the news, and one of the technicians hands him a small cigar which he uses as a prop for the first part of the scene. They act on a bare area under heavy lights which cause both of them to sweat heavily, adding veracity to the scene. "Oh Mrs. Harding," the actor says, "I have terrible, terrible news for you. Your husband has died quite suddenly. I am sorry about this."

According to the instructions in the script, Susan ducks her head, looks at her breasts, runs her left hand indolently across her stomach. "Oh well," she says. "I'm not surprised at all. He had no self-discipline and his diet was terrible. I warned him and warned him."

"Is there anything that I can do for you?"

"Nothing at all," Susan says. "I'm perfectly all right."

"I know that this must be a terrible shock to you and stand ready to do anything I can. Should there be any arrangements—"

"It's no shock. I saw it coming for a long time. At last I'll be able to get out of national politics. I never cared for it much at all, being a very quiet woman, and I begged Warren time and again to go back to the statehouse but it was too late."

"Warren was a very fine man," the actor says and comes over to Susan, puts a hand on her shoulder, runs his fingers across her back. There is some indication in the script now as to a pause for activity and Susan does not know exactly what this demands; she decides to adapt to it simply by relaxing and feeling the actor's hands begin to move all over her body. Shortly there is an insistent pressure around her thighs and she closes her eyes, leans back, feels herself being carried down to the hard wood surfaces of the floor. In her next line she is supposed to ask the actor what exactly he thinks he is doing but she is not sure when she should speak it: should there be a substantial break here for sexual activity, or should she, by delivering the line quickly, indicate that Mrs. Harding is resisting. There is no clue in the script. "What are you doing?" she asks, opening her eyes, seeing the actor above her, his tongue hanging out, gasping, his eyeballs distended as he rocks in a sexual posture, "What are you doing?" The actor says nothing. He is concentrating, really bearing down; his erection is small but it is firm and he is doing his best for the situation. "Hold it!" the director says somewhere in the distance and comes into the scene, the script dangling from his hands. He begins to swear at the actor. "You idiot," he says, "you're supposed to keep on talking, deliver the *lines,* this isn't a goddamned show, you're going to put us all out of business if you don't concentrate." "I'm sorry," the actor says, shaking his head, recovering his feet, "if I only had a little time to prepare—"

"There is no time to prepare," the director says angrily. "We are working here on a very quick time schedule. It is your responsibility to have studied these lines, to know the scene, to act instinctively," and the actor mumbles something shaking his head. "Miserable," the director says. "Absolutely miserable. If we are starting in this fashion, I ask myself, how will we possibly finish? The girl, at least, the girl is acting with a little conviction but you are being absolutely impossible. What you have to do is to play against the script; you must deliver these lines quickly, *con brio, con gioco,* as it were while performing these acts, and the contrast between the lines and the acts will lead to that certain redeeming sense of irony which is the key to our conception. Do you understand? This is comedy, but it is comedy done with substance and style." "All right," the actor says, "all right, I studied, I got some background. I'll do it. If you had told me in the first place—"

"I don't have to tell you anything," the director says, "you must do this instinctively and professionally. I am very unhappy with the level of performance here, very unhappy and this is merely the first scene we are doing. Fortunately we are shooting out of sequence and doing minor scenes first but even so." He leaves the area and drops out of their line of sight. "Wild," the actor says into her ear. "Crazy. I never seen anything like this in my life. If I didn't need the money—"

"Please," Susan says. "I don't want to talk about it. Let's just do the scene."

"If I didn't need the money I wouldn't touch this place with a ten-foot pole. I have dramatic training. I have some *background*—"

"Listen," Susan says, "if it's all the same to you, it's nothing personal, I just want to do the scene."

"You really believe this," the actor says admiringly. "You really are trying to act with conviction."

"Against the lines. Let's act against the lines."

"My name is Murray. I'm—"

"Against the lines."

"All right," Murray says with a sigh. He lifts his head, puts his hands on her, rubs them up and down her arms and Susan feels the damp moving out from his palms to create a kind of perverse warmth. "I'm trying to comfort you, Mrs. Harding," he says as the lights come on full again. Equipment begins to hum, the director makes a foul comment offstage, and the sound of the technicians' laughter mixed with the murmurs of the other actors begins to fill the hall.

CHAPTER XXVI

By the end of the day, Susan has acted in seven scenes and witnessed fourteen others while standing off to the side with her script in hand, learning lines. The scenes in which she has acted have involved roles as Mrs. Warren Gamaliel Harding, Marie Antoinette, Madame von Meck, the patroness of Peter Ilyitch Tchaikovsky, the immortal beloved of Ludwig van Beethoven, Isadora Duncan, the dark beloved of Shakespeare's sonnets and the mistress of Nikolo Paganini. These scenes have been heavily slanted toward the musical, the director explains to her, because they are shooting the unimportant, connective, fringe material first before working into the more basic political and sociological focus of the film as the actors warm up and become more confident in their roles All of the scenes are very short, averaging no more than two to three minutes playing time, and all of them involve sexual activity of some sort, although in the Paganini and Tchaikovsky episodes she has only had to stand to the side and witness the actor simulate masturbation. The purpose of the film is to show the basic sexual obsession of all great lives and events although Susan cannot say that she understands much of it.

Most of her scenes have been with Murray who seems to be basically paired with her throughout, but two or three of them have been with other actors: a thin man named William who played Beethoven with a lisp and an immensely tall, disheveled actor named Frank who under the director's instruction played Shakespeare as if he were a common drunk in search of rough trade. Frank told her in an intense conversation over the sandwiches brought up for a lunch break that he had never seen anything like this in the history of the world but then he was willing to learn. "I think the point is," Frank had said, chewing and gesturing violently, the towel thrown modestly over his lower sections functioning as a napkin as well, "that these people are absolutely *serious;* they may be the last serious people left, they mean business. This is not a gag. You're a very attractive girl; how did you get into this, you look a little young for it," and then, without waiting for an answer, he had gone into an analysis of his background which he said made inevitable what had become of him. He had studied for a doctorate in medieval English at the University of Washington but before the orals had found that he had lost the power to read. "I mean, I looked at the page and it was just letters stuck down in different-sized clumps, but I couldn't make any sense of them at all; I couldn't make out the meaning. I had to use my index finger just to pick out the letters and that's the point at which I decided I had better get out of the business. I mean my subconscious was obviously trying to tell me *something* about taking a doctoral degree in English; so I figured that after hanging around the university for ten years it was time to go. Of course I'm not really interested in acting, I just kind of fell into it." Susan had found his conversation interesting if distracting. She had wanted to read her script and concentrate on the lines and scenes so that maybe she could get some internal comprehension of what everybody was driving at but everyone wanted to socialize, even the director who had gotten on a parapet toward the end of the lunch break and given them a long harangue in which he had talked about the deeper artistic truth and purposes which he hoped to bring out in this film and how he hoped that they would cooperate with one another to cause their performances to flow together. The talk had been almost incoherent. The director seems to have two modes of speech altogether—one of which (abusing actors) makes perfect sense and the other a more ruminative mode in which he cannot make himself understood at all. Susan knows that she will want to think about all of this later on. She will have to think a great deal. She is really stockpiling a lot of experience. The Marie Antoinette scene had been really difficult to get through what with her head being inserted into a strange contraption that entrapped and choked her while unspeakable things were done to her helpless backside. At that the scene had been nothing compared to what the girl playing Man Of War in another scene had gone through. The girl playing Man of War had been dramatizing the celebrated race in which Man of War, that great thoroughbred, had suffered the only defeat of his magnificent twenty-one race career by losing in a head finish to another two-year-old named Upset, and, in the course of simulating the actions of racing while carrying a jockey, this girl had been the subject of certain demented acts by the small actor playing the jockey which Susan simply did not want to watch. That was the whole point. She did not want to think about anything that had gone on that day. It was a day's work. That was all there was to it and tomorrow would be another day and in five or six days they would finish the film and then her career would start. But her career was not something about which she could worry under the present circumstances.

The director let them go at six in the evening telling them that the first day's work had been disgraceful, an absolute abomination and signaled the end of all his hopes if this level of performance continued. He advised them to be back at eight in the morning prepared to act seriously. The technicians, still giggling (they were always giggling) perched now at rest on their equipment like monkeys and sneered at them as one by one they got into their clothing and left the loft. Susan received invitations to go for coffee or drinks from Frank and Murray as well as a third actor whose name she never caught who had played the jockey in the horse racing sequence. She declined them with thanks. Outside, however, turning the corner, she received another invitation from Phil who seemed to have been lying in wait for her, and, for reasons which she could not rationalize, she decided that she better not pass this one up and followed him without a word to the restaurant where he had taken her before, wondering if everybody in New York was looking at her intently, knowing exactly what she had been through that day. She doubted it. You could do absolutely anything at all in New York and then go out on the streets and, for all that it mattered to the people surrounding you, you might not have been there at all because they had been through exactly the same thing. That was why she liked New York and why she hated it.

CHAPTER XXVII

"The industry is at a turning point," Phil says to her, stirring his coffee. He looks down at the table, inscribes small circles with the free hand. "It is at a crucial instance. The next year will turn the tide. This is something that I firmly believe."

"Yes," Susan says, taking some more coffee of her own and trying to look attentive for Phil although he has not looked her in the eyes yet even once. "I think I know what you mean."

"Pornography will either become an art form within the next year or it will collapse," Phil says. "The market has been overextended, it has been overexploited by the worst kind of people, and now it is being reduced again to its natural audience which, as we all know, is composed of freaks. It will not be legislated against; it will merely wither away like the leaves on the branches from winter trees. Unless it can find and hold the larger audience which is now its opportunity. If it can break the limits."

"I agree with you absolutely. I know just what you mean."

"These people for whom I'm working believe that the ship will not sink.

They are not along for a fast buck, they are serious, they wish to do meaningful work. Pornography can be a meaningful art form and can break forth into new areas of experience. That is the intention of this film on which you're working."

"Yes," Susan says. She feels drowsiness overtake her, shakes her head, braces herself in the seat. What she wants is to go to sleep but this is impossible; she is in no position, after this day, to risk Phil's disapproval. "I happen to agree with you."

"The first reports, however, are not good. They are extremely discouraging, in fact. The level of performances are not what they should be. Needless to say, it is hard to find and develop a good level of talent in this kind of film. Nevertheless, there are standards and we try to meet them."

"Well, I tried—"

"They are not good at all and in particular you are not acting up to your potential. I hear unhappy news about you. I am extremely disappointed." Phil rubs his hands together, looks at her for the first time, lowers his eyes and switches the gears of his rhetoric so that once again he talks as he did when she first met him. "This can't be," he says. "We got to keep up to standards. You are a particular disappointment because you begged me for this chance."

"I didn't beg you."

"Don't argue with me!" Phil says and waves his arm with a flourish. A glass of water is upset. Two waitresses, murmuring, appear from the sides to wipe up the water. He says nothing, sits sullenly, hands folded until they are gone. "Trouble is we can't teach you kids nothing these days," he says. "You think you know it all."

"I'm tired. I'm so tired—"

"Don't give me your problems! I got problems; I got to get this thing out. The hell with it," Phil says. "I could tell you things that would make you sit up straight but your whole generation is so selfish that you won't even listen. What do you care? All you can do is take your clothes off and get in front of a camera. You think that's acting? I'll tell you what acting is. Incidentally, I'm not trying to put the make on you. Get that right out of your mind, if you think that that's why I'm seeing you tonight. There is nothing going that way at all because I got other plans. This is purely business and, to tell you the truth, I'm not so hot to put the make on you, if you know what I mean. Of course, if you want to come up to my place to talk—"

"Please," Susan says. She feels that her personality is slowly being pulverized under his weight. She has the peculiar feeling of seeing oneself running out like water upon the table. Of course her father used to make her feel that way; so she has some familiarity with the sensation. "I'm just so tired—"

"I didn't force you to come along. If you don't want to go up to my place, that's perfectly all right; it doesn't make any difference to me at all. Of course I don't know how long we can keep you going in this film. You don't even show any interest in getting advice. You can't even take direction. How long can we ride with you? So it's your decision," Phil says and takes his wallet out of his pocket, beginning to lay bills upon the table. He stops at three, looks at the clock behind them and stands. "So I guess that's it," he says. "You come around tomorrow morning and we'll see if we got anything for you or not. Of course if we don't, we can't guarantee any pay for today because we'll have to scrap everything in which you've appeared; it would be ridiculous to have an actress in a couple of scenes who wasn't woven through the film. I can't tell you people how to live; it's a wholly different life-style."

"You remind me of my father," Susan says. "In many ways, you're just like him."

"That's an old problem. It don't mean nothing to me."

"I didn't say you were."

"I got no time to lose," Phil says standing ponderously, weaving behind the table. "I got things to do so you got to make your move now and not later."

"All right," Susan says. "All right. I'll go to your place if you want me to."

"Not exactly my place," Phil says, putting his arm on her. "No, not my place. There are reasons I can't take you there. We're going to the same place as the other time, the hotel. But I think of it as my place because I've had that room for years and I even sleep in it sometimes and once for three months I even lived there due to certain circumstances which I won't go into now. At a different period of my life now best forgotten. Actually, I am a very complex man."

CHAPTER XXVIII

Under Phil she momentarily forgets the day: he is heavy, he is insistent, there are polarities to his need which force her to split high and low. Bisected she feels like two Susans driven on different courses toward simultaneous ends but as his climax nears it becomes fucking again, simple fucking, heavy and necessitous like everything she has ever known and the feeling of partition goes away. Life is becoming routine, she finds herself thinking: just two days in the film business and she is already in a rut: appear at the loft, participate in scenes of sex for eight hours, fuck Phil, and go back to Timothy. She has always been a person of regular habits; it is astonishing how under any circumstances they seem to reestablish themselves. Phil, predictably, falls away from her in the aftermath, all of him turning inward. He breathes shallowly, looks at his hands, sits. "Well," he says. "I got things to do; I guess I'd better be going."

"I thought you wanted to talk to me."

"We already talked," Phil says. "Listen," he says after a pause, "don't think that you got any claims on me just because of this thing. I go my own way. I'm an independent operator; I got responsibilities and I can't afford to get tied up in any involvements. Your performances are unsatisfactory, you're going to have to do better."

"All right."

"Everything has to be sacrificed for the film, which is the important thing. If you can do the job you stay; otherwise you have to go. I have business," Phil says. "I got to be going. I already spent more time here than I should."

Mumbling he pulls on his clothes, his back toward Susan. Reconstituted he turns toward her, adjusts his tie, says that he guesses that he will see her tomorrow and without any further words goes out the door, reminding Susan to lock up when she leaves. "And don't touch anything around here," he adds. "Don't disturb any of the arrangements. I got things set up a certain way here."

Lying naked on the bed Susan wonders what she could possibly touch; what arrangements Phil could have made in this room. It is spare, ascetic: it contains a bed, a dressing table with a chipped mirror, two chairs, and a tattered rug on the floor. It looks like any one of the rooms she remembers vaguely from college; the kind of motel rooms that dates would take her to although those, for the most part, were much cleaner and had a television console built into the wall. This is definitely an older-generation room. It has no pretensions whatsoever; it appears to be a place for sex and nothing else. She stands, goes curiously to the dresser, and begins to pull open drawers. Under a number of papers with figures jotted on them under columns saying INVENTORY and PRODUCTION SCHEDULE, she finds a stack of pornographic pictures; couples posed in positions of simulated sex, their eyes staring through the camera. The couples appear to have taken little interest in their work; on the back of the pictures Phil or someone else has scribbled names, addresses, and telephone numbers, none of which are familiar to her. She thinks that she may recognize a couple of people in the pictures but on the other hand, people in sexual positions have a way of looking pretty much the same. She replaces the photographs underneath the inventory reports, closes the drawer, puts on her clothes and leaves. She resolves that she will never come back to this room again but, by the time she has reached the lobby, fortunately empty, the edge of that resolve is already blunted and without any strong convictions she takes the subway home.

CHAPTER XXIX

In the subway, hunched into a seat in the corner she is afflicted by a fantasy: everyone in the car is similarly an actor in a pornographic film. As ugly or expressionless as most of them are, they have specialty roles and are coming back from a hard day's work promoting sexual liberalism and an extended consciousness. The tall man carrying a suitcase and mumbling to himself at the edge of the car is a whipmaster in a sadistic film; the heavy old lady banging intermittently on her left elbow is a seamstress for a pornographic film company and makes occasional appearances in perverse segments. Three adolescent girls, chewing gum have performed as a triumvirate in someone's extended fantasy; the conductor, almost invisible in his damp cell, specializes in buggery. It is much easier for her to come to terms with the world in this fashion; it may even be true, for all she knows. The car rockets in darkness through the thin, spreading tube of the underground opening before them; it is all lights and mystery, signals flickering in the void, workmen scuttling like technicians on the tracks to clear the way for the train as it surges uptown.

CHAPTER XXX

At home she finds Timothy in an ugly mood, eager to talk. They are, it seems, on the verge of an emotional crisis. He has done some serious thinking during the day and has decided that they must define their relationship to make some commitment to one another once and for all. Also, he has arrived at the decision that he does not want her acting in the pornographic film business after all; for reasons, which he will not go into, he finds it threatening to his masculinity. "I won't have it any more," he says gesturing rather wildly, knocking some manuscript pages of his novel from the desk top behind which he has been sitting. "We can't just drift and drift! We have to decide right now what we're going to do for the rest of our lives and whether these lives involve one another."

"I'm tired, Timothy," she says. "Can't we talk about it later on or tomorrow?"

"No, we can't talk about it later on or tomorrow. I know why you're tired; I can imagine exactly what you've been doing today. We have to make decisions, Susan, decisions! We must come to grips with our lives."

"Do you want to get married?"

"Married? Who said anything about getting married? Marriage is an archaism; it's only a device through which society entraps us by putting a label on a natural state. I don't think there have been any marriages between intelligent people for five years. I'm talking about an emotional commitment, a commitment to oneness, a feeling of union—"

"I thought we could just go along this way, couldn't we? You were the one who said that we had to maintain our freedom of choices. I don't want to discuss it, really Timothy," Susan says. "I should be relaxing and trying to concentrate on my roles. I've got to prove that I can bring conviction—"

"Conviction! I know what kind of conviction you're bringing! Don't look at me that way, I'm not naive. I deal with the most dispossessed, demoralized, alienated, dangerous, and asocial segment of the population: I have their case records right in front of me and I read things that would turn you white. I used to go to their homes and try to rehabilitate them! I want you to get out of that film, Susan. Emotional commitment is one thing and the film is another. I won't have it! You have to get out of that business."

"You said it was perfectly all right for me to go. You said that each of us was entitled to lead his separate life."

"Well," Timothy says, "that was before I had to come to terms with the effect of this upon my psyche. It's shattering. Tell me what you did today. No, I take it back, don't tell me what you did. It would upset me terribly. Just stop doing it."

Susan looks around Timothy's apartment carefully. She knows it very well; furthermore, every corner of it seems to lurk with sexual memory. There is not a single area of this apartment, it seems, where in one form or another they have not had sex. Say what you will of Timothy, things have been intense in their way. She takes it all in carefully, as if for the last time and then stands. "I'm leaving," she says.

"You're what?"

"I'm going to leave you, Timothy. I can't come back to this. You have no idea of what I've been through today."

"Oh yes I do!"

"All right, maybe you do. I can't take this any more. I can't take any more *scenes.* Probably I'll go into the Barbizon for a while. There isn't that much of my stuff here anyway."

"Now listen," Timothy says, moving over, putting his hands on her shoulders. "There's no need to be hasty about this. I mean, you can express your hostility in some other fashion, I think; you can channel it more reasonably. No one here is asking you to leave."

"I don't care about that. I can't be put through any more scenes, Timothy. I don't have the stamina."

"Well, whose fault is that?"

"I wanted to be an actress," Susan says. "I still want to. At least I've got work. It's a start and an opportunity. I won't have you stopping me." She listens to herself with interest; she sounds passionate and dedicated. "You have no right to interfere in my life that way. Am I stopping you from writing your novel?"

"My novel is an extension of myself. I'm not selling myself—"

"You know something, Timothy?" Susan says. "I'm going to tell you the truth. I can't read your novel. It just doesn't make any sense. I may be wrong; I don't know a thing about writing, but I don't think that you're very good. Which is all the more reason why you have no right to tell me what to do."

After that things get very bad; it is their worst fight yet, which is saying a good deal, and at the end of it it is not Susan but Timothy who walks out, grabbing his coat and saying that he is leaving on personal business and when he comes back at midnight he does not want to see her there. On the other hand, if she wants to be reasonable she can stay, but, if he finds her, he will assume that she will take the relationship on meaningful terms. He leaves, comes back to remind her that she owes him twenty dollars for a personal loan and that she is not to touch the pages of his novel under any circumstances. Then he walks and returns again, picks the manuscript off the desk, slams it into his attaché case, and closing it with difficulty staggers out, this time not closing the door. Susan decides that she feels sorry for him but then that she is not. She thinks about breaking up his apartment but decides that behavior like this is not worthy of a college graduate. She thinks about leaving instantly after scrawling foul notes to him all over the walls and mirrors but does not have the energy. Happily she is saved from all of this by a sudden call from Frank, the Ph.D. candidate who says that he has, with much difficulty, and a few bribes been able to track her down, is right around the corner, and would be delighted to take her to dinner if she has no other plans. Susan says that she would be happy to do this but sex in their relationship is now completely out of the question because of other circumstances. Frank says this is fine; he never had much luck with girls anyway until he got started in the pornographic film business and now he is unable to conceive of sex apart from certain postures made before cameras, a problem which he hopes a psychiatrist will someday help him alleviate. They arrange for him to meet her outside in five minutes and Susan, throwing her clothing into a suitcase, leaves Timothy's apartment pretty much as she had found it, the only difference, in fact, being that his novel is not on the desk where it had dominated the room from the first time she had walked in.

CHAPTER XXXI

Eventually, Susan returns with Frank to his apartment. He has a massive seven-room, rent-controlled place on upper Central Park West whose primary tenant is his mother; it seems that his family has lived here for generations and that they are paying the lowest authorized rent in New York City. Frank concedes that being thirty-four years old and living with his mother is embarrassing and that it puts a certain dent in his social life but, on the other hand, the old lady is the primary tenant and, if she were to leave, his case before the rent control board would be very weak. He has three and a half of the rooms to himself and scarcely ever sees his mother. They meet occasionally in the vestibule but that is all. Or so he says. They are merely tenants with adjoining apartments and she is a rather senile but gentle old lady who occasionally takes too intimate an interest in his toilet habits. Frank leads Susan to one of the bedrooms, neatly if sparsely furnished in materials that seem to be fifty years old and then leaves her, saying that she is welcome to stay. At the door he gives her a meaningful look, full of trepidation and she sees that in a stumbling fashion he is trying to ask for sex. She pretends not to recognize that. The day has simply been too filled with activity of that sort and other kinds, although in the past, she had gone to bed with men like Frank simply because it was less trouble than to do otherwise. The moment passes, the look shifts, and Frank says that he will wake her at seven so that they can go down to the studio together. Susan gathers that he wants, by taking her in with him, to give the impression to the others that they have had sex and she says that that would be fine. He closes the door, she puts out the light, she falls into bed, still clothed and almost immediately begins to dream.

The dream is composed of many things: colors and faces and images of the loft but it coalesces around dinner with Frank; once again he is sitting across from her in the restaurant, looking at her with an intensity in which passion and fear seem intermixed. "I like this, you see," he says to her again, "because in a pornographic film it's right up front, the message and intent I mean. There's no dissimulation, no hypocrisy. People are reduced right away to what the hidden conditioners of society say they are: just cocks and cunts driven toward one another. All that it is is a commercial with the clothes off which makes it less obscene because the only thing the pornographic films are selling is jerking off which is a subject on which I happen to be an expert. Any unmarried graduate student learns a good deal about jerking off simply by opportunity but I am happy to say that as a result of my intelligence and diligent application I probably have mastered more of the fundamental techniques and sophistries of jerking off than anyone who ever lived. At least, anyone from my socioeconomic background." He folds his hands in the dream, regards a glass of club soda before him with an abashed expression, takes a hurried sip and then puts it down, seeming on the verge of saying something, but he is unable to speak.

In the restaurant Susan had said almost nothing; he had gone on like that for hours, but in the dream she is perfectly articulate as she almost never is in real life and she says to him, "All you men talk as if you had invented sex. As if it was meant only for you and you were the only people who understood it. Don't you see that it works two ways? That's the trouble with this film. The women are in it only as a means to satisfy the men."

"That's an old argument and misses the point," Frank says. "Of course pornographic films are for men just as cosmetics are for women. All the men in the cosmetics advertisements look and act just the way women do in skin flicks. That doesn't mean anything more than the nature of the medium. Anyway," he says, knocking the glass of club soda onto the table, small streams and driblets coming at her in waves, "anyway that's all nonsense. I want to make love to you right here in this place." He embraces her, puts his tongue with violence against her lips, and forces it into her; she struggles against him but he is too strong, the situation too compact for flight, and now the restaurant is dissolving. It is coming down upon her in small convulsions of stone and ash; it encircles her and becomes a bed composed of sheets which whip and flail about her as she struggles to avoid Frank but he is insistent, demanding, necessitious. "Get it up!" he screams, "get it up, get it there!" and she fights against him. She does not want to be violated. She has been violated too many times now. "Get it up!" he says, "get up, get up!" and she rises in the bed, her hands flung wildly, to find him standing over her, a puzzled and panicked expression on his face, apology in his eyes. It is seven o'clock, he tells her, and now it is time to go to work. She laughs, laughs with relief and, holding her arms out to him, gathers his confused and joyous form against her. It is not much of a fuck. He assaults her with small circular strokes, quizzicality in his body, a wish not to hurt her, and she can barely feel him coming but can she ever hear him!

CHAPTER XXXII

At the loft the director is in an ebullient mood for reasons that he never explains. He has brought in a large overstuffed chair that he now uses instead of the parapet from which to address them. He sits in it comfortably, his legs outstretched, while they kneel at his feet. "Children," the director says, "children, we were all very short-tempered with one another yesterday and on the first day of production this is understandable, but I want you to know that I looked at rushes later on, after all of you were in bed, and I am happy to say that they are not that bad. There is a certain quality to them, a certain ambience may I say, which portends good things; there is an unprofessional eagerness and lack of pretension, very common to amateurs of course, a certain quality I find most refreshing. It is possible that out of all of this we may get a production. On the other hand, it is possible that we may not. It is hard to tell. In any event, children, I find myself in a more pleasant and patient frame of mind today and hope that you are the same and together I hope that we will be able, as your expression goes, to make music together." He wheels with difficulty in the chair and stares behind it. Phil emerges from the background and stands next to him, a rather uneasy smile casting shadows on his face as he looks past them toward the walls. "Now another gentleman who most of you know would similarly like to say a few words," the director says.

Phil moves forward, leans against the chair with a palm and says, "I don't have too much to say. I just thought that I'd come down on behalf of the management and try to make a couple things clear to you. I, uh, understand that a few of you think that this is just another dirty film and aren't taking it so seriously for that reason. This is not a dirty film. I think that I've told most of you individually that we have plans to do this in commercial run and possibly at major theatre outlets. This is a very serious piece of work and you'll find that, if you do the job, you'll be backed up all the way. I mean," Phil says, "I just mean to say the pornography market is shot. There isn't any room for the dirties as such any more. No one's interested. We got to go out and find some higher horizons if we want to justify ourselves in the business, that's all. We got to have some vision and some enterprise. You'll find that we're not dealing in pornography here, and, if you would give this the same seriousness and respect that you'd give a straight play, we'd all be better off. That's all I have to say." Phil retires, aided to some degree by an amazing spatter of handclaps which come from sources which Susan cannot identify; certainly none of the actors are applauding nor is the director who, eyes on the floor, now seems to be considering his professional future. Perhaps it is the technicians who are clapping. The technicians too are much more cheerful today as they perch on the equipment with elan and ease. Phil, completely disconcerted by the applause, goes back to his office. The shooting day begins. They start at eight fifteen which is even earlier than yesterday and it goes on and on, not ending until well after five. Later on Susan is told that eight hours of final film were made that day which, even for this kind of production, is remarkable.

The scenes blur together and unlike yesterday she does not try to make any sense of the script. For some perverse reason things go much easier this way. It is simpler just to walk through the roles, delivering the lines flatly and performing mechanically without trying to look for motivation or plot. Perhaps on some higher level the script does make sense—Susan wants to believe that all the things the director has said are true and that the film is a serious statement—but scene-by-scene it makes none at all. A group of historical figures, almost always two-by-two, address each other in obscene language and then perform sexual acts. The acts vary. So do the lines. But the scenes all seem pretty much the same. Whoever has written the script seems to believe that a scene has three elements: an initial confrontation, a proposal/refusal, and vigorous sexual activity which usually terminates in anger. Susan does not, despite her affair with Timothy, know too much about writing, but the language strikes her as being rather stilted and the characterizations mediocre. Nevertheless with each moment, she feels she is moving closer to a professional breakthrough.

In one of the scenes she portrays Joan of Arc being burned alive at the stake. Two actors, playing a priest and a politician kneel in front of her as tricks with lighting are used to give the effect of flames surrounding her body. "Burn witch, burn," one of them says. "We've had enough of this nonsense."

"I will burn," Susan says, delivering the lines flatly, "but a higher judgment awaits you. Anyway, I have led France to a greater destiny than you have and you cannot take this from me."

"Heretic," the priest says. "Maid of Orleans indeed. I call you whore."

"I am a virgin. My body has never been entered by a man or by a woman either."

"Well," the politician says, "we'll have to fix that," and, tossing off his robes hurls himself upon her, he begins to simulate vigorous sex while the lights wash over them. "This is nonsense," the actor observes. "How can someone *write* lines like this?" and with a very slight erection mimes an orgasm and emits a low crooning moan. "So much for your virginity," the politician says, and backs off from her, making obscene gestures. "What do you have to say for the destiny of France now?"

"There is nothing that you can do," Susan says, closing her eyes. She puts her back firmly into the cheap, wooden cross that is being used as a prop, feels splinters press into her flesh. "Consider my religious vision," she says. "Consider the question of overthrow."

"Nonsense," the actor playing the priest says and cackles, a thin, high, amateurish cackle and carefully lights a stick of wood which has been handed him. He moves the burning wood toward Susan; she tries not to shriek and to accept her fate with equanimity. After an instant, the director considerately cuts the scene and douses the lights. Susan moves away from the cross shaking; the actor hands the wood to a technician who smiles at it and tosses it into a bucket of water. "There was no veracity there," the director says in the distance. "None whatsoever."

"Now he wants veracity," the actor mumbles. "Am I supposed to burn the place down?"

"Without veracity, without conviction, all of this becomes a travesty. We will have to take this scene again."

"Can I rest?" Susan says. "We don't have to do it right now, do we?"

"Not now," the director says. "In due course. You are projecting fear. You cannot project fear in this kind of a situation; it destroys the entire sense of the scene. Off the area, please. We must proceed."

"Listen," the actor mumbles to her behind as he leads Susan toward the side, "listen, what would you say if you and I just left this place right now?" He is a short intense man with maniacal eyes; excellent casting, she supposes, for a religious fanatic although his acting is completely amateurish. She has not been able to catch his name. "Surely we don't need the money that bad, do we?"

"I'm sorry," Susan says. "I have to study the script."

"You're dedicated, aren't you? Insanely dedicated. I saw that right off."

"I have no time to talk."

"We do need the money then, don't we?" the actor says and wanders away from her, picks his own script off the floor and incongruously reaches under a chair to find a pair of thick glasses. Susan shuts all of this out and looks over the lines of her next scene with fervor. It is hard to explain, but, no matter what she thinks of the situation, she wants to give a rounded performance.

CHAPTER XXXIII

Other shots go better, like the Roman orgy which is one of the major spectacles of the film. The director makes this last scene before lunch so that there will be an edge on their performances. This is a mass spectacle. For the first time, all six of the actors are on the set simultaneously and, in response to bellowed orders by one of the technicians, they arrange themselves in various postures and groupings. Then in response to further orders, they begin to improvise. Susan finds herself in an unspeakable position with Frank who has gravitated toward her, finds equally incredible things being done to her below, but, with several bodies lying across and between her limbs, she cannot localize the source of the disturbance. She can only, in reaction to the suggestions of the director, begin to perform other acts upon Frank. His eyes gleam, his breath comes in rapid gasp, his eyes close, and, in a series of small rolling gestures beneath her, he appears to be going to have an orgasm but the moment of tension goes away. He cannot produce sex on demand he mutters. But Susan remembers that she is constructed differently; on demand or not, strange things are happening inside her and she knows that the camera is picking up all of the details. For the first time she wonders if she really wants to appear in this film—major production or not. Her face is going to be on a lot of movie screens. Was a Roman orgy ever like this? she asks herself as she feels herself impelled from side to side, bodies shuttling around her. If orgies were like this, how did the Romans ever get anything worthwhile done? And what is the point, at this late hour, if reconstructing torrid scenes that didn't happen after all? Isn't the Fall of Rome really too far back in the past to have anything to do with the present situation? Or did Rome fall because of orgies like this? She wonders and feels herself being lifted, feels herself being carried to heights, her back straight to the floor, her arms now over her head, her legs high in the air. She feels the shock of quick entrance, burrowing within her, although not accomplished by whoever has lifted her. He, instead, is doing things to the soles of her feet. She seems to be attracting a disproportionate amount of attention. Looming over her she sees two breasts, above the breasts the face of a girl whose mouth is distended into an o of concentration and surprise. Cold and hard the girl stares at her and then bends down deliberately and kisses her on the mouth. Susan does not even know her name. Unlike the men she has not even had a physical awareness of the girls or their names. This girl squirms, moans, works her tongue between Susan's teeth. Susan thinks *lesbianism.* The kiss builds up in intensity, while other actors manipulate her thighs. Her female partner begins to mutter tensely and incoherently deep in her throat and Susan feels herself rising; something is happening to her. There are hands on her breasts, fingers pressing onto the nipples, and Susan faints. Everything moves far away from her and then she is in a tube of blankness spiraling downward.

When she recovers, she is lying on the floor, surrounded by the other actors and the director who, looking at her in an almost humorous way, says that these kind of problems are inevitable with newcomers but that she is not to worry. Everything is wrapped up now and, besides that, her faint has given much veracity to the scene. "We are looking for the sting of truth," the director says, "and sometimes a price must be paid. We will break for lunch now; it has been a good morning's work. Do you feel able to walk?" he asks Susan.

"I think so," she says, struggling, reaching for her feet. Hands hold her; she finds that she is being supported by the actress who had kissed her, a tall, confused girl now wearing a robe and glasses. "I guess I'll be all right," Susan says and forces herself from the girl's arms feeling revulsion. The girl, however, walks with her toward a corner of the loft and begins to talk softly and intensely. "You don't have to take this so seriously," the girl is whispering, "I mean, it's only a gig, there's no reason to get upset about it." Susan pushes her off, restrains with difficulty an impulse to run screaming from the loft, and finds herself being held by the hand by Frank who walks her off to the side so that she can get dressed. She feels she has to, for this moment at least, be dressed, even though lunch has been brought into the studio and almost all of the other actors, still naked, are collapsed like troops at a bacchanalia, eating with monomaniacal fierceness. Susan finds that she cannot understand a word that Frank is saying to her but she cannot make herself clear to him either. She wonders if she is in a bit over her head. Everyone else seems very matter of fact. Even Frank seems matter of fact. He whispers that this seems a hell of a place to try and get a serious relationship started.

CHAPTER XXXIV

At a particular period of despair and professional insecurity Susan had decided to apply for an investigator's job in the Department of Welfare but she had not been able to actually go through it. In the first place she had had to take a long test about her attitudes with strange multiple choice answers in which the right answer was obviously always the sympathetic one (YOU ARE IN A CLIENT'S APARTMENT DISCUSSING HIS PAST MAINTENANCE AND RESOURCES WHEN WITH NO WARNING HE SUDDENLY PULLS OUT A WEAPON AND THREATENS TO MAIM YOU IF YOU DO NOT DROP THIS LINE OF QUESTIONING. YOUR BEST COURSE IS TO: (A) IMMEDIATELY TERMINATE THE INTERVIEW AND CALL THE POLICE, (B) TELL HIM IF HE CONTINUES IN HIS PRESENT ATTITUDE HE WILL BE PERMANENTLY INELIGIBLE FOR PUBLIC ASSISTANCE, (C) IMMEDIATELY ATTEMPT TO LEAVE THE PREMISES, (D) SOOTHE THE CLIENT AND ADVISE HIM THAT YOU ARE ONLY THERE TO HELP HIM TO THE BEST OF YOUR ABILITY). In the second place, on the completion of this test, she had been taken into a room with a hundred other female applicants and been confronted by a shrewish attendant who said that any one of them with a background of venereal infection should advise them now as there would be a rather demanding physical. Susan had gotten up and left, not without some snickers from the room, because she had decided that no department which was supposed to have an attitude of compassion and respect for people could do any good if it treated prospective employees that way. When she had met Timothy, some months later, she had told him exactly what she had gone through and asked him how he could possibly work for such a department.

"Oh that's nothing," Timothy said matter of factly. "When I applied, I was loaded into a room with twenty other men and we were told to drop our pants so that the doctor could go down the line one by one and check us for hernias. Everybody pretended that he wasn't there at all, just stared out the window or hummed to himself. It's a hell of a thing to go into a room with twenty strangers and start seeing their pricks. Imagine what would happen if you did this kind of thing on the subway?"

"That's terrible."

"One guy started giggling and couldn't stop so the doctor ordered him out of the room, probably nailing him for a fag."

"So you went through with it."

"Of course I went through with it. I needed the job; everyone who shows up at the Department of Welfare, at either end, needs it; he's got no alternative. Of course that was in the good days before the job freeze. Now it takes you about a year to get started working there."

"I think that's terrible," Susan said, "that they would do this to people before they gave them a job; how can they put people through that and expect them to have dignity at all?" Timothy mumbled something about the department, in its wisdom, protecting and conserving itself because the interview and application process pretty well guaranteed that they'd have somebody broken in spirit by the time he got into the job. He, Timothy, had fortunately reconstituted himself through the departmental experience and was sure that he would be out soon, along with almost everybody else who sooner or later went on to good positions or graduate school or the Benton & Bowles advertising agency. Susan had thought less of Timothy ever since then, but, since she had never had a high opinion of him anyway (it was just inertia that got her into the situation) and since there were so many other things to hold against him later, she could hardly blame a hernia examination for the tragic lacks in his character. Right after the welfare interview, a switchboard job had opened. It was not much but they didn't examine her for venereal disease either, so she decided that in the long run she had ended up about even.

CHAPTER XXXV

In the afternoon, Susan plays a scene with the short actor Murray as Millard Fillmore. Millard Fillmore is one of the more obscure presidents of the United States, of course, and the director has taken the trouble to advise them that this is one of his favorite scenes in the script inasmuch as it reinterprets an almost completely forgotten historical figure in terms of modern psychological insights. To the best of her knowledge, Susan has never had any impression of Millard Fillmore. She did not even know that he had a wife but the director seems excited by the possibilities of this character; he says that, although they may not realize this, it is, in many ways, the key scene of the film because it will attempt to make the forgotten fresh and relevant. There is even a little wardrobe. Murray wears a hideous gray powdered wig and a pair of suspenders over his otherwise naked frame; Susan holds a bouquet of artificial flowers and wears glasses. The director seems nervous; he sets the scene several times before he is satisfied and finally flings the props with a crash off the set, telling them that they will have to play this on a bare stage and make the best of it. "I might as well confess," he says, before he withdraws, "your Millard Fillmore is one of my favorite Americans, one of those historical figures of your country most crucial to me. In his stupidity he embodies that which I find the purest and most hopeful about the United States; in his obscurity he sets a standard which all of your leaders should follow. If only all of your presidents, if your recent presidents, were as obscure as this one!" Murray and Susan look at one another in confusion and the director, mumbling something about the hopelessness of educating actors, leaves the set.

Apparently in this scene of renunciation, Susan tells Murray that she is leaving him. "After Zachary Taylor died and you became president," she says, "I had some real hopes for you; at last you'd be able to put your crazy ideas into practice and give me some peace, but you've been worse than ever. You haven't done a thing, Millard! Besides, there are people in Kansas who need me very much."

"That's ridiculous," Murray says, tugging at his wig. "I've never heard of anything so preposterous. I am the president of the United States. You cannot defy me and you cannot leave me facing an election year. Come now Henriette, please leave me alone. There are a number of things on my mind; a new coalition which call themselves the Know-Nothings have asked me to lend my authority and prestige to them in return for their support and I am seriously considering this inasmuch as I do not like foreigners any more than they do. And there's this damnable slave issue, this Dred Scott case. Something must be done about that; there's going to be civil war in this country unless those goddamned darkies and their sympathizers show a little common sense. If they don't, strong action may have to be taken; as little as I like it, I may have to put the troops into Kansas to make a show of force. And furthermore," Murray says, removing his wig, "furthermore, I know perfectly well that you've let sentiments toward slaves escape in the press. You are undermining me and being a grave source of embarrassment."

"Don't you care that the country is going to go up in flames, Millard? Don't you see the injustice of the slave situation? You have to take real, concrete action!"

"Well that may well be," Murray says, "but on the other hand, I believe in circumspection—in taking the long view. Impatience will get you nowhere, Henriette. Poor old Zachary believed in precipitate action, and you see where that got him. Ashes. It was all vanity. The judicious man survives and my obligation is to the country as a whole, taking the long view. This slave situation will pass. Mark my words. If the darkies become too troublesome, they will simply be stopped from reproducing themselves and our peace will remain. It is only a hard core of dissidents, I believe, that are causing the difficulties here."

"You're foolish and deluded, Millard," Susan says, and then, as described in the script, she closes the distance between them, putting her arms around Murray, and shoves her thighs against his rear. "You don't even think of me any more."

"Certainly I do. I have the country on my mind, however, and until that time—"

According to the script, Murray is to show no sexual response to her but, unhappily, he does. Susan can see the outlines of an erection and feels Murray's skin becoming damp; she moves away in slight confusion. The lights go out, convulsively, and the director appears quickly on the set. "You idiot!" he says to Murray, "are you an actor or a rabbit? Where is your sensibility? Are you insatiable; haven't you had enough sex already?"

"I'm sorry," Murray says, covering himself, backing away from the director, finding a wall and putting his buttocks against it while he holds his genitals. "It's not my fault, I mean I can't control—"

"What do you mean, you can't control? The reason you are here has wholly to do with control. Oh God," the director says, "I can't stand it. And you, you bitch," he says to Susan. "You are not free from this disaster by any means. You deliberately attempted to stimulate him. I saw that. I saw your gestures. There is no hiding from me. What you do is very much in public."

"You have no right to talk to me that way," Susan says. "I don't care who you are. And I didn't do a thing to stimulate him."

"Your mind and hands work in only one direction. This is your natural demeanor—"

"Goddamn you," Susan says. "Goddamn you." She wants to say more but she finds her mind blocked. "You bastard," she says and suddenly realizes that she is standing naked in front of five actors, the technicians, and a director, trying to make a point that is essentially impossible. "I wanted to do this; you know how I wanted to do it, but I can't go on this way. I can't stand being talked to like that and I don't even understand the script. How are we supposed to speak this dialogue? I don't know too much about screenplays—I'm not a writer or anything like that— but I know different kinds of dialogue and I know what a play is supposed to be and this is impossible. It doesn't even *flow,*" she cries and walks quickly to the side, finds her clothes, and begins to dress. She has the idea, somehow, that if she can only get dressed and leave quickly it will all turn out somehow. The film will work, the script will work, her life will reassemble itself, and, most importantly, the director will stop shouting at her.

Susan is pursued by the director, by Murray, by various actors and by Phil himself. Phil once again at a critical moment seems to have emerged from a crevice of the loft. They talk to her carefully in low tones, saying things that Susan does not quite understand but at last Phil gets through to her. He puts his arm around her, gently helps her dress and then leads her away from the set. Susan wants to leave, but one persistent thought reaches her consciousness. She realizes that she is now getting an unusual amount of attention for the first time and wonders how the rest of the cast will react to her being in such a privileged position. She hopes that they will feel that she is somehow a more sensitive and talented person than the rest of them. Frank makes a gesture toward them as she and Phil pass. She ducks it. It is the gesture of a blind man, the fingers rigid and uncomprehending, the palm hard and clumsy. She passes him as if in a dream and permits Phil to lead her to his very private office at the rear of the loft. She should have known that. Where did she expect to go?

CHAPTER XXXVI

"It's a very common problem," Phil says, leaning back, lighting a cigar, looking almost patriarchal. "You'd be surprised how many people go through it. You're no exception; you're only the first we've had in this production. It happens all the time; don't worry about it."

"I don't want to do it any more," Susan says. "I thought that this was an opportunity, but it isn't. I just want to leave."

"We can't have that," Phil says gently. "We got you into the film now; we got a whole lot of material on you. If you leave, we got to take too much out to cover for you. We'd have to start all over again. It would cause us a lot of problems, sweetheart. We can't have any problems, not on an operation like this."

"I can't stand it any more. I can't stand being abused."

"That's the way he works. He hasn't got any background in the business; he comes out of art films and this is the way that they treat their actors over in that part of the business. He doesn't have much sympathy. Actually, and this is in confidence, they're not too satisfied with him upstairs either. They're not crazy about the kind of work he's doing. Probably this will be his first and last film for them."

"I don't want to go back there," Susan says. She is not sure that this is precisely the case, but she has noticed that this line of attack has gotten her more attention as well as sympathy from Phil than she has ever received from him before; for that reason alone it seems worth pursuing. "Not if he's going to carry on that way."

"I'll talk to him."

"Who wrote the script? I never had to act stuff like that. It's really impossible."

"Well that's something else," Phil says, his arms behind his head, small patches of dampness being exposed under his arms. "The thing with the script is something else again. It's kind of a joint effort. I had a lot to do with it. I wrote some of it."

"Oh. I didn't mean—"

"No, that's all right, you don't have to apologize. What we're getting at here is a pretty serious point and I'm not too worried whether the actors dig it or not. I got some experience scriptwriting; this isn't my first."

"I didn't mean to insult you."

"You can't possibly insult me," Phil says. "No one can insult me. I've been in this business too long. What we're trying to do is to throw in the heavy historic angle. The message is very important, not only to get it into major production outlets, but because it's time that these bums learned something. We got them in the palm of our hand out there, at least we can teach them a couple of things. You think that's pretty funny, a man like me being serious."

"No," Susan says, "that's all right. Maybe I'm missing something in the script. I haven't had a chance to really work with it, to give interpretations. Everything has been rushed right through."

"Well you don't worry about that," Phil says soothingly. "You don't worry about that at all, that's a technical problem. You just go out there and do your job and everything will look fine after the editing. This is a business of editing anyway. Everything will come out perfect and you'll look wonderful."

"All right," Susan says. She feels better since she has sat in Phil's office. Heavy objects wink at her from the desk and the walls; the drawn curtains and vague smell of smoke give an air of consequence and finality to the setting. Even a kind of dignity. "All right, I'll try to finish it. But can I get the rest of the day off, at least?"

"No, that's impossible. We're on a very tight schedule and the work is moving right along. I think that we can finish this whole thing up tomorrow—we're that far ahead, and that would be good, wouldn't it? You'll only have to come in one more day. Besides, we have a date tonight."

"What?"

"Well," Phil says, with a faint smile, "we've gotten into a kind of schedule, as far as I can see. I look forward to our dates in the evening. I hope that you aren't going to stop now; there's only a little time left before the picture is all over."

"I can't," Susan says. "I mean, I'll go back and try to finish it somehow, but I just can't see you tonight. You've got to let me have that."

"Why? You don't like me?"

"You don't understand. I'm tired. This is doing things to me. I just can't—"

"Well," Phil says. "That's very disappointing. I had really begun to look forward to our little get-togethers. They really mean something to me, even though we haven't known each other very long. It hurts me to feel that you don't have the same emotions." He takes out a nail file and begins to work on his fingers impassively. Susan looks at him intently, tries to stare through him; it is a glint of humor that she thinks she is seeking, some indication in Phil's eyes or face that he is not serious about any of this, that all along their relationship has not only been subterranean but complex. She feels that they have been parodying other relationships that they might have had. Now Phil can, with a wink, put all of this into its proper context and assure her that from the first he was merely collaborating, never demanding, that they were, after all, pursuing the same ends. His face, however, remains stolid and his eyelids, closing slowly, seem to shut him off further. He looks petulant, even accusing. "I can't," Susan says. "I mean, I'd really like to but it's impossible. You've got to show some understanding."

"It works two ways, you know," Phil says. "Understanding has to come from both sides. If it hadn't been for me, you wouldn't have even been in this film. Or you would have been dropped today. I've kept you going on it."

"You're not even *interested* in me," Susan says. "I have a feeling of just being used."

"Now," Phil says gently, "now sweetheart, you just leave the feelings to me. You let me decide how I feel about you and what I want and what I mean and you just do your job which is acting. I wouldn't try to spend too much time figuring out what anything means; you can only get into trouble that way. That's the trouble with you children these days; you try to understand everything and then problems develop. You just stay with me; I know what's best. I'll meet you right here after work."

"There's got to be an end to this," Susan says. "To this *routine—*"

"The shooting could be finished tomorrow," Phil says. "It won't go beyond Friday. So you see, everything works out." He stands quietly, more relaxed, more dominant and puts a tentative but firm hand on her elbow, leading her out the door. "You just go back and finish the day. You really should be quite pleased at your progress. I looked at you last night in the rushes and you're showing up very nicely; you've come a long way. This is an opportunity, a career opportunity," he points the way out and expels her through the door cleanly and quickly, closing it behind her. Susan is left in a small, damp hallway through which she meditatively moves. It is not a very long walk but she feels herself passing through literal levels of insight and experience so profound as she makes her way back to the loft that she truly believes she is a different Susan who comes back on the set. The actors are in the middle of a take. The director looks at her carefully, a forefinger raised, as if he were about to say something. The technicians chatter. Susan walks back to the small space along the wall which has become hers, removes her clothing deftly and perches on her thighs, reading the script, waiting for the call to her next scene. She has decided upon a mode of action.

CHAPTER XXXVII

Susan has always had an abiding faith in the police. She believes that they are fundamental, benevolent extensions of a society which still believes in reason and that they would, if ever faced bluntly with the choice, opt for the right to expurgate the wrong. Part of this faith may have come from her family background in which her mother and father were always threatening to call the police upon her or one another as the answer to misbehavior; part of it may have come from Susan's experiences in college which had taught her that people who had a contempt of authority were fundamentally uncontrollable. Many times in her relationship with Timothy she had had to resist a childish impulse to call the police, identify herself, and ask for help. "I really can't take this anymore; you've got to show him that he can't push me around this way. He's making impossible demands and asking me to perform sexual acts which are illegal in this state," she had imagined herself saying into the receiver, and a calm voice across the wire would say to her, "I understand perfectly, miss; tell me where you are and we'll settle everything." She would hang up and the police would come and deal with Timothy in the way that he deserved, straighten him out, clean up the apartment, tell him the truth about his novel, tell him the facts about Susan's real needs and then leave them both set on the path to a higher, more reasonable life. The police could do that; they were there to enforce order. Any disorder, any fault of behavior or human suffering was their business; they existed to keep society at the status quo.

Of course her experiences in New York and, most particularly her recent experiences in the film business, have made her belief in the law somewhat shaky—if the cops would stop something like this, why weren't they here, and, if they weren't here, did that mean that they approved? But she does not think that this lapse is really a fault in the system. The lawmen are so busy, nowadays, they are attacked by unreason on so many sides that they simply cannot keep tabs on every situation. They need the help of information. If the police truly knew what was going on, they would do their level best to stop it. Susan knows that she is thinking unrealistically, is aware that the pattern of Supreme Court decisions all the way through the 1960s, to say nothing of public desire, makes what is going on in the loft perfectly legal. It is not even worth remarking on any more; but she cannot, with some stubborn pattern of thought somewhere in the center of her head, get over the feeling that if she were to call the local precinct, the police would arrive in droves. If she wants it brought to an end.

CHAPTER XXXVIII

In late afternoon, while she is working on a difficult and delicate scene having to do with John F. Kennedy, Timothy arrives at the loft in an unpleasant mood. How he has found her so easily and exactly how he has actually been able to get into the shooting area with the kind of security Phil must have is beyond her, but there he is, standing in one of the doorways carrying his welfare worker's attaché case and looking at the situation in utter amazement. The setting is certainly worth regarding by this time of day; the technicians have been smoking cigars and working the lights for eight hours and the loft is full of an acrid bluish haze which smells of sweat and metal; the actors have abandoned even the barest amenities and simply sprawl nakedly on the side while they are not being filmed, some of them inspecting their genitals for the possibility of lice. Susan, who is trying to read a part which she deduces to be that of Jacqueline Kennedy although the script here is so obscure that it is difficult to tell exactly who she is portraying, sees Timothy before he catches sight of her and reacts with a gasp. She backs out of the lighted area where Frank, playing a junior senator from Nevada had been attempting to win her electoral support. She reels through cables and stumbles into a wall. At the same instant Timothy recognizes her and shortly after that everyone notices Timothy. The lights go up to full blaze and the director begins to shout rich curses through the chatter of the technicians. Her view of Timothy is suddenly blocked by a wall of actors rising to snatch their clothes. Timothy has always had such an *official* look about him that they assume he represents the authorities.

Susan who knows better turns to run. That would be the best idea; the technicians will be responsible for getting Timothy out of the place and she will not have to deal with him. Her own way is blocked, however, by actors sprinting to the rear, talking about the cops at the same time she hears Timothy's roar. She knows that he is about to charge upon her. There is nothing to do then but face him. Then she sees that he is already being held in check by four or five technicians who have literally fallen upon him. His attaché case drops helplessly to the floor. Timothy shrieks with rage. "Susan! What are you doing?"

"Get out of here, Timothy."

"I'm going to kill you, you son of a bitch. You have no permit," the lowest technician says with flat seriousness and trips Timothy by the leg, bringing him to a scrambling heap on the floor. The remainder of the technicians seem about to leap on and devour him when Susan says, "Stop it! I know him! He's a friend of mine." Susan looks at Timothy coldly and timelessly. She sees something in his eyes that she has never before suspected. It has nothing to do with her nudity although that spurs him on and he emits a cry of primitive and most un-Timothy like fury. "Get out of here!" he shouts, struggling under the technicians, "Susan, you get out of this place right now or I'll call the police; you can't *do* this kind of thing." Suddenly Phil appears; he comes from the same portion of the set that he always seems to inhabit and faces Susan glaringly, hands on hips, a cigarette held like a cigar between his teeth. Everything stops. The technicians shrug, arise. Timothy staggers to his feet, grabbing hold of his attaché case, and says with terrible calm, "Susan, it took me all day to find out where you were and I'm not going to give up now. I'm taking you out of here. Right now."

"No you're not," she says. "I'm working."

"I don't care what you're doing. You can't be in this kind of situation. If you don't come with me, I'll call the police."

"This your boyfriend?" Phil says to her.

"Not really. Not any more."

"Just shut up, Susan," Timothy says furiously. "I'm not going to go into our relationship now."

"Get out of here," Phil says.

"Who are you? What's your authority?"

"I think I'm going to waste this guy," Phil replies earnestly. "I am a temperate man and I do not make waves but this is too much. Get out of here."

"Tell them, Susan," Timothy says, a fascinating flush spreading from one cheek to the next. He looks older, grips the attaché case frantically. "Tell them you won't have any more to do with this obscenity. Get dressed."

"I'm sorry, Timothy," she says. "I can't do a thing for you."

"I told you, I don't want to discuss our relationship now. This has nothing to do with our relationship. Just get dressed and get out of here."

"I hold you responsible," Phil says to her, "for every second of time that we're wasting here. For every minute we lose in the shooting I'm going to dock you twenty." He puts his hands on Timothy with enormous facility, wrenches the attaché case from his grip and hurls it out a doorway. Then he begins skillfully to move Timothy out of the area of the loft. The technicians assist him. Phil with a flourish waves them off and says something about doing the job himself; it is his pleasure. Timothy begins to wail, a high keen wail like the sounds he makes during sex and resists hopelessly. Then he goes limp and allows himself to be pushed off the set. The technicians follow Phil at a distance; Phil seems to be arm-twisting. Susan watches all of this with interest and not without feeling. "He cares," she finds herself mumbling. "He really cares."

"Your boyfriend?" one of the girls asks. She does not regard Susan with compassion.

"Not exactly. I was living with him though until yesterday."

"Oh," she says. "I understand."

"Do you?"

"Men can't be matter of fact about these things. It blows their cool. They take this kind of stuff far more personally than we do. You'll learn about that."

"Will I?"

"Of course you will. You'll learn about a lot of things; you're pretty young now."

"Stop patronizing me!" Susan says. "Stop it! Stop it!" She has meant to disagree with the girl quietly and then drift back to the scene but some element of her control seems to have snapped. "You can't do this to me!" she shrieks, "someone, finally, has got to take me seriously!" And then there are hands on her, soothing hands, and remonstrative voices but they only increase her rage; she begins to struggle against them just as Timothy had been struggling, to fight for some area of quiet in which she can come to terms with herself slowly and with dignity. But they will not listen, none of them will listen, and, the louder she screams, the more unreasonable they become. She throws her script against the wall to quiet them, kicks to quiet them, begins striking out to quiet them but they are simply not reasonable. They throw her to the floor and Susan finds herself buried under a mass of bodies, most of them naked; flesh is to all sides of her and it has no identity other than its own. The bodies are indifferent, expressionless, pressing upon her and Susan wants very much to faint again. Fainting would be fine, fainting would be a great release—it had helped her very much once already and she could look forward to a career of fainting with ease— but she remains very much conscious as the director wrenches her to her feet. Lights cut her right and left. Technicians are pushing her down a hall and she finds herself once again in Phil's office. Phil is not nearly so pedagogical this time but he is looking at her with hatred bisecting his face in the way that sex had torn her body. As he leaps forward to confront her with terrible accusations, she sees behind his left shoulder a very shrunken, very confused Timothy regarding her from a corner. On his face is a look of mild, bland fright which seems to sum up everything that she has ever thought of him, everything that she has thought of herself.

CHAPTER XXXIX

"I thought we had everything nice and settled," Phil says, "but we had nothing settled so we're going to take it from the top. We're going to set this up once and for all. I want to know what you two are up to."

"Nothing," Timothy says. Somehow he has become an agreeable, reasonable Timothy; he hangs on to his attaché case and looks out a window. "I just lost my temper, that's all. I thought I'd come down and get her out of here. But it's her life and your film and I'm sorry about the whole thing and just want to leave."

"In time," Phil says. He sighs, sits behind the desk, checks Timothy's location carefully, and looks at Susan. "There's one thing I don't like," he says, "and that's falling into complicated situations with people who aren't professionals. I can't stand that kind of thing and we're going to settle it once and for all."

"May I leave?" Timothy says. He looks at Phil imploringly, a beaten expression around his mouth. "Really, I don't want anything more to do with any of this. If you just let me go, I won't make trouble again."

"When I'm ready to let you go, I'll let you go. Until then you sit. No one asked you to come here, did they?"

"No," Timothy replies.

"You come busting into a business situation and break up our set and now you want to leave. That isn't very reasonable, is it?"

"No, I guess it isn't."

"We like people to be reasonable. Reasonable people give us our happiest moments. We're going to make you reasonable by the time you leave. We call it shock therapy."

"All right," the new, mild Timothy says. Perhaps this new Timothy is not even a novelist. "I understand that. Okay. I don't want anything more to do with this."

"I want to ask you a question," Phil says, putting his palms flat on the desk and turning to Susan. "Ignore him; he don't matter. Pretend like he's not here, which in every sense he isn't. We'll take care of him later if we have to. What I want to know is something of you."

"I don't want to talk anymore," Susan says dully. "I've been talked at all day."

"That's your problem. Remember who set up the situation; it wasn't me. Remember who wanted to be the actress to begin with. I didn't clobber you and take you down here."

"I want to act then. Let me act."

"When I'm ready. In my time. Let me ask you something and I want it straight. There are no halfway measures here, Susan. Do you want to be in this business or don't you?"

"I don't know," Susan says. She looks for a place to sit, finds no chairs, backs against a wall. Timothy sees her gesture, stumbles to his feet, motioning that his chair is available. She shakes her head; she wants nothing from Timothy and, understanding this, he sits down again and puts his head in his hands as his attaché case drops to the floor. His shoulders seem to shake; he seems to be in even more of an emotional state than she is. "I really don't know," she says again. "I wish I could answer that but I don't think I can. It's not so easy."

"Because there are no halfway measures. This is not a job like any other job. That is the mistake a lot of you people make when you get started; you figure that it's take a couple of sets and do a couple of scenes and pick up your money and go home that it's just another way of making a little. But it isn't like that at all. It is a very peculiar, demanding business. I have been in this business for many years and it is not a question of business but of your whole life. This is something that people learn with difficulty."

"I wanted to be an actress," Susan says. "That was the thing; I wouldn't have gone into this just for money."

"Well that's not the point," Phil says. "We can't talk about your problems and ambitions just now; that's a lot later. The point is, do you want to make it in this or don't you? Because if you don't, you're going to have to get out now."

"I told you before I wanted to get out."

"But it isn't that simple, sweetheart," Phil says persuasively, cupping his palms, leaning across the desk, talking to her now confidentially, almost with affection. For the moment it is as if Timothy were not even in the room and the scene is between just the two of them. "You're already in it. You've been in a movie. You're making another movie. This is not the time to back out. Maybe you should have done this thinking before you got started. But you said you wanted the work and I believed you. So I gave you a chance. Now I am sorry to say that you are beginning to fuck with my business, Susan, and when you fuck with my business, you are screwing around with my life. So certain adjustments must be made. There is no margin for error in this business. All the errors are on the other side, with the people seeing this stuff. They got enough problems; we have to meet them with efficiency. It is very rare that we break someone new into this business. You are under the wrong impression if you think that every person who comes in off the street gets a job in a film. We screen very carefully and we demand more of a person than many find themselves ready to give. We took a chance on you. Twice now within an hour you have been responsible for serious problems. Most of the people who are working with you have been with us for years, do you know that? We trust them. They trust us. But you are making things very difficult."

"I promise," Timothy says, "that if you let me go now, I'll walk straight out of this place and never have anything to do with it again. I won't even *think* about it, that's what I promise you. If someone ever asks me what I think of the blue film business, I'll say that I don't even go to movies. I give you my word of honor on that. And I won't even *think* of Susan. She doesn't mean a thing to me. All that I want to do is to walk out of here and—"

"Isn't that disgusting?" Phil says absently, pointing to Timothy with a shrug. "This is a man who is absolutely terrified and he does not even know why. This is a man who thinks that since we make a certain kind of film, we must all be killers. This is not good thinking. This is not reasonable thinking. This is not the kind of thinking which made our country great. Nevertheless, there are more people like him than you might realize. They are responsible for the way that ninety percent of the people in this country look at things. I think that that is very sad."

"You're not listening to me," Timothy says. "I promised—"

"Shut up. This has nothing to do with you at all; you are just sitting here for safekeeping. In due course we'll find out what we're going to do with you. Right now I'm trying to finish things up with your girl friend."

"She's not my girl friend."

"Nevertheless," Phil says. "Nevertheless. That is your decision to make." Turning to Susan he goes on, "From the beginning I have noticed a certain ambivalence about you. On the one hand, you wanted to act in this and on the other hand you were not sure how much of you could be given to it without beginning to feel that you were a part of the process. This is very common with you young people just starting out and I take it as a matter of course. Sooner or later you learn that you must give almost everything of yourselves and that nothing can be held back. And you are ready to go along with that. But we can no longer put up with this, Susan."

"I don't think I want it any more," she says, after a pause. "If that's what you're asking me. I don't think that it's really the kind of thing I want to do. So maybe we'll just forget the whole thing, after I finish this picture. I'd like to finish this. I mean, I feel responsible—"

"Now, that's where I think you're making a mistake, Susan. Your thinking is not good. It is not thorough. It is not a matter of finishing this film, it involves a lot more than that. Your entire attitude is one of commitment if you are in this business. You cannot take things lightly and you are in it for a long term."

"I don't understand."

"You don't understand very much, Susan. I hate to say this and I do not want you to take this personally, but you are not a very bright girl. You do not think things through."

"I'll go along with that," Timothy says.

"That's not necessary," Phil says quietly. "I told you, we are having a conversation here and it is as if you do not exist. I do not want to hear from you again."

"All right. I don't care for her anyway. I just want to get out of here."

"I have to finish the film," Susan says. "Can't I decide after that?"

"No you cannot. You cannot postpone decisions, Susan; you must face them now. Your attitude is too casual. This sort of thing must stop."

"It's not fair. It just isn't fair."

"Nothing is fair," Phil says gently. "Consider the restraints we have put upon us. Consider what we must go through. We are only trying to give people what they want. We are deeply concerned with the business of appealing to their real desires and what do we get for all our troubles? Contempt and betrayal. Hypocrisy and discontent. Nothing comes easily. Nevertheless, we do the best we can."

"All right," Timothy says from the corner. "If you let me go now, I'll do everything to build you up. I never had anything against this kind of picture. I work with the most dangerous and dislocated segment of the population; I see their pitiful desires and actions before me in cold print every day, mountains of disasters in the case histories recorded in the most horrifying, deadly way. I'm no hypocrite. I'm on your side."

"All right," Susan says, feeling that she is passing over an important boundary. "All right, I see what you're saying and I agree. I'll stay. I'll finish the film and I'll stay."

"Pornography is for the middle class anyway," Timothy says. "Don't you agree? How could a welfare client possibly take this kind of stuff seriously? He has no imaginative power left; it's all been squeezed out of him."

"You know what you're saying?" Phil asks. "Are you aware of what it means?"

"I think so."

"This is for the long haul. There are serious issues here. You are either with us or against us. We do not want the kind of person who is only interested in giving us a day's work."

"All right."

"And not only has the imaginative power been squeezed out of him,"
Timothy says, "but the very belief in alternatives, the very belief in a
whole system of operating choices does not exist. The middle class, don't
you agree with this Phil, the middle class believes in choice. They have
been educated in the truism that they can do almost anything and that,
if they fail, they will be bailed out. That's why most middle class people
go crazy by the time they're forty."

"He talks a lot, doesn't he?" Phil says, shrugging a shoulder toward
Timothy. "He just doesn't get turned off, no matter what. You have that
problem with him?"

"Yes," Susan says. "I did."

"This kind of thing definitely has to stop. If you listen to too much of
that you could go out of your mind."

"I know what you mean," Susan says. She feels detached from all of
it, even Phil now. She stands, adjusts herself, turns away from Timothy
and says, "Can I go back now?"

"I think so," Phil says. "Wait a minute." He leans forward slowly, puts
a hand to her cheek, with a strange, gentle gesture. He looks at her
intently. "Yes," he says. "Yes, I see. I see now. You can go back." He drops
his hand.

Susan turns, walks to the door, leaves. Phil's touch burns upon her,
burns coldly as she returns to the loft. When she reaches the others she
thinks that his touch must have become a stain and that she is glowing
for all of them to see, but they drop their eyes. One by one they turn from
her and continue their work. What Phil has done to her is invisible.
What she has done to herself is invisible. She removes her clothes slowly
and carefully, picks up her waiting script, holding for instructions from
the director.

CHAPTER XL

Later, Phil has no time for the hotel room. He says that he has an
important appointment, people to see, certain contacts who will drop in
shortly; they will have to use his office even at the risk of offending his
sense of delicacy. She submits willingly, easily, finding a familiarity in
his grasp, an accessibility in his need. At last she is comfortable under
him and willing to be led where he will take her, but he goes almost
nowhere at all. His orgasm is only a small quiver inside her, a bare
pathetic act, springing away. He wipes himself in a kneeling position,
his eyes on the wall. She almost asks him about Timothy but decides

that she is not really interested in his whereabouts. Phil volunteers
nothing.

CHAPTER XLI

On the way from the building she intercepts the director who is also
on the steps heading out. She says hello and for an instant he does not
seem to know her; then recognition works slowly across his face and he
licks his lips, touches his eyes, asks her what she is doing in the
building so late after the shooting. She shrugs and he says that he
understands; furthermore he apologizes for shouting at her this
afternoon, but he has been under enormous strain, terrific pressure, and
she must realize that. He has never had to operate under a strict
budgetary situation before while trying to do work of some achievement
and value. "I think that when this is over I will go back to the Continent,"
he says, "the Continent has very little money and an insignificant
audience but there is a respect for serious work built into the culture
and they do not torture you for being an artist. Here it is entirely
different. However I suspect that I am just talking and I will not go back
to the Continent after all because the corruption is already too basic.
It is too late to change; what brought me here has made me
irretrievable. You do not understand that, do you?" Susan says that she
guesses she does not, and the director nods slowly, sadly, going on his
way, a stooped figure afflicted by vagrant flashes of energy so that he
pauses in midstride, every now and then, to commence an erratic skip.
Then each time he immediately gains control of himself and moves
ponderously until the next skip which is more of a twitch than a true
vault. At least he does not seem to be interested in her sexually which
Susan can appreciate. At the corner he turns, kisses his fingers, waves
to her again and she wonders if she can be sure of that. Now he is out
of sight and it is too late for any such speculation. Besides, she has
absolutely no desire for him. She has no desire for anyone anymore.

CHAPTER XLII

She returns to Frank's apartment because there is really nowhere else
to go and most of her belongings are still there. Frank is out but his
mother who is sitting, working out a crossword puzzle in the living room,
says that he only went for a couple of minutes and left word that
Susan should definitely expect him back soon. His mother says this as
if she were reading it off a strip of tape projected on the far side of the
room, then sighs, adjusts her glasses, and goes back to the crossword

puzzle. "I don't suppose," she says, after a pause, Susan having gone halfway to the door leading to her own room, "I don't suppose that there's anything really going on between you and Frank, is there? I would be so happy if there were, but usually there isn't; he finds it impossible to have serious relationships any more. He hasn't been the same boy since he came back from school."

"Nothing too serious," Susan says. "I mean, I like him, but I've only known him two days and the reason I'm staying here is that I had trouble with my roommate. I wouldn't want you to think—"

"Oh I don't think. I haven't had a thought since 1952; I just do these crossword puzzles on instinct. You don't have to worry about what I think, dear. Frank and I have had terrible arguments about this; he thinks that I'm making judgments and of course I'm not making judgments. I don't try to judge anyone least of all my own son whom I don't understand any more. You don't think that there could be anything serious between you, do you?"

"It's not that kind of thing. It's—"

"Yes, I know. It's never that kind of thing. Frank has never had any luck. Of course that runs in the family: luck is inherited like everything else. You're a very attractive girl; you know that."

"I don't think about it too much."

"The attractive ones never do. You wouldn't know a four-letter word for a Chinese hexagon, would you?"

"No," Susan says. "I don't do crossword puzzles."

"I know you think that this is very trivial and obsessive but I'm an old lady and what else is there to do? What is bacchanalian cry? I always forget. I don't even know the easy ones. The trouble is I have no talent for crossword puzzles."

"I don't know what a bacchanalian cry is."

"I didn't think you did, dear. Frank gives me nothing to do; he's ashamed of me and we have this strict arrangement that I won't interfere in his life. But what good does that do if he's always interfering in mine? He has to know everything I do and he doesn't like any of it."

"I'm sorry."

"So I wind up doing crossword puzzles because it's easier than having fights with my son. I'll be seventy-three years old next September. I was really quite old when Frank was born and he was something of a mistake. I never expected to get pregnant at forty."

"Must we talk about this?"

"Well, what's the alternative, dear? We must talk about something and I'd rather that it was basic things rather than hypocritical lies. Frank's an only child, you know. He was born out of wedlock. Maybe I should have married the man; I've often wondered about that. Maybe that was the real problem with Frank from the beginning, that he needed a father. But I treasured my independence and felt that the child would have to come second even though I did want him. Well, you never know. The thing is," Frank's mother says, "the thing is that I had a very dull, uninteresting job as a clerk-typist with absolutely no future and I was fired when Frank was three years old anyway. I wish that I could be resigned and ironic, don't you? That's what old ladies are supposed to be, full of irony. But I'm just as mad now as I was back then. I can have the same feelings. You don't understand that, you young people; you think that everybody over fifty stops feeling. But inside it's always the same, there's just nothing you can *do* about it and that's why old people are so nasty and unhappy. You must be very hungry."

"No," Susan says, giving up on the idea of leaving the room, and sits down on the couch opposite the old lady's chair with a sigh. "No, I don't have any appetite at all, really."

"It must be the kind of work you're doing. Oh don't be embarrassed; I know exactly what you and Frank are doing. He says that he wants to lead separate lives but actually he tells me everything. Sometimes he comes into my room at two in the morning and tells me everything that's on his mind and exactly what he went through. He just can't stop talking. That kind of work keeps you from having an appetite, I bet."

"I never had much of an appetite."

"Well, I neither approve nor disapprove; it doesn't make any difference to me. I guess it makes as much sense as anything else these days and a dollar is a dollar. At least you have a chance to do something creative although I never thought that Frank would become an actor. Somehow he never seemed the type to be an actor in that kind of business. But it shows that the apple rolls further from the tree than you can ever tell. You look a little ill, dear; are you sure that you wouldn't want to get something to eat?"

"No," Susan says and, shifting in the couch, decides that after all she will stand and leave this room, will even leave this house if necessary; but before she can gather herself together Frank walks through the apartment door holding a bag of groceries in both hands. "Hello Susan," he says. "I was just gone for a few minutes; I hope it wasn't long."

"I think I want to leave, Frank."

"Susan and I have been talking," his mother says. "We've had a talk about this thing and that. I'm afraid that I haven't made her very happy though, Frank. Maybe you'd better save the situation."

"I can't stand this any more, mother."

"It's your own fault, Frank; you talk too much. If you don't want me meddling in your life or knowing what goes on, why do you tell me all these things? You can't dump all this horrifying information on me and expect me to take it without a twitch. I'm seventy-three years old next September; I don't have the resources that you young people have."

"Let's go upstairs, Susan," Frank says, putting down the groceries on a table. "Look, we can talk there."

"I don't want to talk," she says, getting up from the couch finally. "I've been talking all day. I just came back here really to pick up my things. I'm going to a hotel. Tomorrow I can look for an apartment."

"There's no reason for you to leave."

"It's your own fault, Frank," his mother says. "You never really knew how to handle a girl. There's something peculiarly self-destructive in you; I've seen it from the first. You make yourself less than what you are and then you want people to take you on those terms to show that they really care. And if they don't care, then you can always say that you weren't trying. You see, I know some psychology too. I've read up on this type of thing."

"Please mother," Frank says. "Please, no more."

"It's all your own fault. If you were a little more secretive about your life then I wouldn't have all these things on my mind and you'd be able to carry on in your own way. But you never could keep your mouth shut, Frank; it's your basic failing. A failing that runs in the family."

"Come on, Susan," Frank says and takes her arm gently, begins to tug her from the room. Susan yields, it seems easier that way. The old lady's glasses glitter in some aspect of light as they mount the stairs. "Are you sure you don't know a Bacchanalian cry, dear?" she asks.

"*Evoe*," Frank says. He leads her out of sight of his mother and into his bedroom. It is the first good look she has ever gotten of Frank's bedroom, an expressionless place with a few pictures of a recent moon-landing taped on the walls, showing astronauts in space suits leaning over the ground. He puts her in the chair facing him on the bed and sits, clasps his hands, looks down at the floor. "I guess that wasn't a very good idea," he says. "Giving her the opportunity to get at you. I didn't think you'd be in so soon. I wasn't even sure you'd be back at all, to tell you the truth. I'm very glad you're back."

"I just came to pick up my things," Susan says. "Listen, seriously, I want to find a hotel. It isn't fair of me to stay here and I just don't want to. I'll pick up what I've got and go somewhere."

"I find it impossible to believe that I'm making pornographic films. It's just an incredible situation, something that I can't adjust to. Here I go to the studio, a man of my background, and make a dirty picture and then I come home at night and back into this. You couldn't possibly appreciate the ironies. There just seems nothing I can do to break this pattern. She was with me all through graduate school, you know. We lived together out there and when I dropped out we used her savings to come to New York and take this place. It isn't even rent-controlled. I told you a lie. We pay four hundred dollars a month for it only because she had some savings. We've always lived together. I had this dream that finally I'd be able to do something so outrageous that it would be inconceivable for me to live with her any more and dirty movies seemed to be the thing, but do you know something? It's the same thing. I don't mean to burden you with my troubles, of course. You have problems of your own. Did you work things out there?"

"I suppose so."

"Did you get rid of your boyfriend?"

"I don't know what happened to him."

"Well," Frank says, "they're efficient. I'll give them that; they do the necessary and they do it very well. They can discriminate between what is important and what is not which is something that intellectual types such as myself have always found difficult. I wouldn't worry about him; I'm sure that they just gave him the message and sent him on his way."

"I'm not worried about him at all. I'm not even thinking about him."

"Well, that's best," Frank says. He grips the arms of the chair, shifts slightly; there is an extended pause. "You wouldn't like to, uh—"

"No," Susan says. "I'm sorry but it's just impossible. I can't do anything now at all."

"I'm not forcing you. It's not my way to force people. I just can't. I was just asking—"

"No," Susan says. "All I want to do is to get my things and go to a hotel."

"It's not as if it would be anything much for you," Frank mumbles. "I mean—"

"What do you mean?"

"I mean, with the filming and all."

"That's different."

"All right," Frank says with a sigh. He shrugs, groans, picks up small bits of litter from the floor. "I understand that. It isn't the best approach possible. There's something in the way I approach girls that always puts them off; it's almost as though I'm driven toward denial and—"

"Frank," Susan says, feeling her voice go slightly out of control, "Frank, I just can't discuss this kind of thing anymore. I can't stand it. I don't want to hear any more of your analyses. All I want to do is to get out of here," and with an act of her will she stands, a feeling of disconnection overtaking her as she does so. She feels the room revolving slowly at a great distance. Only a little while longer and she will be able to sleep. "Now, if you'll help me get my things together and call a cab, that would be all I need. Or you don't even have to help me with the things. I can do it myself." She takes one stride, moving toward her room, feels herself lose her balance, tumble gracelessly backward, grasps a chair, and falls into it heavily. "I'm tired," she says, shaking her head. "I'm really tired. I thought that everything was all right, but it isn't."

"Stay here tonight, Susan. It will be just like last night. I won't do a thing. Tomorrow you can leave."

"You'll just start again. I tell you, I can't listen any more. All that people do is talk to me and talk to me and make me do things. This has got to stop." Susan finds herself thinking that this may well be true; nevertheless, she sounds like one of the characters in a scene she has been playing, perhaps Mrs. Millard Fillmore. Maybe Mrs. Millard Fillmore had this problem; this is why she and her husband are both two of history's most obscure characters. "I just can't," she says, and tries to stand again, does somewhat better this time, moves toward a door. "I should go. I mean, it's nothing personal; I'm sure I like you but—"

"I won't lay a hand on you," Frank says intensely. "I won't say a thing. I just want you to stay; it would be a great thing for me if you would stay. Just to have a girl like you in my house. You don't know how I felt last night, just knowing that you were here; that if I wanted, I could open your door down the hall and look in, could see—"

"Oh God," Susan says. She leaves Frank's room, walks to her own, notices that it is just as she left it this morning and thinks, I've got to get out of here. But she sits on the bed for just one instant trying to decide the most efficient means for exit. This is either her usual mistake or the best thing that has happened to her today because the bed absorbs her, envelops her, and she sinks upon it with a sigh, feeling the sheets close over her comfortably. Susan leans back with a gasp; sleep overtakes her completely. It has been a long day. All of her days since she began to work for Phil have been long; very possibly it is for the best that she use the time allotted her now for rest. Beyond rationalization, beyond the ordering of a vigorous program of activities which will show her to her best advantage, Susan dreams.

CHAPTER XLIII

There are not so many dreams as last night and they are not so hideous. In the worst one her father comes to her after the Academy Award ceremony and says that he appreciates the step forward she has made in her career but now it is time to get serious and think about what she is going to do with her life. "I mean, you're going to have to get married and have a family anyway so you should do it soon so you'll be vigorous in your sunset years," he says to her with an admonitory shake of his forefinger. "This is all well and good and you've certainly had interesting experiences but now it's time to be mature and live sensibly." She turns to him to tell him for the first time what she really thinks of him, holding her Academy Award tightly in her hands. She is ready to demolish him but before she can three celebrities and two major political figures standing near them fall upon her father in the way the technicians had fallen upon Timothy and take him, protesting, into a wing. "You have to live your own life; you must realize that it is a one-way ticket; you must take your life seriously!" her father shouts but Susan is already at the Awards party and cannot listen to him; she is surrounded by hundreds of people who look at her with admiration and come over one by one to fondle her Oscar. They tell her that she has reached the top of her profession. Susan wants to remain level-headed. The Academy Award, after all, has been won in the past by some of the worst actresses in history, but she finds it difficult to maintain her sense of balance. Completely distracted, Susan smiles and talks, gives quick interviews to the press and then suddenly Phil is there wearing a tuxedo and looking at her with a proprietary air. "Come here," he says to her and she tries to indicate with motions that she cannot. She is too busy with the press, but Phil says, "Get over here and stop that nonsense," and she cannot deny him any longer. She goes over to him and he seizes her by an arm, drags her out of the room and into a long, long hallway which looks very much like the one outside his office. "I'll hold that for you," he says, taking the award from her hand and putting it on the floor behind his back. Then, with enormous facility, he lifts her long skirt, pulls down her pants and tearing open his zipper inserts himself into her, beginning to fuck desperately. Susan protests, says that people will come, tries to back away from him but finds herself against a hard, blank wall on which hang the pictures of dead, great movie stars. She tries to move aside under his battering but is paralyzed and Phil finally says, "Just remember who you are; just remember what you are, just remember how you got here." He forces his will upon her, has a fierce orgasm spilling upwards and outwards like a flower and filling her chest with a peculiar warmth while he collapses underneath her, falling to the floor and out of sight. His face, turning in upon itself, folds like paper and Susan finds that her picture is being taken by photographers from *Life* Magazine, the *New York Times, Newsweek, Variety, Women's Wear Daily,* and *Sports Illustrated,* all of whom are using flashbulbs. It is a very embarrassing situation and she does not quite know what to do. Finally she settles for a smile, pulling her hair from her eyes. She realizes that Phil is directing the photographers from the floor, explaining to them about angles of light and her most favorable profile. Despite her justifiable resentment, she feels somewhat grateful for what he is doing. At least she is being kept now before the public.

Much later she dreams that Frank has slipped beside her in bed and is trying to enter her. He acts with a desperate stealth mixed with desire because he is afraid at any instant she will awaken and bring upon him a disastrous failure ... and so his gasps are broken by urgent, piteous little moans and muttered urgings to himself to be quiet ... Susan finds the whole thing rather funny, not that she would want to laugh and hurt his feelings. At length she feels him inside her, wedged tightly, and he begins to work in a simple rocking gesture aided by his fingernails on her back. He attempts to bite her neck. It is inconceivable, she dreams, that he thinks he could carry on in this fashion and not awaken her, nevertheless she lies quietly, letting him work upon her. She has some curiosity about Frank. Also she knows that he can see that she would let almost anyone have her sexually if he only took the trouble to force the issue. As always she minimizes the role of sex. That has never mattered to her. She finds it ridiculous that men should find this act, this series of motions culminating in a sneeze of such unusual value that they will concentrate their lives upon getting it, warp themselves in strange and complex ways in the getting or the failing ... and Frank comes into her slowly with an gasp of pain or maybe simple pleasure. She holds him, rubs a breast against his mouth, whispers to him to be quiet. Throughout he has not touched her breasts; now he buries himself in her bosom and begins to moan. She is now fully awake and knows she has not been dreaming.

CHAPTER XLIV

Perhaps, Susan finds herself thinking, perhaps it would have been for the best if she had submitted herself to the examination and become an investigator for the Department of Welfare. She would then have been spared mornings like this; whatever else she would have had to go through in the Welfare Department, she would not have had to spend an entire day doing for business what she had been doing the previous night to support her emotional life. On the other hand, she would have most likely only met someone like Timothy.

CHAPTER XLV

Frank's mother is waiting for them in the living room, still doing a crossword puzzle, but otherwise vastly changed from last night. Her entire mood is ebullient as Susan, and Frank, laden with suitcases come into the room. Susan will take them to work and look for a hotel in the evening. "Oh I just feel wonderful this morning," she says, "I have this feeling going all through my body that everything's going to work out. Don't you think so, children?"

"We have to go to work, mother," Frank says, dropping the suitcases and, as his mother sees them, her mood seems to shift. She says, "Is the young lady leaving? And just when I was feeling so happy."

"I have to find a place of my own," Susan says. "This was only temporary."

"But I thought that you and Frank were working things out so beautifully. I just have the feeling all through my body that things are all working out for the best. You're not really going to leave, are you?"

"Please, mother," Frank says. He does not seem to be in a very good mood himself; he seems to have accepted Susan's decision to leave very well, very matter of factly. Suddenly a look of rage crosses his face; then his expression settles down to a restrained and civilized revulsion. "Please don't talk any more. I can't stand to listen to it."

"Because I thought that everything was going to be fine between you children. I thought that Frank was finally at the end of his quest. There is an end to every journey and I felt that my son had reached his."

"That's not necessary, mother."

"Oh, nothing's necessary! Nothing's necessary if you want to look at it that way; you can just lie in bed and waste yourself. But I have hopes for you, Frank. Tell me that you're not leaving, dear. He needs someone to love and relate to, that's all. If he can find that, he'd be as normal a man as any you see on the street. He almost had a doctor of letters, you know. He can go back and finish it any time and have a fine career. And you don't have to see me at all; it'll be as though I weren't even living here."

"I can't discuss that now," Susan says. She brushes her damp hair from her forehead, blinks, and tries to look alert. In fact the apartment appears fuzzy to her: fuzzy light is coming through the windows, indistinct figures are moving on the walls, blurred outlines of people in the room are talking to one another. She knows that she could use a real rest, some change of circumstance that would bring her back to herself. Instantaneously she makes a decision: when the film is finished, hopefully today, she will ask Phil for a loan and she will go away for a

week. Phil is understanding; he only wants the best for her. Surely now
that she has committed herself to him, he will be reasonable. Two
hundred dollars will be more than sufficient to take her where she wants
to go. Well, three hundred dollars. No more than two weeks and she will
come back refreshed, ready to do everything she can in the film business.

"It's too late, mother," Frank is saying, meanwhile. He seems to be
gripped in an intense dialogue, the sense of which has somehow missed
her while she was thinking of other things. "It's too late for any of that
shit."

"Watch your language. I don't care what you think of me and what
relations have come to, I'm still your mother."

"I said, stop it! It's too late! I'm thirty-four years old and an actor in
pornographic films, mother. I've never held a full-time, responsible
paying position in my life and I've never finished a single thing I've
started except this relationship with you which *is* finished. Finished, do
you hear me! There is no time for your optimism, no time for your
platitudes. It is far too late for any of this and it is time you accepted
that fact. You can't keep on making these demands of me."

"Well, it's just because I think so much of you and want only the best,"
the old lady says complacently, marking something in the crossword
puzzle. "If I didn't care for you so much, Frank, I wouldn't have stayed
with you all these years. I would have gotten rid of you in pregnancy if
I didn't have plans for you. You can't shock me, don't you understand
that by now? I dealt with you when you were a wee tot."

"Do you think," Susan says, "do you think that we could get going? I
think it's a little late and anyway; I do want to get down there early."

"Yes," Frank says. "I'm sorry. All right. I just can't deal with this
woman any more. She is not reasonable. I can't make her see things."

"Frank gets caught up, dear," his mother says. "He's really very
involved with me and he gets distracted; it doesn't mean that he's
ignoring you or anything like that. It's just that he's known me so much
longer and I annoy him a great deal. Are you sure you won't be staying?
I do think that things could work out wonderfully for the two of you if
you only gave them a chance. You wouldn't even have to get married for
a while; you could just kind of live in sin and have a relationship, as you
people put it. Later on if it's serious you could …"

"It can't be," Susan says. "I mean, I don't have a thing against Frank
but it just couldn't work out. For his sake, it wouldn't be fair."

"Yes, that's what they all say. They always leave him for his sake, not
theirs. Frank brings out all the unselfishness in young ladies, don't you
Frank?"

Frank, however, is already out the door, struggling with suitcases, mumbling and cursing to himself. Susan picks up the two that are left on the floor and follows him. At the door she wants to say good-bye to the old lady but she cannot hold her baggage and turn around. Also Frank seems to be having a great deal of difficulty on the steps and his curses fill the hallway. She settles for a quick nod which she hopes will be interpreted from the rear as being a friendly, if a definite parting and negotiates her way down, to find Frank on the sidewalk sweating in the spring cold and wiping his forehead with a palm. "I can't stand it," he says. "I just can't stand it any more."

"Come on, Frank. We've got to get downtown."

"She uses every excuse to humiliate me and she doesn't understand that life is circular. Do you understand that? Life is a circle. I go downtown to act in pornographic films; I come home to my mother. What could be more reasonable than that?"

"Frank," Susan says with enormous calm, "Frank, now you're getting hysterical," and steps from the sidewalk, waving her arm, hoping for a cab. In the kind of novels which Timothy writes, characters who go into the street to hail a cab always seem to get one immediately, thereby enabling a smooth shift of scene, but she knows that nothing so easy happens in real life; she imagines that she will be standing helplessly in the street for a quarter of an hour, trying to seduce a taxicab while Frank stands amidst her bags on the sidewalk, mumbling about his mother. But, because this is indeed an exceptional day, maybe the first day of an entirely new era for Susan, a cab does come, swaying dangerously toward the curb. It is an old cab with a short driver and a door swings open in readiness. She is on her way, then. She is on her way at last. The trunk is opened, her suitcases are inserted, and she and Frank go off to the studio for another day of filmmaking. In a sulk, he sits at a far corner and holds the spread fingers of a hand over his face. Susan thinks of several possible topics of conversation but she decides that she likes none of them and there is really very little to say. This is Susan's final day of work in the film business.

CHAPTER XLVI

"This is it," Phil says to the assembled, naked cast. The director is off to the side, his head bowed, studying a script, not really in the situation at all and now Phil at last seems to have become the person he always wanted to be. His gestures are assured, he is exuberant, his face glows with vitality. "We're going to wrap this one up today. For some of you this will be good news; for some of you perhaps not because when you work closely together on a project of this sort there is always a feeling of loss when it is over. But today is the day. We're going to do the big scene."

He stops, turns, kneels, and picks up some mimeographed sheets beside him. "I've held this one back until the last minute," he says, "because it was touch and go until this morning whether we'd actually do it or not. Whether we'd get the green light to do this big, controversial stuff. But I'm happy to say that they've decided to go all the way. No holds barred. We're going to have a big film here, a big film. I'm going to pass these scripts out now and let you look at them for a few minutes and then we'll shoot it," he says. "Don't study them too hard, don't worry about line readings, don't worry about anything except getting the general sense of it. What they're looking for here is a sense of spontaneity and truth, that's all, and you should just dive right into it." A curious formality overcomes him, a strange shyness seems to peep at the edges. "I wish you good luck," he says, handing out the sheets "and much happiness." Handing Susan her script he whispers, "You've got the key part here; stop by after filming and we'll talk about a lot of things," and then he disappears, probably once again into the equipment. Phil's comings and goings have always been obscure but there is a definite whisk, even an élan to his means of disappearance this time.

Susan looks over her script without much interest. Her role has been circled throughout with red pencil and seems to have something to do with an argument she is having with her husband. She can hardly make sense of it; she stopped trying yesterday to make anything of these scripts at all. The thing to do in the dirty picture business, she has decided, is simply to go along with the situation. Take the positions assigned, say the lines given, and leave the rest of it to one side. It is a good policy to follow and, now that she has committed herself to the business totally just for this last day, she is glad that she discovered it before it was too late. Murray, the short actor, comes over to her and whispers something about him having just looked over the script and that this is too much, but Susan simply shrugs. Her valises are safely stored in a closet down the hall; the director having given his special permission for this. She will finish the film and have her talk with Phil and find a hotel and then a studio apartment and go on to other things. There is nothing going on here any more that can touch her. Murray says that he cannot believe it; he is an experienced man and has seen almost everything in his time but this is too much, too raw; this, he admits, goes beyond him. Susan says that the work is very interesting and Murray gives her a puzzled look, moves away from her. There is no reason to act with Murray as if there had been any intimacy between them. That too she has learned. She has learned a great deal. Frank squats in a corner, looking at his script, smoking a cigarette and giving her furious looks while he taps ashes onto the floor. Now she is able to look at and beyond him. Frank means nothing whatsoever to her. She has gone as far with him as she needs to go. Once in a psychology class she recalls having learned about something called a disassociate phenomenon. As the symptoms come vaguely back to her Susan decides that that is what she has. Definitely. She has disassociative tendencies. That is perfectly all right with her. She has been through worse. She giggles. Frank looks at her sullenly.

"Places," the director says. "I call for places and no nonsense. This is a crucial scene as you have been told, the most important scene of the entire project and it must be gotten right the first time. Therefore, there will be no nonsense."

"When have you ever done a retake?" someone asks and the director glowers, slams the script against his thigh and says, "There is no time now for nonsense. We are in serious business now. This scene is very close to my heart; it redeems my identification with this project. Do you understand that? The crowd will fall on the perimeter; the four principals please, in the center."

Susan supposes that she is one of the four principals. She moves over, naked, to a group of four chairs under the equipment, sits, folding her legs, still looking over the script. There is a lot more to her part here than she has had thus far; she has always been a quick study but this is difficult. Three naked actors, two men and a girl sit themselves around her. Frank is one of the actors. He sits to her right. The two others sit in front of them, backs facing. "You are represented to be in a car," the director says. "A limousine. This is all highly surrealistic and impressionistic, however, so there is no need to make driving motions. Crowd noises, please."

The surrounding actors begin to groan in a desultory fashion; Susan's view of them is cut off when the lights throughout the loft are knocked out completely. Then the four of them are pinned by a dazzling high spot which arches in from a great distance, blinding her. She raises an arm to her face, trying to block the light and hears the director curse. "Stop this!" he says. "Ignore the lights. Play to one another."

"Listen," Frank says, "we haven't even had a chance to look these scripts over. I don't even think I know the lines."

"Shut up," the director says. Invisible, his voice becomes larger, more threatening, omnipotent as if sounding in an arena. "I have no time for nonsense. You are all professionals. You have studied these parts and they cannot be released further. Music. Commence."

Music comes into the loft. It is the first time that it has been used during filming; Susan supposes that it is dubbed in later for the most part but there is most definitely music here: loud, thundering martial music, in the back of which can be heard the faint sound of strings. "Music down!" says the director and the light becomes even brighter, as harsh as the sun. The actress in front of Susan turns, leaning an elbow over her chair and says, "Well, I guess you can't say that the city of Dallas doesn't love you now, Mr. President."

"That's right," Frank says, "that's right," and then the scene begins, it truly commences: it is a long scene full of colors and screams and many lines for Susan and she says them all, finds it surprising how well she knows the lines right up to the end. At a certain point there is a call for blood, one of them mentions blood and from a great height the technicians toss a bag of something toward the chairs where it explodes with a dull roar and covers them with smears of red. There are screams for this too, screams not wholly in the script, and finally the scene ends. Susan, crawling away from Frank, has only one thought fixed in her mind: if she can make it to the wall, just to the wall and her clothing, she will be perfectly all right; the thing is to get there and from then on she will be able to manage the rest herself but it is very hard, very hard to make this short distance which she has made so easily so many times before. For a while she thinks that she will not succeed, realizes that she cannot somehow stop screaming. Bodies lean over her to talk comfortingly: Frank is there and Murray and the actresses and the director and finally there is Phil ... it is Phil who is the one who calms her, throwing something over her shoulders. Once again he takes her on the long walk to his office where he closes the door. Suddenly it is as if everything is behind her and she will not have to think any more. Phil tells her what a good person she is, what a good actress, how much he appreciates what she has been doing for them and she turns to him to thank him for showing this compassion for her finally. Although she only wants to thank him in the flattest and least emotional terms, she cannot stop laughing. There is no way that she can stop laughing. Then Phil shakes his head and leaves her there, laughing against a wall, and lumbers out of the office, down the hall. Phil is an intelligent man and has been around long enough to recognize what has happened. Susan laughs and laughs. She laughs for six hours but three months later she is much better and when her father comes to take her home she tells him solemnly that she has decided a career in the theatre is not really for her. Her father nods. He says that it is good to hear her finally say that of her own accord. Her father is, like Phil, a sensible man and will do what he can for reason's sake.

THE END

The Commercial Culture
By Barry N. Malzberg

"Pornographic film is just a commercial with the clothes off. And the only product it is selling is jerking off." - Frank, The Director

Manhattan, New York, the East Coast, arguably the country was sinking into rot in the early 1970s; the torrents of mudslide and urban ravaging became more evident in the middle of the decade but the process was already alive and in motion. Vietnam, of course, the plundering of the cities and their polity to keep the War going and the detritus of the Apollo project; one could sniff the outdoors from a window and inhale decomposition. *Cinema*, written in early 1971 and published first as *The Masochist* and then again three years later as *Everything Happened to Susan*, was both product and observation; relevant with decay and my haplessly earnest actress (very similar to the misguided social worker of *Horizontal Woman* in her misguidance if not quite her activity) was refractory and propulsive of that decay in her energetic improvisations on the factory floor on West 26th Street. *Herovit's World*, which was written less than a year later for a classier publisher (but not much more of an advance) also breathed deeply of the urban rot, the equally hapless if not so earnest Jonathan Herovit lived two and a half miles North of the factory and was granted through his living room window a panorama of prostitutes and derelicts across 79th Street, the derelicts derelicting, the prostitutes soliciting. Susan believed that she was advancing her dramatic career through earnest copulation, Herovit had no such illusions surrounding either copulation or composition but both were very much products *and* engineers of the time and place in which they lived. Looking at this novel, re-experiencing it in dull or sharp surges of recollection was looking at the author through the spyglass of half a century and it is as revelatory as it is difficult. Those were the days my friend.

Herovit's World is a novel, I suppose of process and how the form of an activity can well overcome its function. *Cinema* has the same problem; Susan has ambition and she may even (who knows?) have a trace of talent but she is functioning in a commercial medium, a commercial culture and it need not exert much force to overwhelm this delicate and misguided creature, college graduate, mid-twenties, boyfriend who works for the Department of Welfare and envisions himself a novelist: all of the classy appurtenances and ambition of the classless life surging through this young woman who feels too exploited and wants too much from that exploitation to conceive of herself of a metaphor. Pornographic films commercially organized, distributed, paid and sometimes flourishing in their underground were too urgent for such distraction or displacement and what Susan was enacting, what was being enacted upon her were certainly too urgent and painful to be metaphor. Metaphor is defined as one thing working as symbol for another thing or maybe a set of them but the urgency and immediacy of sexual congress do not assist the kind of delicate transplantation which is at the heart of metaphor. Of course *Cinema* has the kind of absurdity, failure of true apprehension, blundering at profundity usually associated with comedy but the heart of comedy has Neil Simon or Shakespeare telling you that the actors therein *do not realize that they are in a comedy*. They take it as social realism and when matters get difficult as tragedy. Lear's Fool goes to sleep at noon because he simply cannot take it anymore but Cordelia and her father are not given the option of desertion.

Cinema was written in the decay of my relationship with Maurice Girodias and his United States version of the Olympia Press; the accompanying novel between these covers, *Screen,* was both the brief ascending rocket and rapidly descending misfire which both began and ended my career as the star in Girodias' new firmament, and that novel, written about three years earlier, was composed in a kind of misguided possibility which in much less time than three years had been burned out of the author and his publisher alike. I wrote and sold ten novels to Olympia within two years but Susan showed up after the feast tables and dyspeptic offering had been cleared. The novel represented a final, cynical attempt to sneak a two thousand dollar advance from Olympia, "I don't know what this is about" was his response, "But it certainly is not attractive" and I could only agree with that. After his rejection of the brief proposal I finished the thing anyway as a kind of purgation or atonement for having once thought commercialized sex was an entertaining sport or a pastime; Belmont Tower in a foreshadowing of the great conglomeratization of publishing was acquired toward the end of the decade by Harry Shorten, Midwood's publisher. Belmont-Tower was a bottom of the line publisher of genre fiction and nonfiction works ghosted by people like me, of adventurous combat or sexual advice; I had already sold the amalgamated publisher two works, *Horizontal Woman* and *The Spread,* already reissued by Stark House and I now speed Susan toward a reunion about which she might have been ambivalent if she were not still imbued with hopeless cheer. The novel ends where it was always meant to—re-enacting JFK's assassination as the nude Jacqueline beside him in the death car, she is central to that utter atomization with which not only the novel but the Republic ends.

So like the decade, like the Kennedys, like Girodias it all ended and that "utter atomization" might as well stand for its most sinister and appropriate legacy; sex did not blow up the decade, Lee Oswald as bumbling agent did and what was experienced through this culture was John Brunner's still ongoing long result, the fire and the fury, the breasts and bush of urban blight, all of it together in that last one great hurrah, blundering like Susan and her actors to the end of National Myth. Which was in fact the beginning of the National Myth. Quantum theory to the degree I understand has everything right, all mashed together, all fire and fury, falling, falling, now a series of flaming skulls upon the living and the dead alike.

February 2020/New Jersey

Barry N. Malzberg Bibliography

FICTION (as either Barry or Barry N. Malzberg)

Oracle of the Thousand Hands (1968)
Screen (1968)
Confessions of Westchester County (1970)
The Spread (1971)
In My Parents' Bedroom (1971)
The Falling Astronauts (1971)
The Masochist (1972, reprinted as
  Everything Happened to Susan, 1975)
Horizontal Woman (1972; reprinted as The Social Worker, 1973)
Beyond Apollo (1972)
Overlay (1972)
Revelations (1972)
Herovit's World (1973)
In the Enclosure (1973)
The Men Inside (1973)
Phase IV (1973; novelization based on a story &
  screenplay by Mayo Simon)
The Day of the Burning (1974)
The Tactics of Conquest (1974)
Underlay (1974)
The Destruction of the Temple (1974)
Guernica Night (1974)
On a Planet Alien (1974)
Out from Ganymede (1974; stories)
The Sodom and Gomorrah Business (1974)
The Best of Barry N. Malzberg (1975; stories)
The Many Worlds of Barry Malzberg (1975; stories)
Galaxies (1975)
The Gamesman (1975)
Down Here in the Dream Quarter (1976; stories)
Scop (1976)
The Last Transaction (1977)
Chorale (1978)
Malzberg at Large (1979; stories)
The Man Who Loved the Midnight Lady (1980; stories)

The Cross of Fire (1982)
The Remaking of Sigmund Freud (1985)
In the Stone House (2000; stories)
Shiva and Other Stories (2001; stories)
The Passage of the Light: The Recursive Science Fiction of Barry N.
   Malzberg (2004; ed. by Tony Lewis & Mike Resnick; stories)
The Very Best of Barry N. Malzberg (2013; stories)

With Bill Pronzini

The Running of the Beasts (1976)
Acts of Mercy (1977)
Prose Bowl (1980)
Night Screams (1981)
Problems Solved (2003; stories)
On Account of Darkness and Other SF Stories (2004; stories)

As Mike Barry

Lone Wolf series:
Night Raider (1973)
Bay Prowler (1973)
Boston Avenger (1973)
Desert Stalker (1974)
Havana Hit (1974)
Chicago Slaughter (1974)
Peruvian Nightmare (1974)
Los Angeles Holocaust (1974)
Miami Marauder (1974)
Harlem Showdown (1975)
Detroit Massacre (1975)
Phoenix Inferno (1975)
The Killing Run (1975)
Philadelphia Blow-Up (1975)

As Francine di Natale

The Circle (1969)

As Claudine Dumas

The Confessions of a Parisian Chambermaid (1969)

As Mel Johnson/M. L. Johnson

Love Doll (1967; with The Sex Pros by Orrie Hitt)
I, Lesbian (1968)
Just Ask (1968; with Playgirl by Lou Craig)
Instant Sex (1968)
Chained (1968; with Master of Women by
   March Hastings & Love Captive by Dallas Mayo)
Kiss and Run (1968)
Nympho Nurse (1969; with Young and Eager by
   Jim Conroy & Quickie by Gene Evans)
The Sadist (1969)
The Box (1969)
Do It To Me (1969)
Born to Give (1969; with Swap Club by Greg Hamilton & Wild in
   Bed by Dirk Malloy)
Campus Doll (1969; with High School Stud by Robert Hadley)
A Way With All Maidens (1969)

As Howard Lee

Kung Fu #1: The Way of the Tiger, the Sign of the Dragon

As Lee W. Mason

Lady of a Thousand Sorrows (1977)

As K. M. O'Donnell

Empty People (1969)
The Final War and Other Fantasies (1969; stories)
Dwellers of the Deep (1970)
Gather at the Hall of the Planets (1971)
In the Pocket and Other S-F Stories (1971; stories)
Universe Day (1971; stories)

As Elliot B. Reston

The Womanizer (1972)

As Gerrold Watkins

Southern Comfort (1969)
A Bed of Money (1970)
A Satyr's Romance (1970)
Giving It Away (1970)
Art of the Fugue (1970)

NON-FICTION/ESSAYS

The Engines of the Night: Science Fiction in the Eighties (1982;
  essays)
Breakfast in the Ruins (2007; essays: expansion of
  Engines of the Night)
The Business of Science Fiction: Two Insiders Discuss
  Writing and Publishing (2010; with Mike Resnick)
The Bend at the End of the Road (2018; essays)

EDITED ANTHOLOGIES

Final Stage (1974; with Edward L. Ferman)
Arena (1976; with Edward L. Ferman)
Graven Images (1977; with Edward L. Ferman)
Dark Sins, Dark Dreams (1978; with Bill Pronzini)
The End of Summer: SF in the Fifties (1979; with Bill Pronzini)
Shared Tomorrows: Science Fiction in Collaboration (1979;
  with Bill Pronzini)
Neglected Visions (1979; with Martin H. Greenberg & Joseph D.
  Olander)
Bug-Eyed Monsters (1980; with Bill Pronzini)
The Science Fiction of Mark Clifton (1980;
  with Martin H. Greenberg)
The Arbor House Treasury of Horror & the Supernatural (1981;
  with Bill Pronzini & Martin H. Greenberg)
The Science Fiction of Kris Neville (1984; with Martin H. Greenberg)
Uncollected Stars (1986; with Piers Anthony, Martin H. Greenberg &
  Charles G. Waugh)
The Best Time Travel Stories of All Time (2003)